COLLISION

COLLISION

SPENCER DUNMORE

WILLIAM MORROW AND COMPANY, INC.
NEW YORK 1975

Published in the United States in 1975.

Copyright © 1974 by Spencer Dunmore

Published in Great Britain in 1974.

Printed in the United States of America.

1 2 3 4 5   79 78 77 76 75

Library of Congress Cataloging in Publication Data

Dunmore, Spencer (date)
    Collision.

    I. Title.
PZ4.D922Co [PR6054.U53] 813'.5'4 74-17488
ISBN 0-688-02886-1

For Thomas Plant
1909–73

COLLISION

1

The right main landing-gear of a Boeing 747 of Anglo-World Airways cut Lee Chan's general store and hardware shop in half.

The incident took place a few minutes before midnight. The shop was closed but Lee Chan had remained on the premises to work on his accounts and to tag and display a new shipment of faded Levi's just received from London. Lee Chan had been out of faded Levi's for more than a month—a sorry state of affairs for they sold briskly. Lee Chan was constantly vexed by the inordinate time it seemed to take to move a few goods from London to the West Coast of Africa.

It was raining hard but through the drumming on his sheet-steel roof Lee Chan heard the approaching aircraft. He took no notice. Aircraft were always flying over his shop on their way to or from the International Airport. The aircraft, it was said, brought traders and tourists; but none ever seemed to come to Lee Chan's shop. The people who travelled in big aeroplanes kept to the city. They weren't interested in Lee Chan, therefore he wasn't interested in them.

He continued to tag the Levi's.

Then he looked up, frowning. The aircraft was making an uncommonly loud din. The roof was shuddering. Lee Chan shook his head, annoyed. Aeroplanes should not be permitted to make such a din so late at night. There should be a law. Perhaps indeed there was such a law.

Then the 747's undercarriage sliced through the timber and corrugated-iron structure like a razor through butter. A slow-motion film would have shown the building staggering, bending, folding, finally splitting and disintegrating almost explosively.

Had it not been for the chimney, the jet's gear might have gone straight through without incurring a great deal of damage. But the chimney was built of solid stone. (It had belonged originally to a colonial gentleman's house which had burned to the ground under slightly dubious circumstances. Lee Chan had built his store on the site, retaining the chimney which had stoutly survived the holocaust.) Thus, when the gear struts encountered the chimney they shattered, despite the 300,000 p.s.i. yield strength of the heat-treated, vacuum-arc milled steel from which they were made. A 4-foot diameter landing wheel hurtled free, missed Lee Chan by 18 inches, demolished 5 Raleigh bicycles, 6 transistor radio sets, 50 L.P.s by Harry Belafonte and James Last and took out the shop's end wall. The roof sagged and collapsed.

Lee Chan, dazed but unhurt, stood in the wreckage of his shop and watched as the 747 hit the ground a thousand yards beyond him—five miles short of the runway at the International Airport.

The 747 touched down in tolerably good landing attitude even though most of its right undercarriage had been shorn off. As it happened, the loss of the gear was fortunate. It caused the huge machine to veer wildly to one side the instant it touched the ground. The nose gear and the left main unit crumpled and snapped at once. Skidding, one gigantic wing thrust forward like an exploring arm, the Boeing flopped down on the scrub. Its broad, swept-back wings and engines took the weight. And the punishment. Metal buckled and ripped. Earth sprayed back as if it was water at the bow of a speeding yacht. One entire JT9D engine unit—8,450 pounds of it— went spinning and bouncing between two shacks. Another skidded along until it vanished with an explosion of steam into a river.

Blindly, like a suicidal beast, the aircraft plunged across the scrub, scything through bushes and trees. Three-quarters of a mile later it came to a stop.

The 364 passengers, 15 cabin crew and 3 flight crew members were shaken but unhurt.

There was a minimum of panic among the passengers. The fact implies commendable self-control, even heroism. But the truth is that the passengers reacted typically. A few kept their wits about them and were galvanized into instant, intelligent action the moment the 747 stopped sliding. Most, however, were benumbed. The total unexpectedness of the whole thing, the shattering bumping, the cacophony, the wreckage: all combined to create a momentary stupor. Minds seemed incapable of absorbing the fact that this had really happened. Passengers stared stupidly as crew members dashed through the 747's cavernous hull, exhorting everyone to move, to escape via the chutes and the emergency exits. The passengers listened in amazement, as if witnessing an extraordinary performance on the stage. Some had to be pulled bodily from their seats. And when they were on their feet they had to be restrained from searching for hats and paperback novels.

'Hurry! Please hurry! She might catch fire!'

Everyone, it seemed, came to their senses simultaneously. There was a scrambling. Shoving. Clutching. When a woman slipped and fell her husband openly cursed her for a fool. A stewardess helped her to her feet. A Scot kept telling everyone that everything was going to be all right. A woman screamed for her daughter. A child screamed for its father. At the exits there was courage and there was cowardice—and courtesy too: standing back and nodding and permitting the very old or the very young to jump out first.

At last the 747 seemed to be empty of passengers. But she wasn't. A stewardess discovered a man behind one of the first-class seats, looking for his spectacles. He said he understood the danger but it was frightfully important that he find his glasses because he was going on a lecture tour in Africa and it would be awfully inconvenient without them.

Then the enormous jet was truly empty. She didn't burn. Mute and still, she lay in the dirt, gamely enduring the indignity of it all. She had no engines; they had been ripped from her wings and scattered. She was creased and bent and she was bleeding oil. Great strips of her metallic flesh had been torn from her. Her ribs were exposed to view. The heavy raindrops hit them with odd, ringing thuds.

'I say, it's raining,' observed a tall man. He sounded surprised although he was already drenched, his hair plastered across his forehead.

A woman opened her umbrella; for some reason it struck a portly man as hilarious. He pointed at the woman and laughed unrestrainedly.

The passengers were gathering in confused little groups, asking

3

each other what had happened and whether everyone was all right and agreeing that everyone should stay more or less where they were and not stray too far because one could easily become lost in strange territory. An African gentleman with gleaming white teeth and shirt declared loudly that it wasn't strange territory at all.

Members of the crew hurried among the passengers, assuring them that everything was under control. No need for further alarm. Everyone was safe. A few cuts and contusions were apparently the worst that anyone had suffered. Yes, it was indeed a good show but, no, it shouldn't be considered a miracle exactly; soon, very soon, transportation would be arriving to take them on to the airport. No, Anglo-World would not be charging them for the ride. Yes, the Customs people would undoubtedly want to do their stuff in spite of this, er, incident. And yes, Anglo-World Airways was extremely sorry about the whole thing, but, no, it couldn't be said at this point in time precisely what caused it or what the Corporation might be prepared to do about it.

By now, many passengers were smiling, some laughing. The realization was making its impact: they had survived a veritable disaster. What had just happened would be read about and discussed all over the world. They were celebrities, in a manner of speaking!

But there were other reactions. A seventeen-year-old girl from Ealing suddenly vomited on the left sleeve of a lawyer from Accra. A muscular, six-foot man who was moderately well known as a 'bad guy' in Hollywood westerns fell over in a dead faint, having at last comprehended how incredibly close he had just come to losing his precious life. A couple who in three years' time would be celebrating their golden wedding anniversary held hands and laughed at each other as the rain streamed over their faces, blurring the marks of age. This would *really* be something to tell the family!

Anxiously, like fretting shepherds, the airliner's crew kept trying to herd the passengers into manageable groups. But by now the rain was so heavy that it was impossible to see more than a few yards. And the passengers kept straying, most of them apparently half asleep.

A tractor materialized through the deluge. Its driver, cowled like a monk, asked in hesitant, sing-song English if there was some assistance he might be.

4

'Aye,' said a man with a Lancashire accent. 'Do you have any petrol? We've run out.'

Then the official traffic began to arrive, sirens wailing, lights blinking importantly.

Roger T. Thorne dabbed at his forehead with a spotted handkerchief. Nervous tension always made him perspire, no matter how high he turned up the air-conditioner. A plump man, he was Anglo-World's local manager—a job that under normal circumstances was only moderately demanding since the Corporation had but a score of flights touching down at the International Airport per week. Suddenly, however, he had become the most important man in town. All the world's news agencies wanted to talk to him; the local papers wanted to photograph him. All very flattering of course, but Roger T. Thorne knew the drill. No statements to the press until Head Office in London gave the nod. A crash had to be handled like the public relations dynamite it most assuredly was. The Corporation's reputation and the ticket-buying decisions of God knows how many people were at stake. Thank the Lord for the Procedure Manual; it told a fellow precisely whom he had to tell and what he had to do, and in what order. Number One: inform Regional Headquarters by telephone. Number Two: inform the nearest Corporate Public Relations representative by telephone. Number Three: inform the Flight Safety Co-ordinator by telephone. Number Four: inform Regional Personnel by telephone. 'Be helpful to the Press,' the Manual advised, 'but do not permit them to interview members of the flight or cabin crews. When talking to the Press confine your remarks to facts of which there is no doubt. Avoid speculation. Do not reveal the names of any passengers.' It was easier said than done, Roger T. Thorne had discovered. Reporters after information—even the Mickey Mouse locals —were like sharks who had tasted blood.

He scowled at the buzzer on his desk.

'A Mr Parrone on line one.'

'And who, pray, is Mr Parrone?'

'I don't know.'

'Perhaps you would be good enough to ask.'

'OK.' A moment later: 'He's with Reuter's.'

5

Thorne sighed long-sufferingly. 'Just give him the statement I dictated to you. And tell him we have no more information at the present time. Then hang up.'

'Right-oh,' said Miss Swayze.

'God, the bloody office help is atrocious around here,' said Roger T. Thorne to the man sitting opposite him, a man in a dark blue uniform spattered with white mud. 'Can't wait to get back to civilization. It's impossible to get anyone who gives a damn. Bone-bloody-idle, the lot of them. Of course, that's the trouble with the whole world these days, if you ask me. Everyone is bone-idle.'

'I'm sure you're right,' murmured the man in the uniform.

'The media will be hounding me now,' said Thorne. 'Absolutely hounding me. You watch, they'll be ringing me at home in the middle of the night, hoping to catch me off guard, trying to get me to say something that'll make a nice, sensational story. No respect for the truth—nor a man's leisure hours. Merciless, they are, quite merciless, when they get their teeth into a story.'

'I'm sorry to cause you so much trouble.'

'No trouble, old man. After all, it wasn't *intentional*.'

'No, it wasn't intentional.'

'Are you feeling all right, old man? You look a bit pale.'

'Do I?'

'Yes, although under the circumstances ...'

'I often get pale when I crash-land 747s.'

'I ... yes, quite.'

Roger T. Thorne sniffed. Sarcastic sod, this Beatty. No need for it. Didn't help the situation one bloody iota. Thoughtless, too. A chap had problems enough representing Anglo-World in the Colonies without having his compatriots taking the mickey.

The buzzer again.

Thorne scraped his lower lip with his upper teeth. It was something he had once seen Bogart do in a film; quite unconsciously he had adopted the habit.

'London on line one,' said Miss Swayze.

God.

Thorne cleared his throat, jabbed the line button with a pudgy forefinger and reached for the telephone.

6

2

For the first time in ten years Frank Beatty regretted having given up smoking. He was tempted to reach for the Tareytons on Thorne's desk—but no, after a decade of abstinence, they would unquestionably taste frightful.

They might even make you sick, he thought.

He rubbed his eyes. Why did his mind persist in dwelling on trivialities? Didn't he have a sufficiency of critically important things to think out? Wasn't his entire future in the balance?

A tall, spare man in his late forties, Beatty had a face that an aunt had once described as 'patrician'—the result of high cheekbones, a prominent though well-formed nose and lines of unusual severity framing his regular features. At Anglo-World he was considered a somewhat reserved and caustic individual. The truth was that Frank Beatty was shy, and he tended to over-compensate for his shyness by speaking directly and sometimes curtly. It was known to only a few of his intimates that he possessed a lively sense of humour. He looked rather younger than his years; only in the sunlight was it noticeable that his thick hair contained as much grey as blond.

They're going to crucify you, he thought. They have no choice. There are no extenuating circumstances. You were in command and you flew the bloody aeroplane into the ground. It's that simple. What isn't so simple is *why*. He shook his head. He didn't know. He recalled Forrest who had piled up a Britannia at Orly. No one had been hurt. But that fact didn't help Forrest. The enquiry had revealed confusion on the flight deck, an unforgivable buggering-up of communications. Forrest had instructed his first officer to handle the landing. But he had failed to make it utterly, completely, perfectly, crystal clear that he, Forrest, would perform all the

7

duties normally carried out by the first officer. The result was that shortly after touchdown a misunderstanding led to the undercarriage being retracted instead of the flaps. A great deal of extremely expensive machinery was, in pilots' parlance, badly bent. Poor Forrest. The last anyone heard of him he was flying a Dove for a washing machine company that went bankrupt.

Airline captains who made mistakes were cancers that had to be sliced from the corporate body as rapidly and cleanly as possible.

I wish I had been killed, Beatty thought. Characteristically, he reviewed the thought. Did he really mean it? He came to the conclusion that he did. Oblivion seemed infinitely preferable to a future full of explanations and questions. A future full of sidelong glances. There's Beatty. Remember him? Flew a 747 into the deck. Good man in his day, but ...

He thought how, a few hours ago, he had longed for sleep, yearned for the chance to close his eyes and relax. Now he had that chance: a comfortable chair, a relatively quiet office. But he was fiercely, thumpingly awake.

He thought: Diane will be an absolute brick. The soul of loyalty, Diane. Not for an instant will she entertain a suspicion of a hint that any of this might have been my fault. She will *know* that I did everything that anyone could conceivably have done. But did I?

He couldn't remember. The events were curiously blurred and foggy; it was hard to separate fancy from reality.

What of Vincent? Beatty shook his head. Would the boys at school make it hard for him, flail him with the sins or omissions or whatever-the-hell-they-were of the father? Schoolboys were cruel little bastards. At least they used to be. Savage, merciless. These days, the kids seemed different with their ridiculously *femininely* long hair and their asinine rock music. They were all wrapped up in *causes*—at twelve years of age, for God's sake ...

On the wall before him hung a photograph of the Corporation's first DC-2. Parked on the apron at Croydon with a boxy little mid-'thirties Austin nestled under one wing. In those days the Douglas must have seemed huge. But by today's standards it was diminutive, a mere fortieth of the 747's weight, carrying a load of passengers fewer in number than the 747's normal complement of stewardesses. As a boy, Beatty had spent numberless hours travelling by bus and tube across London, from Wembley to Croydon, to be intoxicated by the sights and sounds and smells of the Ensigns and Albatrosses of Imperial Airways, the Dewoitines of Air France and the Junkers of Lufthansa. A teacher had asked his pupils' ambitions. To be an airman, Frank Beatty had replied. He was eight, but his decision was immutable. He learnt the fundamentals of flying ten years later on the Downs at Dunstable, strapped into the hard tin seat of a body-less glider, hurled into the air by the perspiring bunjie-launch team of fellow-enthusiasts. When the war came, there was no question of his intentions. He progressed through Tiger Moths, Oxfords, Ansons and Wellingtons. He flew a Halifax on a dozen ops. When the war ended, the squadron converted to transport duties. Beatty applied for a permanent commission. He stayed in the air force half a dozen years, flying coal to Berlin and paratroops to Salisbury Plain. In the early 'fifties he presented himself and his log-book (a wonderously worn affair detailing some six thousand hours of flying aloft) to Anglo-World Airways. The Corporation was pleased to accept him as a probationary pilot at £625 per annum plus £99 Daily Allowance. His was just the sort of experience the line wanted. But he had to work hard. Manuals by the dozen. Procedures, check-lists. Endless tests and reviews and examinations. He progressed to first-officer rank. Seven years ago he made the all-important leap up to captain at £10,000 a year. He had arrived at the peak.

And now this.

Thorne was talking earnestly to London, assuring them that he was in command of the situation and that everything was being handled the Corporation way. By now, Beatty reflected, the powers-that-be would have been informed of the erring captain's identity. In their minds he would have become a kind of non-person, part of the wreckage that the authorities would examine and eventually cart away. He would be labelled as the part that caused it all. The component that failed.

'Captain Beatty?'

Thorne was holding the telephone at arm's length as if afraid that it might explode. His hand covered the mouthpiece.

'The Chairman wants to speak to you,' he announced breathlessly.

Beatty took the telephone.

'Hullo, sir. Beatty here.'

The voice from London was crisp and well tailored and seemingly undismayed by the fact that a ten-million-pound aeroplane had been written off. The Chairman said that he was most frightfully sorry to hear what had happened but he was gratified to learn that no one had been seriously hurt. He hoped that the local authorities were taking care of everyone satisfactorily.

'Yes sir,' said Beatty. 'They have been quite efficient. All the passengers and crew have been examined. Most of them have already been released.'

'Delighted to hear it, delighted. I understand our man there is making all the necessary arrangements. Have you been in touch with your wife, captain?'

'Yes sir, I spoke to her on the telephone.'

'Excellent. I'm sure she must have been most relieved to hear from you. I believe you are coming back to London tomorrow morning.'

'Yes sir.'

'Good, good. Well, the important thing is that everyone is safe. Most gratifying. What you should do now is to get a good night's rest. Have they given you something to make you relax?'

'Yes, I have some pills.'

'Good. Take them, my boy. You'll feel as right as rain after a good night's rest. As right as rain.'

'Yes sir,' said Beatty, suddenly realizing that the Chairman was hesitating, awkwardly unsure what to say next.

'Well ... delighted that everyone is safe. Pleasant to talk to you, Captain. Goodbye.'

'Goodbye, sir. Thank you.'

Beatty handed the telephone back to Thorne who re-announced himself, only to find the line dead; the Chairman had rung off. Thorne was annoyed; he still had much to tell London. He commanded Miss Swayze to get London back on the line.

Beatty thought it considerate of the Chairman to telephone him halfway around the world. A kind man, the Chairman. But naïve to suggest that there was nothing to worry about, that all would be forgiven. Didn't the Chairman know the ground rules? Didn't he know what would happen? Or was it part of the Chairman's duties, to telephone the surviving captains of Corporation crashes? Was it written into his contract?

Beatty massaged his right wrist. It ached. Tomorrow he would be flown back to London. To the questions.

You've got to think up some bloody answers, he told himself.

You've got to remember.

3

It was easy to remember the departure from New York. An utterly normal departure. The pre-flight routine: external checks of the aircraft's vitals, its control surfaces, flap mechanisms, fuel-dumping chutes, access doors, inspection hatches, navigation lights; ensuring that fifty thousand gallons of mixed petrol and kerosene gurgled into the tanks in the correct sequence. The ritual of before-engine-start checks: INS switches, probe-heat switches, window heat, beacon lights, data selectors, galley power, upper-deck temperature, pack-valve recorder, annunciator lights, fuel booster pumps—the three flight crew members responding dutifully as they pored over their operations manuals like clerics over prayer books. 'INS to NAV.' 'Probe heat on.' 'Auto, TK/GS.' 'GPU disconnected.' 'Recorder switch guarded.' The starting of the four engines—first number three, then four, followed by two and one—was a ticklish business, with starting levers and pressurizing controls adjusted to suit the conditions of the place and day, because of the JT9D's tendency to overheat. After starting there were the checks of electrical power, air switches, galley power, aft cargo heat, hydraulic switches, door lights, ground equipment, fuel heat, INS mode switches, nacelle anti-ice, aileron trim, flaps, rudder trim. And while trundling out to the runway (carefully watching the INS ground-speed indicator because it is easy to underestimate one's velocity when one is sitting three stories high) still more checks: oil quantities, pressures, temperatures, pressurization differential pressures, pack temperatures, hydraulic pressures, weights, yaw dampers, transponder. 'Take-off flap selected. Green light.' 'Anti-skid light out.' 'Annunciators checked.' And at the threshold of the runway, a rapid review of the take-off arithmetic: gross weight of the aircraft, ambient temperature, pressure altitude—all of which had a direct influence on the ability of the 747 to haul itself and its passengers and crew into the air.

'Anglo-World Seven One Two, ready to roll.'

'Anglo-World Seven One Two, you are clear for take-off.'

A quick glance right and left. Coast indeed clear.

'Set take-off power.'

The brakes were released. The 747 began its roll, three hundred tons propelled by the power of air being compressed, expanded by fuel combustion, then ejected in a furious, bone-snapping stream to the rear. Quickly the enormous machine picked up speed—although from the lofty height of the flight deck, the pace still seemed positively lethargic. A light pressure on the rudder pedal corrected a tendency to wander away from the runway's centre line. The white strips became a single line. Engine nacelles trembled beneath swaying wings.

'Vee-one,' said Dowling, the first officer. One hundred and twenty knots. Now or never speed. Time to rotate, to ease the nose wheel off the deck, time to coax the whole colossal contraption into the air.

A gentle easing back on the control column—gentle because the aircraft's tail was bounding along more than two hundred feet behind; too enthusiastic a heave on the controls could result in banging and scraping the rear underside of the fuselage along the runway, to the dismay of passengers and Corporation alike.

The rumbling of the main gear ceased. Airborne.

'Undercarriage, please.'

'Gear up, sir.'

At an angle of fifteen degrees to the horizontal, the jet thrust her nose up through the haze and scattered cloud into the clean sunshine. Fifteen hundred feet: flaps up a notch. Climb power. Flaps fully retracted. Speed: two hundred and fifty knots as required by Federal Air regulations, up to ten thousand feet. Effortlessly the JT9Ds propelled her to her cruising altitude.

'Speed coming up to Mach point eight, sir.'

'Roger.'

Now the aircraft was controlled by a complex of computers, accelerometers and gyroscopes collectively known as the Inertial Navigation System. On the ground, the INS ('the little black boxes' to the crew) had been fed the latitude and longitude of the starting-point and those of the destination and half a dozen waypoints between. Armed with these data the INS was able to keep an electronic eye on the auto-pilot, adjusting heading for wind, compensating for in-path turbulence, maintaining a phenomenally accurate course and altitude.

The three-man flight crew did little more than supervise the workings of the aircraft's systems. Beatty, the captain, and Dowling, the first officer, sat side by side in the forward seats. Between them, before them and above them were the dials, levers and switches that controlled the entire aircraft. Behind the two pilots, facing to starboard, sat Milden, the second officer. He was a fully qualified 747 pilot but his duties were those of a flight engineer. He ensured that the engines were being fed the correct quantities of fuel, that oil was flowing satisfactorily, that the aircraft's hundred miles of electric wiring was doing its job.

Frank Beatty stifled a yawn. He took a deep breath. No time for dozing. He watched the control column moving gently in obedience to the nagging demands of the little black boxes. Insulting, the sheer damnable efficiency of the things. The truth was that the little black boxes could fly a smoother, more accurate path than any human pilot. And it could land the 747 by itself. Superbly. A greaser every time. A cynic once quipped that the only advantage of human pilots over the mechanical variety was that the former could be made by unskilled labour.

But the little black boxes sometimes went wrong. Upon occasion, all three sets of little black boxes could tell three completely different stories. Then the humans had to come in and sort out the mess; they still had their uses.

Beatty was aware of the glances from Dowling. He pretended not to notice. He had flown with Dowling before. Nice enough chap, but appallingly loquacious. Give him the slightest encouragement and he would chat the rest of the way to Africa. About his days on Beaufighters and of the aircraft's proclivity for charging off in odd directions if one wasn't absolutely firm with it. About Dakotas and how they were wont to do much the same sort of thing on landing if you tried to get the tail down too soon. About Vikings on the London-to-Paris run and how the passengers and crew had to yell at one another to make themselves heard above the engines' din. About run-away props. About icing. About turbulence. About fog. About how flying wasn't that much fun any more since the advent of the little black boxes. About the 747 crew set-up: how BOAC had four pilots on the flight deck and Anglo-World (and practically every other line) had only three. Oscar Dowling was never at a loss for something to talk about.

But Beatty preferred a quiet, contemplative trip. It was therefore important not to let Oscar get started.

Dowling's face was a good-natured study in convexities: a series of jolly but rather over-fed curves bubbling out of his wilting collar. He was a year or two older than Beatty, a veteran of three decades of flying, a superb craftsman. At his age he should have been a captain. No one—including Dowling himself—seemed to know why he wasn't. Perhaps at some point he had said something ill advised; perhaps it was simply his girth. Or his garrulity. Whatever the reason, Dowling had been a first officer for *centuries*, first on DC-3s, then Tudors, then Tridents, now 747s. He had applied for the superjets, attracted by the higher salaries and by the possibility that the Corporation might soon have to rush out and buy more of the huge aircraft—at which time they would find themselves desperately short of 747 captains. So far it hadn't happened. And the portents weren't particularly encouraging; the Corporation had trouble enough keeping the original fleet of three operating at a profit.

The clouds began to thin. Now the Atlantic could be seen, restless, merciless. As he often did, Beatty spared a thought for the doughty souls of the 'twenties and 'thirties who had attempted to span the ocean in their underpowered and overloaded crates. Somewhere in the waters below a sixty-three-year-old lady of noble birth had gone to her death, dressed in a bright blue suede flying-suit. Aboard her aircraft she had been carrying half a dozen hat boxes containing the millinery she intended to wear on her triumphal tour of the major North American cities as the first woman to fly the Atlantic. Something had gone wrong; they never found a trace of her, her aircraft, her two pilots or her hat boxes.

The big jet sped on, becoming lighter at a rate of four hundred and seventy pounds per minute as the four JT9Ds thirstily consumed the petrol and kerosene fuel.

The passengers ate, watched a film, then ate again. One woman had four cocktails and fell deeply asleep, locked in one of the dozen toilets. A man wearing a check suit made a series of indecent propositions to a married stewardess from Dundee, at one point offering her one hundred dollars ('or the equivalent in pounds, baby, if you prefer; it's all the same to me') to meet him at his hotel that evening. Milden, the second officer, had to go aft and inform the man that he would be clapped in irons for the balance of the trip if he didn't behave. The man said Milden was bluffing. Milden produced the key to his front door in Wimbledon. 'This opens the forward hatch,' he said. 'It's twenty degrees below zero in there. You won't feel randy very long in there, I can assure you.' The man thought about it and then mumbled that he didn't mean any harm, for crissake. Two dinners were spilt in laps. One hold-all crammed with holiday funds was lost. And found. It was a normal trip.

An hour from the African coast Beatty told his passengers, 'I expect you are interested in hearing about the weather ahead. Not very good news, unfortunately. It's been raining on and off all day. So I do hope you've all brought your macs and umbrellas. The latest temperature they've given us is ninety-seven degrees Fahrenheit—with a humidity of ninety-four. A trifle sticky, I'm afraid. We expect to be parked in front of the terminal building in fifty-eight minutes.'

He released the intercom button on his mike, glad to have the tiresome little PA duty done. He disliked talking to invisible people who didn't respond. He was no David Frost, he told himself, and had no wish to become one. Besides, there was always the awful possibility of leaving the intercom button on and letting the passengers in on the truth—which at times could be disquieting even to the crew. Hearing the captain's voice was said to be good for the passengers' peace of mind. In the piston-engine and early jet days their peace of mind was assured by personal visits from the great man. It was a popular practice. But during one trip across the Atlantic, a jet-liner's auto-pilot had become disengaged. The captain was aft on his goodwill tour of the passenger cabin. The first officer, engrossed in a Henry Miller novel, didn't notice the problem until the jet snapped suddenly into a dive. Its speed escalated at a terrifying rate, because of its great weight, its highly streamlined form and its swept-back wings. The captain managed to drag himself back to the flight deck. Together he and the first officer coaxed the machine out of its plunge. And only just in time. The tossing Atlantic waves were said to have slapped the undersides of the jet's wings as it levelled out. From then on, captains were required to remain on the flight deck throughout every flight, leaving only for calls of nature.

Beatty's reference to the estimated time of arrival was also in accordance with Corporation requirements. 'Don't be vague. Don't tell your passengers, "We'll be there in about half an hour". Tell them, "Twenty-nine minutes" or "thirty-one minutes",' advised the Marketing Department. 'Precision suggests efficiency; efficiency implies safety.'

Shortly after Marketing issued this directive, an Anglo-World captain was reprimanded for repeatedly telling planeload after planeload of passengers that the aircraft would be arriving in 'twenty-nine minutes or thirty-one minutes'. He informed Management that that was what he had been instructed to say. Management said he was being childish. The captain informed the Association. Scores of letters and telephone calls ensued. The arguments dragged on for several months. Eventually everyone became bored and forgot the whole thing.

Beatty's eyes scanned the instrument panel. It was an automatic procedure. He did not deliberately study each dial and gauge, but had any of them indicated trouble the fact would have registered on him like a red light on a day-dreaming motorist.

Another weather report: rain, torrential at times, visibility ranging from five hundred yards to two miles—according to the questionable opinion of the airport officials. And hot as hell. Far too hot to put on one's raincoat and far too wet to leave it off. Why, Beatty wondered inconsequentially, is it unthinkable for an airline pilot to carry an umbrella?

His eyes prickled with fatigue.

He told himself: You're not the least bit tired. It's simply mind over matter. You're as fresh as a daisy. Repeat after me: fresh as a daisy, fresh as a daisy.

But his body wasn't convinced.

After this trip there would be thirty-six hours of utter indolence, recuperation time in which his body could sort out whether it was day or night and whether it should be demanding breakfast, lunch or dinner, or nothing. A deck chair by the hotel pool, a tall, frosty drink in one hand, a good book in the other. And when the eyes became weary of reading and surveying svelte bodies in bikinis, deep, delicious sleep. Hour after hour after hour of it.

Why was it that sometimes one could sleep like a top in a strange bed and at other times it was impossible? Surely someone who had been flying airliners for rather more than twenty years would have become accustomed to it by now. Of course, this time it could all be blamed on the weather in Hong Kong that delayed Mathews' departure and resulted in Beatty's spending the better part of an entire day waiting in the sweltering mid-summer heat at Kennedy. Then, compounding the problem, there had been the maintenance crews' work-to-rule campaign. Fuelling had suddenly become a half-day operation. When at last Beatty had taken off, he was eighteen hours behind schedule. And he hadn't slept for thirty-four hours.

He had gone to bed at midnight, leaving a call with the desk to call him at 6.00 a.m. But it was already 6.00 a.m. in London where Beatty had last slept. As far as his body was concerned, the new day had already begun. He closed his eyes but sleep eluded him. At first it didn't concern him. Although he was tired he was also alert. Sometimes the machinery took its own sweet time in winding down. You had to be patient. You had to think of Lake Windermere on a tranquil evening or a Hawker Hart performing fifty loop-the-loops. And if that failed you had to relax each bone, each muscle in succession. You started with the left little toe. Usually, by the time you reached the knee you were fast asleep. But not this time. When Beatty rose at six he hadn't slept a minute. He felt groggy and slightly dizzy. But there was nothing for it; he had to go to work. He showered, dressed and left for the airport.

Now the clouds were thick again.

Dowling was chatting to the ground controller in his cheery way, announcing Anglo-World's position and intentions. The controller answered in sing-song English.

'You are cleared to flight level two four, Anglo-World.'

Dowling repeated the clearance. Unexpectedly the controller thanked him. Dowling grinned at Beatty. 'The Wogs are jolly polite for a change.'

Somehow he managed to say it without sounding patronizing.

Throttles back, nose down a few degrees.

Now the airport was reporting visibility down to half a mile. Which probably meant fifty yards, in Beatty's opinion. Someone would have despatched the most junior member of the control tower to stand at the end of the runway in the downpour and esti-mate the visibility. Now the results of this exercise were being reported to incoming aircraft and pilots were making up their minds whether to land or divert to another field. Some airports in Africa— and elsewhere—were notorious for their sanguine reports on local weather conditions. It was understandable if not admirable. Land-ing fees were, after all, a major source of income.

According to the ground, the visibility minimum was well above the A-W minima.

'Anglo-World Seven One Two, continue on heading one niner fife until you intercept the ILS for runway one six. Over.'

The Boeing had to be slowed with flaps and air-brakes: barriers to interrupt the smooth flow of air over the great wings since jet aircraft do not lose speed as rapidly as propeller aircraft when their engines are throttled back.

'Tell the passengers we'll probably be encountering some tur-bulence, will you.'

'Roger,' said Dowling who always seemed to enjoy declaiming into the PA.

In the clouds, the 747 rocked and swayed in her dignified way. Beatty watched the ILS dial. The vertical needle indicated direction, the horizontal needle represented the angle of the descent towards the runway.

'Anglo-World Seven One Two, you are cleared for an ILS land-ing on runway one six.'

'Pea-soup,' said Dowling, peering ahead.

The ILS indicator still showed a neat cross. Descent rate and direction were bang-on.

'Outer marker,' Dowling reported.

'Roger. Undercarriage please.'

'Gear down, sir.'

Green lights confirmed the statement.

Still nothing to be seen outside but swirling, dank greyness that smeared wet fingers over the windscreen.

'Middle marker.'

'Roger.'

'Altitude is ...'

Beatty didn't hear the altitude.

He knew that he wanted to know it. But other matters were capturing his attention. ILS needles wandering, stating dumbly but with dreadful clarity that the aircraft was pitching and tumbling through the murk. His hands moved to wrest control from the auto-pilot. Not an instant to lose. He knew it. But there was a gap somewhere. Moments seemed to drift by. Voices were low and languid; even the ILS needles now danced at a weary tempo. Lights kept flashing, although the mechanism of the flashing was somehow lethargic: a protracted gathering of forces, a build-up of effort for the moment of brightness, followed by a step-by-step diminution. The control column kept exerting back-pressure, but it was a gentle, undemanding kind of pressure. Beatty saw Dowling turning, a plump arm reaching, hairless hands clutching. One of his front teeth was lighter in colour than the others. Was it false? The noises faded, almost disappeared, then they returned, amplified until they were stunning, deafening, stupefying.

He saw the building, dead ahead.

Suddenly the noise ceased.

He felt the wrenching, twisting thump of impact.

Dowling's hand grasped the panel as if he alone could keep the front of the aircraft from exploding upon him.

Beatty was aware that his mouth had opened.

But no words came. None was adequate.

The ground swept up at him. Metal screamed in pain.

4

A few minutes after 8.00 p.m., Eastern Standard Time, a DC-8 touched down at Toronto International Airport. Eye-catching in the red and gold livery of TranState Airlines, the jet taxied to Terminal One and parked beside a Wardair Boeing 707. The passengers disembarked, followed by the crew. The captain—his rank was denoted by the four gold rings on each sleeve of his tunic—was the last to leave the aircraft. Of average height, he moved in the easy, fluid way of one who exercises regularly and thoroughly. The dark blue TranState uniform flattered his trim frame. He had a pleasant face, good-natured rather than handsome; he had a strong, well-formed jaw; his eyes were blue; his dark-brown hair was touched by grey at the temples.

His name was Charles Vaughan.

Vaughan's great-great-grandfather had journeyed from Dun Laoghaire to Liverpool and thence to America, eagerly seeking the rich, full, free life that was said to be had for the taking in the New World. What he found was a labourer's job on the construction of the Brooklyn Bridge. During the first winter he slipped on ice and fell two hundred feet into the East River. They never found his body. His widow did not remarry in spite of half a dozen offers and repeated assurances by her priest that the Church would look with favour upon a new union. She was convinced that Patrick O'Hagan Vaughan would return. She was wrong. She was a tough, incredibly narrow-minded individual who adored her family without reservation, firmly believing them totally faultless in a sin-sodden world. She lived to the age of ninety-eight. Charles Vaughan knew her in her last years. She wanted him to take the cloth. She was horrified when he confided that he had ambitions to fly. 'Only angels and birds can fly,' she declared, resolutely refusing to accept the evidence of her own eyes. She died the day before a B-29 named Enola Gay dropped a bomb that killed 130,000 people.

'In my entirely unhumble opinion,' said Walt Przeczek, 'your average airport has as much gorgeous stuff walking around it as your average Playboy Club.'

He looked around the terminal building, smiling at females of every age. An astonishingly high proportion of them smiled back.

'You're horny again,' said Vaughan.

'The sight of females always makes me horny,' said Przeczek.

'Are you boasting?'

'Hell no, just stating a fact.'

Walt Przeczek was also a TranState captain, although junior to Vaughan. He had been promoted to captain from first officer six months before. The vagaries of Crew Scheduling frequently meant that junior captains found themselves back in the right-hand seats for a trip or two. At a few hours' notice, Walt Przeczek had been asked to fly copilot for Vaughan to Chicago, Toronto and New York; the scheduled first officer was down with the 'flu. The arrangement suited both men; they were old friends. They had joined TranState within weeks of one another and had attended the same Constellation class for probationary pilots. They had flown together dozens of times; now they lived within five miles of one another in the San Bernadino mountains near Los Angeles. Rumours at TranState had it that Przeczek would have made captain a couple of years earlier if only he had agreed to change his name to Peck or Prez or something equally pronounceable by the average citizen. But he had refused. Vociferously. He was a large man, well over six feet in height, exceedingly ugly and yet quite remarkably attractive, with an overwhelming smile and a winning charm. He was fond of telling junior crew members that flying was a futile way for a man to make a living. It was dull, repetitive and likely to result in piles and lung cancer because pilots spent their lives strapped to seats and breathing in mechanically produced air. Walt Przeczek claimed that he stayed in the business only because the uniform made him irresistible to women.

'Put me in a double-breasted Terylene and wool,' he told Vaughan, 'and I'm just another big, ugly Polack. Put me in the uniform with the golden wings and suddenly I'm an exotic experience too fascinating to miss.'

Together they made for the office TranState maintained at Toronto. There, they heard for the first time about Beatty's crash.

'Did anyone get out?'

It was the first, urgent question.

'They all did,' said Adler, the company's Toronto traffic manager.

'What happened?'

Adler shrugged. 'All I heard, the guy undershot and hit a house or a store or sump'n.'

'And they all got out?'

'Yep.'

'Wonder how.'

'Rapidly, brother,' said Adler, 'rapidly.'

Vaughan smiled and handed him the flight documents, the way bills and passenger manifest that represented the official existence of Flight Twelve. The flight was due to leave on the last leg of the trip, from Toronto to New York, in fifty-one minutes.

Adler reported that there would be forty-three passengers joining the flight at Toronto. Vaughan nodded; Toronto-to-New York was usually well patronized. Forty-one more souls would put him well over the magic sixty-two per cent occupancy figure which, according to the Sales Department, was the point at which TranState started making aviation pay. Vaughan often wondered what he was supposed to do with such tidbits of information. Did Sales hope that he might scout around the airports on slack days, signing up additional passengers?

According to Met, the weather was so-so. The east coast had been hit by severe thunderstorms earlier in the day. They were weakening, however. By the time Flight Twelve reached New York, the worst would be over, although there would be rough going in the turbulent air left by the waning storms.

The 747 crash in Africa was a major topic of conversation. The TranState aircrew, like those of every other line, felt directly involved. Any accident was the worst possible news. It didn't matter whether the aircraft involved was American, British, French, Russian or Chinese. Any crash had the same effect on the way the travelling public thought about flying as a means of getting from point A to point B. The story was told in the records of bookings and cancellations on days following accidents. People in their thousands suddenly decided to drive, take the train or stay home. The public seemed able to accept forty or fifty thousand road deaths a year as the inevitable tariff for the convenience of the automobile. Somehow the same people found it impossible to be a fraction as philosophical about air travel.

Walt Przeczek was fond of declaring that a crack-up was simply an infinitesimal possibility lurking within inevitable statistical limits.

'But it still smarts like hell,' said Lindsay, the flight engineer.

'We are slaves to the doctrine of chance,' said Przeczek. 'We *know* someone is going to get it in the next twelve months, most likely the next twelve weeks. Something is going to go wrong for the simple reason that we depend on far too many things for our own good. But it's going to go wrong for someone else, right? Some other guy is going to set his altimeter wrong and fly into a hill; someone else is going to get screwed up in a DC-10's vortices. Always someone else.'

'It's a comforting thought,' said Vaughan.

Przeczek said, 'The thing is, it'd be simple as hell to eliminate accidents. They're all caused by bad weather, inadequate or faulty equipment and/or stupidity. So all we've got to do is stay on the ground when the weather's lousy, refuse to use any field that has bad lighting or an unserviceable ILS—and never, ever, let a copilot touch the controls. I just hope,' he added, 'that the guy who cracked up the '47 has got something good and solid to blame. Spoiler malfunction or a runaway stabilizer. Something. And I hope he can prove it. If not, the poor son-of-a-bitch is in one hell of a lot of trouble.'

Vaughan agreed. Investigating committees seemed only too eager to heap Everests of blame upon the captains of crashed airliners, especially, it seemed, those who weren't alive to defend themselves.

'Pilot error' was the all-too-frequent conclusion of weeks and often months of investigation.

Light rain was falling when Vaughan and Przeczek walked out to the DC-8 and commenced their routine external inspection. It was Przeczek who observed the fluid on the underside of the left wing. He touched the stuff and sniffed it. No question. It was jet fuel. The leak appeared to be located in the corner of a small inspection cover. Przeczek reported the leak to Vaughan; they examined it together. All wings of jet liners tended to leak, especially when they had recently been topped up. But it was a question of degree. How much was acceptable?

'Better get in touch with Dispatch,' said Vaughan. 'Tell them there could be a delay. I'm talking to Maintenance.'

Irwin, the chief mechanic, said there was a gunk that would do the trick.

'I'm familiar with the stuff,' Vaughan said. 'But this is more than a dribble.'

'The gunk'll fix it, Captain. No sweat. If it was a big leak, why, we'd have to strip the wing. They'll probably want to do that when you get back to LA. But in the meantime the gunk'll do just fine.'

'How do you know it will?'

'Used it lots of times before. No complaints.'

'What does the Manual say?'

'It says use the gunk.' The mechanic noted Vaughan's thoughtful expression. 'You want to look at the Manual, Captain?'

Vaughan nodded. 'I think I'd better.'

'OK by me,' said Irwin. He wiped his hands on cotton waste and reached for the voluminous company maintenance manual. Yawning, he flipped through the pages. 'Here it is. "Fuel Leaks".'

It was as he had said. But was the leak really 'minor'? The Manual was no help on that point.

Vaughan watched a BOAC jet take-off without really seeing it. 'What happens,' he asked Irwin, 'when the gunk sets? Does it get dry and hard?'

'I guess so. It's a sort of plastic, you know.'

'What happens if the wing flexes more than usual in flight? In turbulence, say.'

Irwin pondered that one for a moment. 'Reckon the leak could open up again,' he admitted. 'But I never heard of it. Always worked just great.'

Vaughan walked slowly back to the office. 'I'm sorry,' he told Adler. 'I'm cancelling.'

'Got a problem, Captain?'

Vaughan was tempted to say, No, he just didn't feel like going flying. He stopped himself. Sarcasm wouldn't help the situation. 'We've got a leak. Maintenance are going to be on it for hours.'

Adler clicked his tongue as he studied the passenger manifest. He seemed to be silently counting the money TranState was going to lose.

'Can I use your office?'

'Be my guest,' said Adler.

In three minutes, Vaughan was talking to the company's Flight Director in Los Angeles. He explained the situation. 'Maintenance can only provide a temporary plastic filler material to plug the leak.'

'And does Maintenance say the stuff will be satisfactory for the trip to New York?'

'Yes, sir.'

'Then I don't believe I understand your problem, Captain.' The Flight Director had a terse, incisive way of expressing himself; the front-office grapevine had him heading for a vice-presidency. 'Maintenance rarely says things without meaning them.'

Vaughan paused a moment to collect his thoughts. 'You see, the stuff just plugs the hole, sort of like chewing-gum.'

'Hardly like chewing-gum, Captain.'

'Sir, it's turbulent all the way from here to New York. We've been advised that we can expect moderate-to-severe turbulence. The wing is going to flex more than on an average flight. If it does, and if that stuff has dried and hardened, then the leak will open up again.'

'Yes, but if Maintenance——'

'Maintenance isn't flying the aircraft, sir, I am.'

'If you'll permit me to get a word in edgewise, Captain.'

'Excuse me.'

'If Maintenance says the repair is in accordance with the company Manual, then my advice would be to take the flight, Captain.'

Vaughan felt the irritation bubbling within him. 'To a guy in a hangar, a leak can easily be classified as "minor". But it can look as major as hell to another man thirty thousand feet up in the air. I'm cancelling the flight, sir.'

When Vaughan emerged from the office, he felt drained. He had had basically the same conversion with three of TranState's senior executives. All three had urged him to think of the inconvenience to the passengers, the damage to the company's reputation as a reliable carrier, the expense of rescheduling, of accommodations, of meals. All three had talked smoothly and professionally, assuring him of the high quality of TranState maintenance, testifying again and again to the dedication and experience embodied in the Manual's pages. All three had succeeded in implying the threat of disciplinary action without actually using the words. All three were practised euphemists.

But in his own way Charles Vaughan was as stubborn as his great-great-grandmother. He knew he was right to cancel the flight. He refused to be swayed.

Adler went off to inform the passengers assembled in the boarding lounge that their flight had ceased to exist. On the way he stopped by Air Canada and American to check on their availabilities to New York. There were half a dozen seats, no more. Adler sighed. Sometimes he wished he had stayed in the chain-link fence business.

Vaughan completed the Flight Cancellation documents. Under 'Reason for Cancellation Decision' he wrote: 'Moderate to severe turbulence was to be expected en route. (See Met report attached.) This condition made temporary repair of wing leak a safety hazard. In my opinion the leak could not be classified as "minor". A steady loss of fuel could be seen. In view of the weather situation, the possible danger to the aircraft and passengers was in my opinion completely unacceptable. (Signed) C. J. Vaughan, Capt.'

He reread his statements. They were accurate and to the point. No wasted words. No pussyfooting. He had mentioned the weather twice. Good. The weather was the factor that made all the difference.

He rubbed his eyes. No matter how carefully he phrased the thing, there would be trouble. Cancellations were about as popular at TranState as FAA inspectors. On countless occasions, TranState aircraft had flown when other lines had opted to stay put. Management was fond of reminding employees that the company was in business to make a profit and the only way to make a profit was to keep flying. Airplanes sitting on the ground, they pointed out, were liabilities not assets. The big international, government-subsidized lines might be able to afford to cancel because of dirty windshields and full ash-trays but not TranState.

In the five years since he had become a captain, Vaughan had cancelled only a dozen flights. And in each case the circumstances were such that even the gung ho TranState management couldn't complain. But this time the whole thing was open to interpretation. It was essential that he present his side of the matter as lucidly and forcefully as possible at the inevitable company enquiry. He decided to write down the complete sequence of events while they were still fresh in his mind.

He was engrossed in this task when Przeczek came bursting into the office, grinning delightedly.

'Great news, buddy.'

Vaughan looked up. 'They've fixed the aircraft already?'

'No, much better than that.'

'Well?'

Przeczek declared, 'There's no need, old friend, to spend a lonely evening at the movies or in your hotel room——'

'I wasn't planning to go to a movie——'

'Because, you lucky devil you, they've invited you too!'

'They?'

'The luscious ladies from Air Canada.'

'Oh Christ, no, Walt——'

'But you can't disappoint them, Chuck. One of them is getting married or engaged or divorced or some damn thing. I happened to bump into a bevy of them down the corridor and they told me all about it. They're having a party in Toronto somewhere. They've invited us!'

Vaughan smiled despairingly. 'Can't you ever stop bumping into strange women?'

'God, I've tried,' said Przeczek, back of hand to forehead. 'But some evil force keeps egging me on, maddens me with its insistent throb——'

'Count me out.'

'You're coming, Charles.'

'No, I'm not. And remember, we're leaving bright and early in the morning.'

'But you must come.'

'Why?'

'Because I said you would.'

'No, Walt.'

'They particularly asked for the cute captain with the blue eyes and the Rock Hudson profile.'

'Get lost.'

'I insist that you come.'

'Walt, under no circumstances whatever will I come. It's definitely no. Absolutely, irrevocably no!'

The room was packed. And noisy. And infernally hot. Vaughan talked briefly with an actor who complained at length that he had been cheated out of a part—a *juicy* part—at Stratford. It was, he explained, the work of the *clique*. Then there was a smooth-faced young man who went off with the actor, holding hands. A plump young woman with big feet asked Vaughan when the action was going to start. A draft-dodger from Philadelphia was worried about his status if Canada became part of the United States—an event which he seemed to believe imminent. Seven people asked him if he had heard about the crash 'someplace in Africa'.

Vaughan put up with it for a couple of hours. Someone trod on his left foot; someone else spilt a gin-and-something down his tunic front. A very young man called him 'sir' which depressed him a little; then he reasoned that the young man was merely showing respect and being properly polite to someone approximately twice his age. Wouldn't he, Vaughan, say 'sir' to a man of eighty? He listened politely to a guitar player with a ginger beard who proclaimed that the only way to stop those goddam skyjackers was to erect goddam gallows at every goddam airport and hang every son-of-a-bitch of a skyjacker and leave the bodies dangling, rotting away. 'Then,' he declared, 'your goddam skyjacking will lose its goddam popularity, I'm telling you!'

'Possibly air travel would too,' Vaughan murmured, moving on. He wondered what had happened to Walt Przeczek. But not for long. It was practically certain that Przeczek had decided upon his prey and was at this moment hard at work seducing her. Vaughan edged towards the door. He stumbled over a couple kneeling on the floor in passionate embrace. The girl's left breast was free of her dress; it was a handsome breast. Two men in kilts lay propped against the wall in the corridor leading to the front door. One of the men had something of urgency to tell Vaughan but he fell asleep during the telling. His companion smiled beatifically. Vaughan sighed. He was out of his mind to have come. Wasn't he in enough trouble already? What if the Toronto Police suddenly burst in? Mass arrests. Pictures in the papers. Singular coincidence, wasn't it, Captain, that you decided to cancel your flight on that very same evening. . . .

'Are you Martin?'

'I beg your pardon.'

'I suppose you're Martin. You are, aren't you?'

A girl was asking the question, a girl with very fair hair that fell straight to her shoulders.

Vaughan shook his head. 'I'm not Martin. Sorry.'

'I thought you were.'

'No.'

'I haven't met him yet, you see.'

'Nor me,' said Vaughan.

'Really?'

'Really.'

'You don't know him either?'

'No. Should I?'

'I though he might be a friend of yours.'

'I don't think so.'

'Then you must know Peggy.'

'Peggy?'

'She's the one who's marrying Martin.' The girl frowned, puzzled. 'Are you at the right party, for goodness' sake?'

Vaughan chuckled. 'You might say I was invited by proxy. I don't know anyone here, except the screwball I came with and he's vanished somewhere—with someone, I rather imagine.'

'She's invited too many guests,' said the girl. She had an intriguingly husky quality to her voice. 'Typical Peggy. Always overdoing everything. Imagine bringing all these people to a little apartment like this. It's crazy.'

'It does make things a little over-intimate,' Vaughan admitted.

'Peggy and I were stews together.'

'What line?'

'Air Canada. Is there any other?'

'Sorry for asking, ma'am.'

She smiled. 'What line are you with?'

'TranState. Out of Los Angeles.'

'What do you fly?'

'DC-8.'

'Do you like flying?'

'It's better than working for a living.'

She smiled again. She had heard the adage before; it was traditional among airline crews. Her teeth were white and even except for the front left incisor which angled very slightly away from its mate. Curiously, the imperfection failed to detract from her looks; it seemed to add a quality. The girl had a remarkably lively and alert way about her.

'You're not a stew any more?'

'No,' she said. 'I quit when I realized waitresses on the ground were making more money. And I got tired of travelling. Funny, I never thought I would. But I liked the flying. I wanted to learn; I started taking lessons but it was too expensive. So I took up gliding.'

'Gliding?'

'We have a little club about forty miles out of town.'

'And you fly?'

'Surprised?'

'In a way.'

'Typical male.' She shook her head reprovingly as she reached into a brown leather purse and withdrew a billfold. The licence, issued by the Canadian Department of Transport, was made out to PRINGLE, Rosalie.

Vaughan apologized. 'I'm sorry, but you've got to admit that there aren't very many pretty girls who are glider pilots—at least there aren't many in the States.'

'Nor here,' she admitted.

'Anyway, I'm envious.'

'Why?'

'I've never flown in a glider.'

'You're kidding.'

'Cross my heart.'

'If you're willing to part with four dollars, we can fix you up with an introductory student familiarization flight.'

'I might take you up on that.'

'OK, and under the circumstances we might even let you take the controls for a minute or two.'

'I'd be honoured.'

She sipped on her drink. 'Do they know what caused that crash, where was it, in Africa?'

'I haven't heard,' said Vaughan. 'But everyone survived it. That's the important thing.'

'Have you ever crashed?'

She asked the question seriously, a seeker of important information. Her soft blue eyes were upon him as he recounted an incident from his days in the air force. He was copilot on a C-47. During the take-off run, just as the wheels left the ground, the aircraft's cargo shifted back towards the tail. The C-47 had staggered into the air, but it was fatally tail-heavy. The two pilots were unable to force the nose down. They half-landed, half-stalled into a ploughed field.

'Was anyone hurt?'

Vaughan shook his head. 'We were shaken up, but not half as badly as the crew chief who loaded the ship. The major went and had a long, heart-to-heart chat with him. I believe they discussed the guy's ancestry a lot.'

Her smile was momentary. 'Were you scared?'

Vaughan thought about it. 'I don't think so, not at the time. I was too busy. I don't think it ever crossed my mind that we wouldn't get down OK. But afterwards, when I had time to think what might have happened, yes, then I was scared. And I wasn't too crazy about going up in an airplane for a while, either. I had mysteriously lost my enthusiasm for the air.'

She said, 'I wonder sometimes how I would react if I was crashing.'

'That's a hell of a thing for a pretty girl to wonder.'

'There you go again,' she said. 'Pretty girls should only think about ice-cream sodas and the colour of the dress for the Saturday night prom, right?'

He apologized. 'But you've got to admit that that's what most pretty girls *do* think about.'

She nodded, smiling. 'Do you live in LA?'

'About eighty miles outside the city. Up in the mountains. A little place called Blue Jay.'

'Sounds nice.'

'I like it.' *Why, mister, didn't you say: 'We like it'?* He asked her: 'Do you live in Toronto?'

'Yes. The west end. Near High Park. Do you like Toronto?'

'Sure do.'

'Why?' She was engagingly direct.

'It has ILS on every runway.'

'What?' She frowned, then laughed. 'I meant the city.'

'I know you did. I was trying to be funny. And failing. The city's great too. Good places to eat. Two or three theatres. You can walk around without getting mugged. And there's usually some real fine jazz in town.'

She looked up. 'You like jazz?'

'Uh huh.'

'Me too.'

'No kidding.'

'You're surprised.'

'I guess I am.'

'Why?'

'It's just that most people who like jazz—I mean, *really* dig it— are men.'

'There you go again.'

'Yes, I realized it as I was saying it. And by then it was too late. I apologize.'

'Accepted,' she said.

'Who do you like on trumpet?'

She grinned. 'Testing me, huh? OK. I like Miles and Clark Terry and Louis and Wild Bill Davison and Ruby Braff and Maynard. Enough? Satisfied?'

'And impressed,' he said.

'I also dig Oscar Peterson, Cannonball Adderley, Woody Herman, Erroll Garner and Stan Getz. By the way,' she added, 'he's in town.'

'Getz?'

'Yes, at the Colonial.'

'I just had an idea,' said Vaughan.

5

When Vaughan landed at Los Angeles he was requested to report to the Chief Pilot. But not immediately. The appointment was set for 9.00 a.m. two days hence. It meant making the ninety-minute drive from Blue Jay into the city during his off-duty period.

'The corporate needle is at work,' Walt Przeczek observed. 'Anything I can do?'

Vaughan shook his head. The cancellation was his responsibility alone.

'Be seeing you,' said Walt.

I hope so, Vaughan thought.

His white Cougar sat baking in the sun at the western corner of the parking lot where he had left it three days before. At that time, he reflected as he eased himself into the driver's seat, you were in pretty good standing with the company. And you weren't an adulterer.

'You're a stupid bastard,' he thought, starting the engine. He flipped the air-conditioner fan switch and stared at the grille until the rushing air began to cool. The last time he had sat in this car life had seemed an orderly, predictable business; now uncertainties loomed like threatening avalanches.

Christ!

Is it . . . ? No. He sighed. The slim young blonde driving the rent-a-car bus had, for one heart-thumping moment, looked like Lee. ('It's really Rosalie. Rosalie Pringle. Isn't that a hideous name? I hate it. Everyone calls me Lee. Which isn't a hell of a lot better, in my opinion, but I'm stuck with it.')

I'm honestly sorry, Susan, he told his wife silently. I didn't want to hurt you. You don't deserve to be hurt. I really didn't *mean* to do what I did. I didn't set out with the *intention* of doing it. You

34

might say that circumstances outmanoeuvred me. He grimaced. Then again, he thought, you might not. In daylight the whole thing seemed inconceivable. There were no words that would assuage his guilt so he might as well stop looking.

He drove along Century Boulevard then turned north, accelerating into the bunched, speeding traffic of the Harbor Freeway. After the orderly patterns of aerial traffic, the freeways always seemed terrifying. Umpteen tons of metal hurtled along at a mile a minute: a formation of neurotics, alcoholics, day-dreamers and just plain incompetents, none of whom knew what the other might do next.

That day, Vaughan was as preoccupied and potentially as dangerous a driver as any. He dreaded the confrontation with Susan. Would she *know*, the instant he walked into the house? Would the guilt in his eyes blurt out the whole sordid story as surely as words?

But it wasn't sordid. He shook his head as if to dispell that notion. What happened was wrong; there could be no denying that. It wasn't sordid, however. But how, for God's sake, could he attempt to convey that fact to Susan? Should he even try? He squirmed as he pictured the scene: red-faced, stumbling husband; icy, scornful wife. Susan could make her tongue bite when she wanted to. 'You're right, Charles, of course you're right. There was nothing the slightest bit sordid about it. Now let's just review the circumstances. You met her at a party. I won't say that you picked her up because you say it wasn't like that at all. It was a simple meeting. And rather delightful because you found you had common interests. Flying and jazz. Charming. And so you slipped away to a jazz spot to hear Stan Getz who happened to be in town —how very fortunate, wasn't it? You had a few drinks—not you, of course, because you were flying in the morning—must be faithful to TranState, mustn't we? In fact, Charles, you were utterly sober throughout the entire operation. After a little hot music— or should I say *cool* music?—it's off to your suite at the Park Plaza. And there you bedded her, Charles, you took her clothes off and your clothes off and you had sexual intercourse. Now what could possibly be deemed sordid about that, Charles?'

She always called him Charles when she was mad.

Perhaps he should deny everything. And keep on denying. What could she prove? The evidence, so to speak, was three thousand miles away.

Perhaps he should throw himself upon her mercy.

Have pity on the poor first offender.

He edged across the lanes as the Route 10 exit neared.

Was all this really happening to *him*? Square old Chuck Vaughan? The guy whose idea of a big time was to curl up with a Budweiser and the *Journal of the American Aviation Historical Society*? He was the one who had been seen to shake his innocent head at the pilots who maintained discreet little pads in Chicago and Atlanta and Montreal. He had been heard to say that extramarital sex wasn't worth the risk or energy.

Now he was an aging Lothario, just like the others, and just as despicable.

The traffic began to thin. The mountains were near. Blue Jay was up there, 6,000 feet above sea level, way above the rat race and the smog. At Blue Jay the air was still crisp and the water clear. Vaughan had bought the cottage almost ten years before, soon after Janet's birth. At first it had been strictly for weekends and vacations, an escape from the apartment in Inglewood. Then, as tensions in the city mounted, the decision was made. The cottage became a home. Rapidly. Huddled against the hillside, defying gravity and the restless earth, it had doubled in size, sprouting bedrooms, patios, sun-decks. Once neatly Spartan, it now sprawled in complacent amplitude.

He said to himself: You're damn' nearly old enough to be her father. But you conveniently neglected to mention that fact, didn't you? She told you she was twenty-four. Did you figure she'd take you for thirty? Thirty-five tops? You're a bastard; you know that, don't you?

Yes, he replied to himself, I know that.

But the fact that Lee was almost sixteen years his junior proved to have a curious elasticity. The truth of it was undeniable. It was a fact with which to berate himself. And yet it seemed to possess about as much significance to the permanent state of affairs as a passing shower.

He wondered why he was incapable of saying to himself: Boy, that was one hell of a good party. And I scored. And aren't I lucky.

And forget it. Wasn't that what the roués did?

In a few minutes he would see Susan.

She would *know*.

He sped up the mountain road, his tyres squealing, complaining, as the car took the tortuous curves. He didn't spare a glance for the views of the valley or the labouring vehicles he overtook. All the way to the top he far exceeded the 40-m.p.h. speed limit. It was as if he craved to hasten the moment of confrontation—and yet his stomach churned in apprehension.

She would *know*.

Six-year-old Lynn met him on the driveway. The Carters' cat had had kittens. Could she have one? Vaughan said he would think about it. Lynn sighed and nodded. She had guessed that would be the response.

'Hi, Chuck.'

Susan was in the doorway. Her jeans and check shirt were in becoming contrast to her rather dainty features. She wore just a touch of make-up. Her dark hair was prettily short. She could still turn heads on Wilshire Boulevard.

'Good trip?'

He smiled. 'Fine.'

He kissed her. As if nothing had happened, nothing had changed. It was easy. Damnably easy.

6

Captain Fisher stoked his pipe, slowly, methodically, working the nubs of tobacco between his fingers until the shreds came loose and could be eased gently into the bowl. It took several minutes to complete the job. It took several more to light the pipe and tamp the mixture and get everything glowing and drawing evenly.

Sometimes the act of getting his pipe operational helped to solve problems. This time it hadn't helped a bit. What faced him was a vile job and there was no getting out of it and there was no way to select the words to soften the blow.

But, damn it all, there was no choice. Everyone involved knew it. Everyone was acquainted with the rules of the game.

He put the pipe on his desk. He was a solid-faced man of sixty, Chief Pilot for Anglo-World Airways. He watched the smoke curling up from the fading glow in the pipe's bowl. Why did smoke conjure up memories? Driffield, Yorkshire, 1940. A wrecked Whitley. Inexplicably, Ronnie Porson had side-slipped in from the cross-wind leg of his landing circuit. Had he fallen asleep or been taken ill? No one would ever know. The wreck had burnt all night. In the morning a long, lazily-curling pillar of smoke still ascended from the remains of the bomber and its occupants. Fisher shook his head. Ancient history. Ronnie Porson and his crew had been dead more than thirty years. Nowadays the satirists made jokes about RAF officers and their monstrous moustaches and diminutive brains, and about their bumbling missions over Germany. But it hadn't seemed very funny at the time. On the contrary, it had seemed quite vital. And dreadfully dangerous. In those early days the casualties daunted many a stout heart. But everyone pressed on. And some continued year after year, miraculously evading the fighters and the flak. They were the types who had a talent for survival, a knack for avoiding trouble. Airline pilots had to have that knack. Just as Napoleon demanded lucky generals, airlines demanded lucky pilots.

Beatty, it seemed, was unlucky.

Fisher sighed. It was a damnable business. For so many years, Beatty had been such an excellent fellow in every way.

Why the devil did this have to happen?

Thank God no one was killed. It was incredible that there hadn't been a single fatality, absolutely incredible.

Perhaps, Fisher mused, Beatty was a lucky pilot after all.

But, dash it all, he had flown the thing into the ground when it was apparently in good working order. It was true that conditions were poor. And possibly there was something wrong with the ILS. Torrential rain could affect the glide path and localizer beams. Such things did happen—although it was practically impossible to get any government official to admit it.

But every airline pilot knew of such problems and was ready for them. Montreal's Runway 24-left had an ILS peculiarity; it dipped for a few seconds just before the outer marker. But everyone was aware of it and compensated for it.

The first officer, Dowling, had been of little help. Busy with his check-lists and his instruments, he had been unaware of any problem until instants before the aircraft hit the Chinaman's shop.

Dowling said he considered Mr Beatty one of the finest pilots with whom he had ever flown.

A commendable expression of loyalty. And predictable. Most pilots were as bad as doctors where criticism of colleagues was concerned.

Fisher relit his pipe.

Should Beatty's superb record be taken into consideration?

No, of course not. Beatty was paid superbly to handle aircraft superbly—indeed his hourly rate was absolutely phenomenal. In return a masterful performance was expected at all times. Beatty knew that as well as everyone else. He had spoken of extreme fatigue; he had slept poorly the night before the flight. But the Corporation rules were straightforward: a pilot had to ground himself if for any reason he felt physically unfit for flying. No excuse to be found there.

But was there a *reason* to be found?

Was Beatty so tired that he fell asleep during the landing?

Hardly likely. Who ever heard of a brain surgeon falling asleep during a lobotomy or an acrobat during his act? No; totally occupied minds don't permit themselves sleep.

But was it possible that fatigue might have affected Beatty's ability to cope with an emergency? Was he, in fact, slow-witted because of lack of sleep?

Let's hope Fleet Street doesn't light on that angle, Fisher thought. According to far too many newspapers, the sky was full of jets manned by crews stupefied by exhaustion because they had been flying for impossible numbers of hours without relief. Long-distance transport drivers, it was said, had better working hours.

Another favourite newspaper story was that the crews were engrossed in orgies on the flight deck and let their aircraft crash.

Both angles made good copy.

Captain Fisher's pipe didn't seem to be drawing well today. It had started to fade; he had puffed vigorously, making it too hot; and it had gone out anyway. Today was one of those infinitely bloody days.

A knock on the door. Miss Abbott announced in her demure way that Captain Beatty had arrived and wished to see Captain Fisher.

Fisher didn't respond for a moment. If only the aircraft had had something wrong with it. Something blameable.

Damn! He had bitten through his pipe stem.

'Ask Captain Beatty to come in, please.'

'They were really very nice about it,' Frank Beatty told his wife. 'Very reasonable. Couldn't have been fairer, actually. But the fact remains that I have now joined the ranks of the unemployed.'

'They are rotters,' Diane declared, her fists clenched as if she intended to take on A-W in hand-to-hand combat. 'After all the years you've given them—'

'I've hardly *given* them any years,' said Beatty. 'They bought them, at a pretty high price. Besides, they had no choice but to let me go.' He smiled wryly. ' "Let me go". It sounds as if I was anxious to be gone.'

'It's beastly of them,' said Diane. 'If it hadn't been for you, everyone would have been killed.'

'That's a loyal wife speaking. It was because of me that everyone very nearly *was*. You do see that, don't you?'

'If you say so.'

'I don't suppose it's any consolation but I wasn't actually given the sack. They permitted me to resign under my own steam. Nice of them, really. They didn't have to do that.'

But Diane wasn't placated. 'It was the least they could do. God, how I hate big companies. They expect their employees to be loyal, but they don't think twice about dropping you....'

'It was hardly an impulsive move on their part, darling.'

'Don't defend them. They're absolutely rotten. All they think about is profits.'

Beatty smiled. Diane's view of the situation couldn't possibly be described as objective. She was frightfully worked up about it. Understandably, of course. The question was: why wasn't *he* frightfully worked up about it? He reminded himself: It isn't some other poor soul they're sacking; it's you. And you can't fly for three months. The licence you worked so bloody hard and long to get is officially revoked. You are grounded. What do you have to say about that?

The worst had happened, yet here he was, looking out of the drawing-room window at the Cambridge Road. A bus gusted by. Nothing had changed. The world still tottered on.

Diane asked: 'Are you going to talk to the Association about it?'

He said: 'I don't think so. I haven't been denied any rights. I can't honestly say I've been unfairly treated or victimized. The company did what it felt was necessary.'

'Why do you defend them after what they've done to you?'

'I'm not defending them.' Wasn't it odd how women tended to see things only in black or white? 'A-W has to do a great deal more than just sell tickets for rides on aeroplanes. The company is also in the business of convincing the general public that everything possible is done to ensure passengers' safety. It isn't always, of course, but that's beside the point. Let's suppose for a moment that A-W decided to let bygones be bygones and they kept me on as a captain. Let's suppose I had another crash. Just suppose. Think how the newspapers would love it. Imagine the headlines. BEATTY

PRANGS AGAIN. After that, how much confidence would the travelling public have in Anglo-World?'

'It's horrid and unfair.'

He took her hand and held it between both of his. By degrees, her anger evaporated. Then she became the comforter. Everything was going to be all right, she told him. There were dozens, hundreds of other airlines. Scores of them would jump at the opportunity of obtaining a captain with his experience and skill. And they would recognize his abilities as A-W had never really done. (True, A-W had made him a 747 skipper but they could have done so much more.) In the long run it would all turn out to be a blessing in disguise. Hadn't he often groaned at the ponderous way A-W approached every problem? Hadn't he often said they had become too big and prosperous for their own good?

He nodded. Yes, indeed he had. And the matters had seemed burningly important at the time. He had boiled with indignation. But now that he had something to be indignant about, he felt nothing. Zero. Life had become dead calm. Would he, he wondered, be much upset if some idiot flew a 747 into this very house and flattened it just as he had flattened Lee Chan's shop? Or would he regard that disaster in the same torpid way as he was regarding the disaster of the loss of his licence and job?

Diane suggested a drink. He agreed. No need to concern oneself with the number of hours until one ventured aloft.

The whisky tasted good. Possibly, he thought, this is the first step to a brand new career as a hopeless alcoholic.

Vincent came in. Noisy as hell, as usual. He burbled hullo and dashed upstairs, his long hair floating in the self-made wind. Beatty wondered whether he would succeeded in getting him to cut his hair before his return to school. He would be at home until early September—until twenty-nine days before licence reinstatement. Funny, Beatty thought, how he had worried over Vincent's reaction to the crash. But there had scarcely been a reaction: just a kind of mild annoyance, a suggestion that Father had done something not terribly bright, like taking the wrong turn off the M.1. The kid was so unbelievably secure under that idiotic mop of his.

'Another one, darling?'

'Why not?'

Why not indeed.

He watched her as she poured the drinks. She was taller than the majority of women, slightly over five feet ten. She carried her height well. She had a balance, a grace that set her apart. Beatty had first noticed her at a Corporation Christmas dance. A navigator named Kellaway had brought her. Shortly before midnight, he went off to replenish drinks, leaving her alone. Beatty, never at ease with strange females, persuaded his curiously awkward limbs to transport him across the floor as the band groaned into action. A clearing of throat. Would she care to dance? Yes, it seemed she wouldn't mind at all, thanks very much. To the laboured strains of 'Moonglow', he cleared his throat again and said he knew it was a bit of a cheek but might she care to come and have a spot of dinner one night? Absurdly, he added that he was sure Kellaway wouldn't mind. He had no idea why he said it. The words simply tumbled out of him. But, happily, she was amused rather than irked. She would love to have dinner with him, even if Kellaway *did* object. Seven months later they were married. No flutter-brained kids, they; he was thirty-six; she was twenty-eight. Twelve years later, Diane still carried herself like an international beauty queen, although her features were unremarkable: pleasant but unremarkable. Beatty loved her and considered himself lucky to have found her. But it never crossed his mind to tell her.

'I was talking to Mother,' Diane said. 'She asked how you were feeling.'

'And what did you say?'

'That you were in good form.'

'She didn't believe you.'

'Of course she did.'

'It's rather a difficult thing for people,' said Beatty. 'They don't know how to behave. They are familiar with the correct thing to say when someone dies or has a baby. But what is one supposed to say to an airline pilot who smashes up his aeroplane? "Sorry you bent it but glad you're OK"? It isn't in any of the etiquette books. It really should be, don't you think? After all, lots of chaps are pilots these days.'

Diane smiled. Her eyes were upon him, deep with kindness. 'She's frightfully sorry about it. She's very fond of you, you know.'

'And your father?'

'He said it ... it was a shame, or something.'

'He was right. It is a shame or something.'

Beatty's own parents had died more than ten years before, within twelve months of one another. His mother had died first, a victim of Parkinson's disease. After her death, his father seemed to lose interest in the tiresome business of being alive. He had died quietly one day in June, a still day of sun and droning bees. Vincent had found him, sitting in the garden, holding a cup of cold tea in his lap. He had been dead more than an hour; he hadn't spilt a drop. A very neat and orderly man, Mr Beatty, a lifetime employee of a gigantic insurance company, an earnest student of probabilities, a kindly man who knew his place in the scheme of things and was apparently content.

Beatty's parents had hated his flying. Medicine, they said, was the profession; the world needed doctors and accorded them respect and magnificent livings. You were right, Beatty thought. I should have listened to you. I won't let Vincent make the same mistake; the hirsute little rock-'n'-rolling bastard will do what I say ...

He smiled to himself. The whisky was working well.

He awoke. Why? He listened. Nothing. He lay still.

Then reality assaulted him. It was as if he had been awakened for the express purpose of receiving an accounting of his situation. It was half-past four. The vulnerable hour.

You're grounded, he heard himself say. Chances are bloody good that you'll never fly for an airline again. Never. Ever. You'll keep on applying and they'll keep on turning you down. And you can hardly blame them, can you? You pranged. And you're damned nearly fifty. *Fifty*, for Christ's sake. Face it: most airline pilots have had it by the time they reach fifty; their eyesight has given out or they've got heart murmurs or high blood pressure.

You're *ancient*.

When they say 'old boy' they're speaking literally.

What then? A job in an office, pushing paper? Who on earth would be so stupid to take him on, at his age, with his experience?

What then? Selling cars? Insurance? Investment funds? Vacuum cleaners?

God, no.

What then? What then? You've got to do *something*, he told himself. You've got responsibilities.

Instructing? Surely to God, they would let him do that.

But he didn't want to instruct. He had no patience for it, no yen to create pilots out of groundlings.

Damn it to hell!

If it hadn't been for that bloody crash-landing he could have expected more than ten years of active airline flying before reaching the mandatory retirement age.

Ten more years. A lifetime.

He could spend it writing to every airline in the world, filling out their application forms, being interviewed and rejected.

Perhaps the feat would earn him a spot in the *Guinness Book of Records*: The Longest, Most Hopeless Attempt to obtain a Job Flying for an Airline.

Beside him, Diane stirred gently, then resumed her soft and regular breathing. No sound from Vincent's room. Why the hell was everyone sleeping so bloody soundly? Didn't they realize there was a family crisis?

Don't work, he told himself. You have insurance money and savings. Sell the house. Get a place, a tiny, cosy place in Cornwall.

Then what? Gradual deterioration? Slow-but-sure decomposition?

He had failed his wife and son. That much was undeniable. He had proved inadequate, unable to meet the challenge ... He grimaced. The weary platitudes kept floating before him like head-lines from religious advertisements.

Fear lay on his stomach like a cold hand.

Hell, man, you'll be lucky to find a job earning you a thousand a year outside the world of aviation. What good are you? What do you have to offer except the ability to fly several types of large aeroplanes?

The last veneer of hope seemed to peel away. Perhaps *nothing* would turn up. Perhaps he would keep looking, without result. It was possible. Probable, even.

His heart pounded. He could hear it. Loud, panicky. In a moment it would disturb Diane.

How long was a woman supposed to rally behind a total failure?

Why did I survive the crash? He stared at the ceiling and its mottled pattern of shadows. Why couldn't I have been the one casualty? It would have been so much simpler and neater. The investigators could have labelled the thing 'Pilot Error' without any qualifications. Diane would have found herself a moderately rich woman with the insurance proceeds. And he wouldn't have had to face an utterly bloody future.

To make matters worse, he still didn't know why the crash happened. Uncertainty nagged at him like a toothache.

How could a pilot of your experience, Captain Beatty, permit an aircraft to fly into the ground?

Doesn't it strike you as strange, Captain Beatty, that no other aircraft reported any problems with the ILS equipment that night?

Captain Beatty, isn't it your job as captain of an airliner to be prepared for emergencies?

Surely, Captain Beatty, you don't have to be reminded that a jet engine becomes over-fueled and will thus over-heat or surge if it is abruptly commanded to go from low rpm to maximum thrust?

Would it not have been prudent, Captain, to have declared yourself unfit to fly?

But, Captain ... Surely, Captain ... Why, Captain ...

Endless questions. Righteous voices.

Something had caused the bloody crash. Something. There was always a reason. In Kent, a light aircraft had crashed vertically into an orchard, killing the 5,000-hour pilot. Incredible, everyone said, unbelievable. Until they found the reason, the stupidly simple, fatal reason. The rear seat hadn't been fastened correctly. It came off its runners during the flight and jammed the rear-seat joystick forward. The unfortunate pilot had probably never thought to look behind to find the source of his problem. A murderously indolent factory workman hadn't taken the trouble to tighten a tiny bolt on a rate-of-climb indicator. The instrument was installed in a jet airliner without anyone noticing its deficiency. During a climb in foul weather, the indicator needle had caught on to the slightly protruding head of the bolt. It had stuck, registering a totally spurious angle of climb. The pilot had no reason not to accept the reading. His aircraft stalled. Forty lives ended suddenly. There was always a reason for a crash.

'Darling, are you awake?'

Diane spoke softly, sleepily.

He didn't answer. In a few moments he felt her relax. She slept.

Beatty left the house at eight, wearing his loose track garb. He told Diane he would be back for breakfast in thirty minutes. He headed for his usual route: the path beside the river, then over the bridge, through the wood and back to the house by the railway lines.

It was a fine morning after an overnight shower. The world smelt fresh and good. Beatty set himself an easy pace. Soon he was responding to the rhythm of his limbs. He enjoyed jogging; it had been a part of his life since an A-W doctor had observed an increase of seven pounds between the six-month medicals. Beatty had been aghast. For the first time he had faced the appalling possibility of becoming fat. He immediately initiated a strict regimen of diet and exercise. At the next medical he was ten pounds below his previous weight. The doctor advised him to gain a few pounds.

His running shoes beat a pleasantly insistent tattoo on the gravel path. His body seemed particularly well balanced today, everything pulling and pushing and pumping in splendid concert. It was curious how very much more efficiently one's systems seemed to work on some days than on others.

He reached the wooden bridge. Hardly breathing hard. Lungs like a lad of eighteen! With constitution to match! A phenomenal specimen! No use leaving your body to medical science, good sir, for truly it will never wear out!

Cinders crunched softly beneath his running shoes. Still he breathed easily.

Not bad for an old chap, he thought delightedly. Optimism now warmed him. He *would* get back into flying. Nothing would deter him. Others had bounced back from adversity, hadn't they? Churchill, for example. All washed up, everyone had said, back in 1920. But what were they saying twenty years later? Take Bader; smashed up a Bristol Bulldog doing fancy aerobatics at Woodley; lost both legs in the process. Did he permit that minor inconvenience

47

to prevent him barging his way back into the RAF and subsequently shooting down twenty or more Jerries? No indeed. Losing one's legs was a damn' sight worse than losing one's licence for ninety days. Could that fact possibly be denied? No, Beatty thought as he jogged, that fact can't possibly be denied. Dash it all, he reasoned, airlines *need* people like me. There's always a shortage of really competent, really experienced captains. I have lots to offer. I'm really rather a rare species. It may not be an easy matter to become re-established but I shall do it. I shall keep on trying until I do.

He was aware of the sun as he ran. It was strong and it came splashing down through the trees above him. The branches kept interrupting the light. It fell on his face and then vanished, like the flickering light from an old film projector. An instant of glare. An instant of gloom. Glare. Gloom. Light. Darkness. Black. White. Blackwhiteblackwhite ...

Black.

He had no recollection of falling.

'Are you all right, young man?'

Young man?

'You appear to have fallen down.'

A man with white hair was speaking. He smiled hesitantly.

'Did you hurt yourself?'

'No,' said Beatty. He rubbed his eyes. 'I don't think so.'

'I'm relieved to hear it,' said the man. 'Would you like me to help you get to your feet?'

'Help me? No ... no, thank you.' An absurd question. The man with the white hair was obviously an idiot. Why was it that his features were slightly blurred?

And why was it that a tree was necessary to hold on to, in order to pull oneself to one's feet?

The coarse black bark seemed to pulsate beneath his hands.

'If you are quite certain you are all right, I shall be on my way.'

'What?' Beatty had momentarily forgotten the man's presence. 'Yes, of course, thank you. I tripped. I'm OK now.'

'You came quite a cropper.'

'Yes, quite a cropper.'

'I shall be on my way, then.'

'Thank you.' Go, for God's sake, Beatty thought.

'Good day to you.'

'Good day.'

He watched the old man walk back towards the river. Decent of him to stop. The Good Samaritan, and all that. Must have thought I'd dropped dead. Must have tripped. Quite shaken up for the moment. Rest a jiff. Be right as rain.

He winced, remembering a kindly voice over the telephone telling him he would be as right as rain.

He shook his head. Enough of all that. Forget it. He took half a dozen deep breaths, then attempted a gentle trot. But it was no use. For some extraordinary reason he had been robbed of his strength. He had to walk, slowly.

Diane asked what had happened.

'I fell down,' he told her.

'Are you all right?'

'Perfectly.'

'I was getting worried.'

'Why?'

'Because you've been gone over an hour and you said you would be back in half an hour.'

'Don't be ridiculous,' he snapped.

She frowned, stung by his tone. 'I'm not being ridiculous, Frank. It's after nine. You've been gone well over an hour. Did you go a different way?'

'No,' he said. 'But I went around twice.'

'There you are then.'

She was smiling now; everything had been explained and was in order.

He went upstairs to change. All the clocks in the house said the same unbelievable thing. It was an hour and ten minutes since he left the house. And, despite his explanation to Diane, he knew he had travelled the course only once. Forty-five minutes had been lost somewhere. Evaporated. Vanished.

He was suddenly clammy with the fear of something that he could not explain. What the hell was happening? Was he losing his mind? How could three-quarters of an hour disappear?

He clenched his fists. Hang on, he ordered himself. Remember the time the two starboard engines of a troop-laden Hastings cut out moments after becoming airborne. And the time a great blanket of fog suddenly descended on the runway's end just as you were ready to touch down. If you'd panicked then you'd probably have killed dozens of people. But you didn't panic. So don't panic now.

But those situations were ones for which he had trained himself. He had reacted precisely as countless hours of conditioning had instructed him to react. His hands and feet had shifted controls and levers semi-automatically, performing complex series of operations with scarcely a moment's thought. But how was one supposed to react to finding great chunks of time missing?

Had he indeed run the course twice? Was he so used to it that he simply hadn't been aware of it? Or had he fallen and knocked himself out for forty-five minutes?

But if he had knocked himself out, why didn't his head ache? Why did he have no cuts or bruises? Was it possible to knock oneself out without a mark? It had to be possible. It was the only explanation. Therefore, it had to be what happened.

Diane called up the stairs, asking if he would please hurry; breakfast was ready.

'Be there in a mo!'

All very casual. Not-a-care-in-the-world Beatty. He changed into a sports shirt and slacks and went downstairs. He managed a gentle quip about the length of Vincent's hair and he sniffed appreciatively at the bacon and eggs.

But he had no appetite.

7

Haze obscured the ground. Tall trees and transmission towers thrust up through the murk like the masts of ships sunk in shallow waters.

The runway lights were two lines of glowing balls, fading as they merged in the distance.

The middle marker indicator glowed on the panel.

'Middle marker.'

'Roger.'

The runway was a mile ahead.

The misty carpet was close now. Houses could be seen, semi-submerged, ghostlike. A car crossed the DC-8's path, its headlights carving twin tunnels through the fog.

Vaughan checked the altitude and airspeed for the last time. Now it was his turn to take the controls. Ackroyd, the first officer, had been flying the instrument approach, his eyes glued on the instruments. Beside him, Vaughan had spent most of the descent concentrating on the outside. Now he watched the approaching runway lights. His hands touched the controls lightly. A glow on the panel. Minimum descent.

'I have control,' said Vaughan.

Ackroyd raised his hands a few inches above the yoke.

The lights beckoned, brighter and braver with every speeding yard.

The threshold of the runway swept below. The white centre line stretched away into the mist. Black tyre marks stained the concrete.

Vaughan eased back on the control column, lifting the DC-8's shapely nose. Her speed dropped as the broad undersurfaces of her wings met the rushing air.

'One twenty-five.'

Vaughan held her off by progressively raising her nose. Her speed slackened. She was almost a creature of the earth again as she was systematically robbed of the velocity she needed to stay aloft. Vaughan held her off until she could fly no more. The air flowing over her wings and tail lost its strength. She stalled; she fell. But at the moment of stalling, her wheels were within inches of the runway. She touched down silkily with scarcely a bump on her main gear. A moment later her nose gear settled.

'Reverse thrust.'

With a howl from her four JT3D engines, the hundred-ton jet slowed to a moderate pace.

'A smoothie, Captain,' said Ackroyd.

'Got to get it right once in a while,' said Vaughan with the modesty the occasion demanded. He turned the aircraft on to a taxi-way. The terminal building lay ahead, shrouded in the mist.

'How do you rate it?' Vaughan asked. The company was checking out the instrument landing system which he and Ackroyd had just used: one pilot flying the approach, the other handling the touchdown.

'Good,' said Ackroyd with enthusiasm. 'I've never liked that moment when you suddenly have to adjust to looking at a runway after you've had your eyes on a little dial for the last fifteen minutes. I'd say this idea is good. How about you?'

'It's OK,' Vaughan agreed. 'I guess the only problem is that the control of the aircraft is being taken over at the most critical instant. Suppose the trim is a bit off but the pilot who's done the instrument approach just happens to like it that way. It could be a shock for the pilot who takes over—at a bad time.'

'Is the company going to make it standard?'

'It depends on how the crews rate it.'

He closed the telephone door behind him.

Chances are, he thought, she won't even remember you.

Charles who? Ah, I recall now—the elderly airline pilot.

I hope she does say that. I deserve it.

He assembled a small heap of nickels, dimes and quarters. No credit-card calls this time. Such calls were itemized on monthly statements, complete with names of cities and the numbers. Evidence for the prosecution.

'Operator. Can I help you?'

'I want to call Toronto, Canada.'

He gave her the number and waited, betting that the phone would be slammed in his ear the moment he identified himself.

But she most likely wouldn't be in. Why the hell *should* she be in? She was an attractive girl, wasn't she? Why wouldn't she be out having a good time? One thing was for sure: she wouldn't have been spending the last three weeks waiting to hear from one Charles Vaughan.

Probably hates my guts. Can't blame her.

Big of you.

'That'll be sixty cents for the first three minutes.'

Vaughan injected the coins. Soon the dull, far-off sound of the ringing could be heard. The operator asked the number of the telephone from which Vaughan was calling. He was absurdly alarmed. Should he tell her? Would the call be recorded in some black book somewhere? Stupid! They always asked the number on call-box long-distance calls.

'Hullo.'

One word. And he could picture her face in every detail (after twenty-one days of trying to reassemble the parts in his memory).

'Lee?'

'Yes. Chuck?'

'Yes——'

'Chuck!' She laughed in her open way, without reserve. 'You bastard!'

'I——'

'Ever since I met you I've had a crick in my neck from looking up at every damned jet that goes by.'

'I'm sorry about that but——'

'Where are you calling from? Are you here in town?'

'No, Buffalo.'

'That's not far. Are you coming to Toronto? How long have you got? God, but it's good to hear your voice again, you know that?'

It disintegrated. It was as if her ebullience was a projectile that shattered the whole silly assemblage of logic, of phrases, the step-by-step apologies and explanations, the reasons, the protestations. Now the words had become, quite literally, unspeakable.

'I'll rent a car,' he said.

'Take care. There's gobs of fog about.'

'I noticed.'

'Yes of course! Stupid of me. Was it bad?'

'Not very. How long does it take to get to Toronto from here?'

'Hour and a half to two hours. Take the Peace Bridge and just follow the Queen Elizabeth signs to Toronto. But hurry.'

Frosty martinis. Good gin in cheap, thick glasses. Posters for art shows and bullfights. A veritable jungle of plants, tumbling over shelves and tables. Teak and junk furniture in equal proportions. Matisse prints and two earnest original oils. A highway STOP sign over the bed. The warmth of her, her vibrancy, lingered in every corner of the little apartment.

She tossed her purse on to a chair. 'Should we have a drink first? Or should we get laid right away?'

White skin against black velvet cushions. The soft down on her arm. Her hair falling against her breasts. Her welcoming smile. The touch of her long fingers on his back, pressing insistently, urgently. Clothing sliding untidily to the floor. The electricity of flesh against flesh. Gasps. Tastes of ultimate pleasure, akin to pain. Blood on fire.

They lay in silence. Vaughan dozed momentarily. He awoke to find his head between her breasts. They were rubbery and smelled deliciously of her sweat. He told her one nipple was erect, the other flaccid. Then he kissed her, slowly, methodically, from head to toe.

She said, 'Did I say anything obscene?'

'I didn't notice,' he said. 'Well, maybe I did. But I couldn't repeat what you said, not in the presence of a lady.'

She smiled. 'Was it very obscene?'

'Unbelievably.'

'That's because our sex was so good. I can't hold back when it's good. It probably means I'm a rather terrible person, all those vile things locked up inside, bubbling away, waiting to burst out.'

'You're marvellous.'

'You wouldn't have thought so if you'd called a half hour later.'
'Why?'
'Because I was all set to go to dinner with a public relations man named Felix. A very dull public relations man.'
'Why go out with him if he's dull?'
'It's mid-week.'
'So?'
'Mid-week is a very slow time for bachelor girls. All the interesting men are getting set up for next weekend. Or still recuperating from the last one. A girl can't be choosy mid-week.' She grinned. 'Felix is dull but he's easy to handle. As mid-weekers go, he's not all that bad.'
'How did you get out of your date with him?'
'I said my uncle from California flew in unexpectedly. Wasn't that clever.'
'Brilliant,' said Vaughan.
'I like my lies to have a measure of truth,' she said. 'It makes them so much easier to remember, so I'm not so likely to get caught out. I mean, if I'd told Felix you were a cousin from Winnipeg, you can bet your bottom dollar this would have been the one day in the year when not one plane flew in or out of Winnipeg.'
'You're really quite devious.'
The grin became a laugh, a delighted laugh. 'You're sore because I said you were my uncle.'
'It's better than being your grandfather.'
She nodded as if agreeing with herself. 'Yes, you're a nice man,' she said. 'I like you.'
She kissed his nose.
'You're OK yourself,' he said.
She stood up suddenly. It was imperative, she said, that they had music. Naked, she walked back into the living-room. A moment later the sound of piano, bass and drums filled the room. Peterson. Lee had not only a beautiful face and a magnificent body, but also splendid taste in music. And she was a glider pilot. What a girl. A rare and wondrous specimen. Vaughan found himself thinking how great it would have been had they met thirteen years before. He checked himself. It was disloyal. And ridiculous; Lee would have been only eleven years old.

She returned with two glasses of cold beer.

'Beer's marvellous after intercourse,' she said.

He glanced at her, but she wasn't attempting to shock him or make him laugh. It was a simple statement of fact, a valued truth that she had discovered.

'You quit your job with Air Canada,' he said. 'So what do you do now?'

'Work for an advertising agency.'

'Doing what?'

'Writing ad copy.'

'Clever girl.'

'Not very,' she said. 'I do copy for toilet paper and sanitary napkins. All the things girl copy-writers usually get to work on.'

'Do you like your work?'

'Most of the time. But one day I'd like to do an ad for a tractor or a Boeing 747 or a blast furnace. Something durable. Everything I write about goes down the drain. Literally. I'm starting to get a complex.'

'Do you have family?'

'My parents are divorced. My mother remarried. She lives in Brampton, not too far from Toronto. My father lives in Calgary now. I was married once.'

'You were?' He was surprised; he wasn't sure why.

'I was eighteen,' she said. 'He was twenty-one. A nice-looking weakling. Cute curly hair but no backbone. I despised him after six months. Horrible, isn't it, how you can change? That marriage was a disaster from the start. I went to bed with his best friend and then described the whole thing to him, in lurid detail. I guess I must have a nasty, sadistic streak. But Geoff wanted to forgive me. It was pathetic. He cried—actually cried—when I told him I couldn't stand him any more. And the thing is, I really didn't give a damn for the best friend. I can't even remember his name now. He was a nice guy and nervous as hell. That's all I remember about him.'

Vaughan glanced at a neat row of paperback books on a shelf. Their spines were cracked from steady use. Had Lee learnt her startling honesty from those books? Or was it instinctive?

'I'm married,' he said.

'Of course you are,' she said quietly. 'And you have children.'

'Two. I'm also forty years old—or I will be in a few weeks.'

'So?'

'So I thought I should tell you.'

'OK, you've told me.'

'Don't you care?'

'What, about your being forty or being married?'

'About either.'

'They're truths,' she said. 'Facts. You're dumb if you try to pretend they don't exist. But you're just as dumb if you let them mess your life up. I'm quite a realistic person.'

'I had noticed,' he said.

They caught a taxi at the corner of Queen Street and University Avenue.

'I'll tell you an odd thing,' said Vaughan.

'What's that?' She nestled against his shoulder.

'We've just had a great Italian meal and listened to some good jazz at that place—what was it called?'

'Bourbon Street East.'

'Right. And I'll be damned if I can remember what I had to eat or what the band played.' He brushed his lips against hers. 'I was paying too much attention to you.'

'That's sweet—but you can't possibly pay a girl too much attention. We have infinite capacities for absorbing attention.'

Yonge Street was a narrow Broadway: garish and crude, massage parlours and adult movie houses jostling one another in their eagerness to entice customers out of the ceaseless pedestrian throng.

'Were you born in California?'

He shook his head. 'New York City. Queens, to be precise.'

'When did you move west?'

'Right after I was ...'

'Married?'

'Yes. Married. It's hard to avoid the subject.'

'Don't try.'

Gently he stroked her long hair. He felt her head pressing against his hand in a touchingly feline manner.

'Maybe it's as well,' he said. 'It reminds me what a son-of-a-bitch I'm being. To both of you.'

'Not to me,' she said. 'I'm here voluntarily. I know the score. You haven't deceived me, Chuck, at least I don't think you have. I'm here because I like you one hell of a lot and because you're fun to be with and because I'm attracted to your body. I know I'm going to get hurt, but that's life, isn't it? Just about everything seems to wind up hurting you in some way or another.' She looked up at him. 'You know what my motto is?'

'What is it?'

' "Screw Tomorrow!" '

'That's a very brave motto.'

She wriggled free of him as if seeking space to express herself. 'Chuck, I know you and I aren't going to come to anything. I know it. OK? It's impossible. So I'm not even thinking beyond tonight. Now a lot of girls would say I'm stupid. Maybe I am, wasting my time with you when I've got others around who are eligible and want to go out with me. OK, then I'm stupid.'

'You don't look stupid.'

'I probably am,' said Lee. She patted his hand. 'While we're on these delicate subjects, I may as well say that I'm sure your wife is a nice lady. I'd probably like her if I met her. But I don't want to meet her. And I don't want to know anything about her.'

'I wasn't going to tell you anything about her.'

'Are you mad at me for saying that?'

'No.'

'Honestly?'

'Honestly. Mind you ...'

'What?'

'I think if anyone else in the entire world had said it I most likely would have been mad. Mad as hell. But you're a very unusual person. I admire your way of looking at life. You're very honest. It's hard not to have respect for honesty.'

To which she said, loudly enough for the cab driver to hear, 'If you've got so much respect for me, how come your left hand is on my right tit?'

'Will you be back soon?'

'I think so,' he told her. 'But I can't say when. My schedules are chaotic. They've got me on stand-by duty until further notice.'

'So it could be a couple of days.'

'It could be.'

'Or a couple of months.'

'Not that long, I'm sure.'

'God, I hope not.'

'It's almost six.' He rubbed the sleep from his eyes. 'I've got to get going.'

'You can't.'

'I see that. You know it's liable to break off if you do that.'

'Christ, will it? ... You bastard, you fooled me!' Laughing, she flung herself on him, burying her head in his chest. She relaxed with a sigh. 'Aren't mornings hell? I think I'd like the North in winter where it's dark all the time. You could spend the whole winter in bed, sleeping and screwing.'

He kissed her. 'You've got a foul mouth.'

As he was shaving, she called to him.

'Chuck?'

'Yes?'

'I want to tell you something.'

'All right.'

She appeared at the bathroom door, her arms crossed over a loose, Oriental-style robe.

'I didn't think I'd ever see you again.'

He looked at her reflection in the shaving mirror. Her eyes met his. She half-smiled.

He said, 'To tell you the truth, I wasn't sure what sort of a reception I'd get when I called you.'

'You didn't get the one I intended.'

'Oh?'

'I had promised myself that if you called me, I would tell you to get lost.'

'Why?'

'Because I was mad at you, in a way.'

'What way?'

'You were obviously married—although you hadn't told me then. So you were a lousy prospect. And you made me a hell of a lot too easily the first time.'

'I see.'

'It's upsetting for a girl, to be made too easily.'

'I guess it must be.'

She grinned, showing her bright teeth. 'But all my good intentions flew out the window the moment I heard your voice. The very moment!'

'Imagine that,' said Vaughan.

8

It was a sentence, a term to be served. Ninety days of enforced idleness. Ninety days of reading newspapers tense with trepidation, afraid of finding yet another righteous story on the A-W 747 crash. Ninety days of thinking the same weary thoughts, struggling with the same unanswerable questions. Ninety days of petty irritability, of bitter, unreasoning tempers. Ninety days of shame: of avoiding neighbours and tradesmen. Ninety days of envying the unseen crews of every aircraft that passed over the house.

Faced with similar circumstances, many men might have taken part-time jobs or completed long-delayed projects around the house or embarked on courses in Spanish. Beatty considered such endeavours; he even agreed with Diane that some form of activity would be beneficial. It would keep his mind occupied. But in fact his mind was totally occupied—with his licence and with his profession. It was as if flying were a part of him; without it he was incomplete, only partly alive. Once, Diane said that flying wasn't the *only* thing in life. It was an innocent remark. But Beatty had reacted ferociously. She had no idea what she was talking about; she was an idiot; she should stick to kids and periods and cooking and clothes, the only subjects she was capable of passing an opinion on.

Afterwards he had been desperately contrite. He was the idiot. Would she ever forgive him? She told him she understood; she didn't mind what he said because she knew he didn't mean it. They tried to make love. He failed, miserably, abjectly. Gently she said it was hardly surprising; he loved her more at that moment than at any time since the Christmas dance and Kellaway and Moonglow.

Beatty's worst nightmares involved thin-lipped judges declaring his licence revoked for a further six months, a year, ten years, for life. He would wake, sweating, fearful like a child, the sound of his pleas still echoing in his brain. A dream, only a dream, thank God.

But it wasn't all a dream. He *was* grounded. No longer the admired skipper for A-W, he. Unemployed, he. Of distinctly dubious future, he. Of questionable health, he ... No! No, damn it, he wouldn't allow that. Absolutely not. He was in perfect shape. Always had been. Always would be. Admittedly he had been under one hell of a strain recently, and strain always took its toll. But he would get over it, once he was employed and flying again....

Vincent had returned to school (his hair uncut). The leaves turned. The weather cooled. Sluggishly the days passed, a tedious, tiresome procession, wearisome bundles of hours whose only value was that they constituted components of a total that had to be attained. Diane, splendid Diane, was courageous. She ignored Beatty's savage moods. She pretended not to hear his insults. She went about her work as if he was not in the house.

During the second-to-last week, the telephone rang. Diane took it, as had been the custom since the crash.

'It's Oscar Dowling,' she said.

'What does he want?'

'I don't know, dear. If you speak to him, possibly he will tell you.'

He took the telephone. 'Frank Beatty here.'

'Oscar Dowling, old man.'

The voice evoked memories of a catastrophe, of questions.

'How are you?'

'Same as ever,' said Dowling with a chuckle. 'And you?'

'I'm well,' said Beatty. 'Taking it easy, you know.'

'Jolly good. Envy you, old man.'

Beatty frowned. Was this one of those duty calls? Did fat old Oscar imagine that he was doing a good turn, cheering up the black sheep, bringing him up to date on Corporation gossip? Or was the sod merely gloating, laughing up his sleeve?

Dowling said, 'Look, this is absolutely none of my business, old man, and you probably won't want to follow it up, but I thought I'd give you a tinkle about it anyway.' He cleared his throat. 'A chap I used to know quite well during the war rang me up; he's starting up a new line and he thought I might be interested. I wasn't—well, you know, I'm a bit of a fixture at A-W now. Want to hang on for the pension if nothing else. But I thought of you.'

'I see,' said Beatty. Flatly, noncommitally. No point in getting eager, not yet.

'The chap's name is Amory,' said Dowling. 'A Canadian. Used to run Provincial Airways till the big boys bought him out. Had a nice operation all over Quebec and the North-West Territories. Made a hell of a good thing of it, I understand. I believe the old rascal is a millionaire several times over. And now he's decided to make room for himself over here. It's charter business he's going after, old man, no scheduled stuff at all.'

'I see,' said Beatty.

'He told me he's got an option on two or three 707s, and now he's getting his personnel sorted out. If I know old Don he'll make a success of it. He's as tough as they come. Barges his way through everything. Hell of a good pilot too. Could make a Beau sit up and beg. Treat to watch him when he was showing off. Bit of a rough diamond, of course, but a good type when you get to know him. Anyway, he's in the market for some crews, old man, so I thought I'd tell you about it.'

'It was thoughtful of you,' Beatty said. 'I'm much obliged.'

'Don't mention it, old man.'

'Of course, I have feelers out with several lines.'

'Of course you do.'

'But nothing has been signed and sealed as yet.'

'Quite so.'

'No harm, then, in having a chat with your Mr ...'

'Amory.'

'Yes. Amory. Where can I get in touch with him?'

'He's at the Savoy. Nothing but the best for old Don. Give him a ring there. I took the liberty of mentioning your name already, so he's expecting to hear from you.'

Amory was a craggy-faced man in his fifties with broad shoulders and gigantic hands. He greeted Beatty at the door of his suite wearing a striped bathrobe. His feet were bare; his thinning hair was rumpled; he needed a shave.

'Eaten lunch yet?'

Beatty said he had.

'I haven't. You mind if I eat while we talk?'

'Not at all.'

Amory telephoned room service and ordered a steak and two pots of coffee.

'London's one hell of a good town,' he said. 'Had some wild times here in the war. Really wild. Always enjoy coming back. Especially if I leave Judy at home. London broads are sensational. I have a different one 'most every night. Go home rejuvenated. A change sure as hell is as good as a rest, believe me. Or maybe you know. Uh?'

'No ... I ...'

Amory chuckled throatily. 'Never mind about that. It's none of my business anyway. So you're the guy who piled up with old Ossie Dowling, eh?'

'Yes sir, the actual circumstances——'

'I know all about the circumstances,' said Amory with a smile that was surprisingly warm. 'I don't waste my time talking to people until I've done some checking. You were with A-W a long time.'

'Twenty years.'

'When do you get your licence back?'

'Next week.'

'Do you figure you were unfairly treated?'

'Not really.'

'Not really?'

'I think if it were possible to unearth *all* the facts, in other words if the investigators knew a lot more about what happens to aeroplanes—and pilots, I suppose—under certain circumstances, then, yes, I think it might be found that I was unfairly treated. But under today's conditions, no. They could find no mechanical failure, therefore the pilot was blamed. It's the rules of the game. I knew them and so did everyone else. But the fact that my licence was revoked for only ninety days is an indication, I believe, how doubtful the decision was.'

'You figure you did everything possible to prevent the crash?'

'Yes, I think so, sir.'

'So does old Ossie. He thinks highly of you.'

'It's good of him.'

'Did he tell you what I'm planning?'

'Yes sir, a charter operation.'

'That's right. I guess he told you I had a line back home.'

Beatty nodded. 'Provincial. I remember seeing some of your aircraft at Montreal.'

'Had a lot of fun building that one up. A ball. Did all right out of it, too. I was lucky; I started it at the right time and I sold it at the right time. I guess running airlines gets into your blood. I should be golfing in Florida but here I am, starting over again, risking everything again. Dumb, eh?'

'I wouldn't say that, sir,' said Beatty, unsure how to respond to the bluff Canadian.

Amory grinned. 'There's a lot of business around. I've already got some lined up. May have to do some sub-contracting; depends how soon we can get things rolling on our own. You want to show me your log book?'

He slipped on a pair of rimless glasses and studied the log book in silence.

'Spent a little time on Halifaxes, eh?'

'Yes sir.'

'I was on Beaufighters, but I guess Ossie told you.'

'He said you could make it sit up and beg.'

'He's full of shit,' said Amory, obviously pleased. 'That Beau could be a mean airplane. You had to show her who was boss.' He read on, then handed the book back to Beatty. 'You've got a lot of air-time, mister.'

'Thank you.'

'You think you'd be interested to come and work for me?'

'I ... I think I might, sir. I'd have to consider ...'

'Not too sure about it?'

'It's just that ... there are a couple of other companies ...'

Amory raised a hand as if to express complete understanding. 'Sure, after flying for Anglo-World for twenty years, a little charter operation seems like real small potatoes.'

'It's not exactly that, sir....'

'Lots of prestige, I guess, working for A-W. Lots of respect; must be kind of like flying for the Vatican. And now there's a wild man from the Colonies with no offices, nothing but a whole lot of talk. I know how you feel. But remember, I've been a pretty successful guy in my time. It might not turn out so bad for you in the long run. I've got a hunch this charter thing will be OK. So in the end you might wind up farther ahead than if you'd stuck with A-W. Then again,' he smiled, 'it could turn out to be a real stinkin' bust.'

When Beatty left the hotel an hour later he was simultaneously elated and alarmed. It was marvellous to think that he might be flying again in a mere matter of days. But for whom? And for what? And for how long? Amory might have been a crackerjack in his time in Quebec and the North but he could easily turn out to be a dismal failure in Britain. After all, things were done differently here. Then what? Would the Canadian simply cut his losses and head back across the Atlantic? In all probability, yes. And he'd hardly give the matter a second thought. They were like that, those entrepreneur-types.

Old Oscar is staying well away, he thought. Smart fellow.

He stopped outside a travel agent's. The window was full of BOAC and Pan-Am and El Al. And cut-away models of their aircraft with little wooden crew-members seated at the controls. Posters lured one to hot and glamorous places; all offered bathing-suited girls of varying hues with neat little rivulets of water dribbling between generous breasts.

He thought: BOAC, Pan-Am and El Al aren't exactly queuing up for the privilege of employing you, are they? The letters had been arriving in a steady stream, all with dashing logotypes on the envelopes and basically the same message inside. Thank you, Mr Beatty, but no thank you. Amory was offering a *job*, which was infinitely more than any other line was doing. Indeed Amory might be the *only* one to offer a job. But what sort of a job? It might last only a few months. And it would mean flying in the right-hand seat for a 'while', according to Amory. And that could mean for ever. Back to copilot on a 707 after being a captain on a 747. Marvellous, he thought bitterly, what a bloody success story.

He walked along the Strand. In Trafalgar Square the inevitable tourists were feeding the inevitable pigeons. The sun appeared and played on damp stone lions. Deep in thought, Beatty strolled up Charing Cross Road. It became warm. He took off his raincoat and carried it on his arm.

How seriously could one take a man like Amory? Dash it all, airline presidents were well-spoken gentlemen in Savile Row suits, not middle-aged sex maniacs in bathrobes. And airlines were established organizations in offices, not ideas in hotel suites. Hell's bells, Amory didn't even have a *name* for his bloody airline!

Beatty had told Amory that he wanted a couple of days to think the offer over.

'Sure thing,' Amory had said. 'So if you don't get a better offer by Friday I can expect to hear from you, right?'

'Er, right,' Beatty had said, 'sir.'

But was there really anything to think over? If you don't have any better offers by Friday, he told himself, you've bloody well *got* to accept his offer. You've got no choice, chum, not if you want to fly. The simple truth was that he was branded. Every personnel manager of every airline had his name filed away in a private list of untouchables. If the airline world had been short of captains, it would be a different matter. The laws of supply and demand applied in the airline world as in every other. At present, with the introduction of larger and larger aircraft, capable of carrying more and more passengers, pilots were in plentiful supply.

The fact is, he decided, the Don Amorys are the only sort who are going to offer you jobs. You can forget BOAC and BEA. You've left that plateau for ever, chum. He took a deep breath. All right. There were plenty of opportunities in smaller airlines, weren't there? More, probably. Nothing to be ashamed of, flying for a smaller line. Lots of chaps spent their entire careers doing it. No one ever thought the less of them. The small carriers were as much of the total airline scene as the big boys.

As he walked, his enthusiasm grew. Yes, it was going to be all right. Amory would succeed brilliantly with his UK charter company just as he had succeeded in Canada. And everyone involved would prosper. The whole thing, Beatty thought, may well turn out to be the luckiest break of my life. Things often tended to work that way. It was one of the odd things about life, good luck coming disguised as disaster. The trick was to be able to recognize it for what it was.

He turned into Coventry Street. Cheerful now, he strolled in a leisurely manner—something he realized he hadn't done for ages. Why had he walked only when he wanted to get somewhere? How pleasant to walk simply for the pleasure of walking.

It was warm enough to sit awhile on a bench in Leicester Square. Gentleman of leisure.

He smiled, savouring the warmth of the Autumn sun and the glow of satisfaction within him. Good old Amory; good old Oscar Dowling.

Everything's going to be all right, he thought. It will be a breeze to convert back to 707s. He spent a few enjoyable moments trying to recall the exact positions of the instruments on the panel: ASI, Machmeter, compass comparator, horizon switch ...

He seemed to doze. The instrument panel became rubbery, the dials went floating away, wandering, bumping into one another.

Pressure. Something was crushing his shoulder. Something heavy, insistent. He opened his eyes. An empty cigarette packet, a dead match, yesterday's evening paper.

'Go home and sleep it off, chum.'

'What?'

A burning pain seared through his skull. The light of the sun hurt his eyes.

'Come on, now, let's not have any trouble with you.'

Beatty discerned a policeman, a young fellow with a kind face.

'Trouble?' He moved his shoulder but the policeman's hand remained. 'What do you mean, officer?'

'You know full well what I mean.'

Curtly Beatty told him to talk sense.

The policeman stooped lower. Now his tone was less assured. 'Now you've 'ad one or two too many, sir, 'aven't you?' He asked the question quietly as if afraid it might offend the nearby listeners.

Beatty snapped, 'I haven't been drinking, for God's sake.'

'Are you ill then, sir?'

'My head hurts like hell.'

'I'll call for an ambulance.'

'No!' Beatty shook his head. 'I'm all right now, Constable. I must have fallen asleep.'

The policeman nodded gravely. 'You were almost on the ground, sir, you were, lolling half off the bench. I really did think you'd 'ad a couple too many. But ... if not, I beg pardon.'

Beatty swallowed. His stomach churned. 'It was good of you to be concerned, Constable.'

'Not at all, sir.' The constable seemed reluctant to leave. 'You think you'll be all right now, do you?'

'I'm sure I shall. I'll take a taxi.'

'Very good idea, sir. There's a rank over there.'

'So there is.'

'I'll walk over there with you, sir.'

'No thank you. I'm perfectly capable of walking there alone.'

Christ, would the sod never go? Beatty clutched at the iron arm-rest. At last, ponderously, the policeman moved off. Beatty stood up. For a frightening instant, the world revolved. Beatty wobbled. He caught hold of the bench arm and steadied himself. A deep breath. The policeman glanced back. Beatty took another deep breath and began to walk. His legs felt oddly disconnected, as if they belonged to someone else. Sweat beaded his forehead. He longed to collapse and allow his limbs to relax utterly. There was another bench only a few feet away. But no, damn it, he would keep going. He wouldn't give in. Nothing the matter, he kept telling himself. All that happened was that I fell asleep and my head lolled forward which made me feel a bit sick.

Then he remembered the man with the white hair.

I wonder, he thought, whether I'm going mad.

9

Henry Peel found he had trouble controlling his lips.

He had an almost overwhelming desire to smile, to chuckle, to laugh, even. But this was hardly the time or place. A guy had to look serious, intent and intelligent when he was embarking on his very first flying lesson. Above all, he couldn't break down and burble about this being a lifetime ambition and about it being unbelievably gratifying to get his rear end in the pilot's seat of a Piper Cherokee, after all those years of waiting.

Henry Peel was nineteen.

'You got to be comfortable and relaxed.'

'I am ... really.'

'OK. Put your hand up there over the dash. Feel the grip? Grab it and pull yourself forward until your feet set on the rudder pedals. That's better. You're not driving a sports car. OK, now put your left hand on the wheel. Your right hand's free for throttle, switches, trim adjustment, flaps and a couple 'other things I'll tell you about later.'

The instructor's name was Joe Machin. His face was weathered like old stone; he looked old enough to have been fighting over the Western Front with Billy Bishop. His mouth was set in a long-suffering pout of disappointment at the ineptitude of his pupils. But his voice was incongruously gentle.

'See, the wheel moves the ailerons out there on the wings. One goes up, the other goes down. It's a little safety device; it prevents you raising both wings simultaneously.'

Henry glanced quickly at Machin, ready to laugh at what was presumably a joke of sorts. But the long-suffering pout remained.

'Pull the wheel back and it raises the elevator back there on the tail and the aircraft goes up. Push it forward; the elevator is depressed. Down she goes. Whole idea of flying an airplane is to keep her balanced. Kind of like a bicycle.'

Henry nodded gravely as if absorbing brand-new information. In fact, however, he knew it all by heart. He had read it a thousand times. Ten thousand times. Ailerons, elevators, flaps, slots, rudders, trim-tabs, variable-pitch propellers, stub exhausts, oleo legs, pitot tubes, nacelles, spats: the terminology of flight was more familiar to him than were the names of his cousins and aunts. For as long as he could remember, Henry had wanted nothing in the world more than the opportunity to fly.

'We'll take a little ride around,' said Machin. 'See how you like it.'

'I'll like it,' said Henry fervently. And the smile popped on to his lips like a nervous twitch.

Expertly, Machin's fingers danced over the instrument panel. Master switch, fuel pump, radio, mixture control, throttle setting.

'See the ignition switch? Right there in front of you. Just turn it to the right, through the two magneto settings to ignition. Now push her. OK.'

The machine trembled as the engine heaved, caught and sent the propeller hurtling into motion. Machin checked the oil pressure, fuel pressure, ignition, controls. He sniffed, then called the tower, identified the aircraft's registration letters and requested permission to taxi. A voice crackled something in reply.

'The brake's right there under the dash,' Machin told Henry. 'Press the button to release it and away we go. You steer with the rudder pedals. No need to hang on to the wheel; it's all done with your feet. Try it.'

For a moment it seemed impossibly unnatural; Henry found himself reaching for the control yoke. Then he discovered that steering by foot was easy.

'OK,' said Machin. 'We're taxiing via Alpha; that's the first taxi-way on your right. Just ease off the throttle a little as you get near, just like you would in your car, only this time you're adjusting the throttle with your hand and steering with your feet. You can use your other hand to slow us up a bit more with some brake.'

Run-up at the threshold of the runway: revs up to 1700, the Cherokee straining like an impatient hound, noise battering at the

71

windshield, sending shivers of anticipation through every component. A check-list of tests: ignition, mixture, carburettor heat, slow idle, lights, trim, flaps, controls, altimeter setting, directional gyro. . . .

'Always make sure your door's latched,' said Machin. 'It's a son-of-a-bitch to do in the air. OK, now we switch to tower frequency from ground frequency and ask 'em if we can go. When we do, you keep your hands and feet on the controls—but gently, mister, gently. Follow me through. OK? Give you an idea how she feels.'

He showed Henry how to apply pressure on the right rudder pedal during the take-off run in order to correct a tendency to swing to the left, how to ease back on the yoke to get the nose-wheel off the ground. 'See, she just floats off herself, pretty as hell. Up she goes. Best climbing-speed is about eighty-five knots.'

At 3,000 feet over Southern Ontario, Henry took control of an aircraft in flight for the first time. He noted the time; he would record it later. Machin told him to fly straight and level, to try to keep the horizon in the same place.

It was a delicious hour; it escaped in great chunks, ten and fifteen minutes at a time.

When they landed, Machin asked Henry how he liked it.

'Fantastic,' said Henry, breathless. 'Can I have another hour now?'

Machin shook his grizzled head. 'Got another student waiting. How about Wednesday first thing?'

'I'll be there,' said Henry.

They walked back to the office.

'You want to get your licence?'

'More than anything,' said Henry. 'You think I'll be able to?'

'Sure. You have a good feeling for the controls. Mind you, you've got to get your medical but you should be OK. Then we'll apply for a student licence for you. You figure on making a career in aviation?'

'I might; I don't know. I just know I want to fly. I've been saving up. I have enough for my lessons and by the time I get my licence I should have enough to buy a small plane. Would you be able to advise me what to buy?'

Machin nodded. 'I think we should be able to handle that for you. Wednesday at 8.00 a.m.?'

'I'll be here,' Henry said.

Possibly it was pure luck; more probably, however, Flight Scheduling arranged it intentionally, on order from above. For most pilots it would have been a drag: a late Saturday-night trip into Toronto with a lay-over until Monday afternoon. For Vaughan it could hardly have been bettered. Sunday morning dawned bright and mild. Lee's little MG whisked them to Brockton, a small field with a single hangar, a club house and an assortment of gliders leaning sideways into the wind. Two Piper Cubs were the only powered aircraft in evidence. Glider pilots, Lee explained, defined powered aircraft as appliances for the purpose of towing gliders; they tended to have much the same distaste for power as did yachtsmen. The club members appeared to range in age from sixteen to sixty. Many had British and German accents. They comprised a congenial group and talked endlessly of cumulus clouds 'popping' and 'rates of sink'. They all knew Lee; some greeted her with a reserve born of shyness, others with the exaggerated courtesy born of lust. The weather was delightful; it was an unusually busy late-season day. They watched the students on their 1,000-foot tows, practising landings and take-offs. Towards noon some of the higher performance sailplanes were pushed out to the flight line.

Lunch was a soggy, grilled cheese sandwich in a tiny shack of a restaurant across the road from the field, sharing the table with a burly metallurgist who was building his own sailplane in his basement at home and a red-haired college kid who was still on dual instruction. There was only one subject: flying, and, more specifically, soaring. Through the window the tow-planes and the student glider pilots could be seen, wobbling into the air, tiny engines bleating gallantly, the training gliders seeming to flap their wings as they corrected and over-corrected in the turbulent air close to the ground.

Vaughan observed with pleasure Lee's delight in explaining the club's procedures: the circuit rules, the hand-signals to the wing-man and to the tow-plane pilot, the penalties for staying aloft too long and keeping other members waiting. He met a youthful Air

Canada second officer named Larry who flew tow-planes for fun at weekends and a jovial Luftwaffe veteran of the Russian front who now instructed for the same reason. He examined the gliders: the Schweizer trainers, sturdy as trucks, the advanced Blaniks and Libelles, sleek and delicate. Shortly after two, he strapped himself into the front seat of a metal Blanik; Lee climbed into the rear seat. The canopy closed over their heads—like a transparent coffin lid. The tow-line was fastened beneath the sailplane's nose. Arms waved; the Cub tow-plane wormed forward, pulling the bends from the line. Then, a burst of throttle; a jerk as the line took the strain; the grass flattened behind the Cub's whirling propeller. As the Blanik started its roll, Lee explained how it was necessary to ease the stick forward to get the tail off the ground and balance the sailplane on its central wheel. For a few yards, the wingman ran alongside, supporting one wing. He let go. A moment's wobble, then, almost immediately, the rumbling of the wheel ceased. Airborne.

'We get off before the tow-plane,' said Lee, 'but we have to stay close to the ground or we'll drag his tail up and he'll be in deep shit.'

Vaughan nodded, his eyes on the rocketing ground just inches away and the Cub careering along the bumpy grass strip. The glider's metal bones were creaking. Audibly. Did all aircraft's bones creak? Was it just that with power aircraft the engine noise drowned it out?

Then up, into the sparkling Fall sunshine, obediently following the Cub, always turning in a wider arc to keep the tow-line taut. Lee flew well, with the smooth assurance that is the mark of the natural pilot. He found himself feeling an intense pride in her skill. He turned, awkward in his constraining harness. She grinned at him. Her eyes were grey behind circular sunglasses.

'You're good!'

She coloured prettily, nodding and smiling her thanks.

What a girl, he thought. A goddamn marvel.

At 2,000 feet she asked him to lean forward and pull on the tow-line release knob. The umbilical line went snaking away behind the turning Cub. Suddenly it was quiet but for the sighing of the wind against the canopy.

'Like it?'

'Great,' he assured her.

She succeded in finding a modest thermal which won them four hundred and fifty feet. Vaughan tried the controls and promptly lost the thermal.

'Keep turning tightly,' she told him.

But it was too late. Laughing at his incompetence, they turned gently over the flat countryside, in perfect peace. They landed ten minutes later, side-slipping in to a gentle touchdown opposite the flight line. The Blanik rolled for only a few yards before settling on to one wing-tip. Vaughan unfastened his harness, twisted around in the narrow seat, leaned back and kissed her. She squirmed, laughing, aware of the interested onlookers.

They drove to Niagara-on-the-Lake, saw a Shaw play and ate at The Pillar and the Post. They talked of the day, and of flying and living and loving. There was so much to tell each other: likes, dislikes, memories, fears, hopes. The words tumbled out, to be recalled and cherished. Hours slipped by, each moment replete with a marvellous intensity. That night there seemed to be another dimension to being alive. And only they were privy to its secret.

The air was crisp and fresh for the drive back to Toronto. They huddled cosily in the narrow confines of the MG, the roof flapping eagerly above them. An Ontario Provincial patrol car stopped them near Grimsby. Sixty-nine miles per hour in a sixty zone. It was a charmed night; the policeman let Lee go with a not-very-stern warning.

Love-making was a tumultuous experience. A sweat-bathed marathon in which fatigue and satiation could again and again be converted magically to fresh desire. It was as if they wanted to consume one another; they revelled, wallowed in each other's closeness. Their bodies were territories to be explored and adored. Every square inch. In the morning they clung to one another and grinned like veterans who have won yet another hard battle.

'We should have invited the policeman,' said Lee. 'He was so nice.'

'Your average adult male,' said Walt Przeczek with enthusiasm, for this was one of his favourite topics, 'is a creature with a very low boredom point in matters sexual. He needs a change of female every now and again. Note that I said *needs*, not wants or fancies. *Needs*. That is,' he added darkly, 'unless the poor soul lacks a spark plug or two.'

'I see,' said Vaughan who wished Walt would keep his voice lower in the airport coffee shop.

'I've done some research on the subject,' said Przeczek. 'Fifty-seven point four of the interviewees admitted that they would welcome a change from time to time. The rest were lying. Or lacking. Now, I can't pretend to speak for women, although I do pride myself on understanding the sweet things rather better than the average man. My educated guess is that the vast majority of them would welcome an occasional change of partner too. In fact if we could really get to the bottom of it, I'll bet we'd find that even *more* of them craved a change than men. But the great problem with females is that they are such shocking liars—they avoid the truth at all costs; in fact, they are so accustomed to avoiding truth that most of them become incapable of recognizing it when it stares them in the face. A good example is the relative charm and intelligence and good looks of their offspring.' He smiled thoughtfully. 'Ah, but they are darling things. I adore them. Always have. I'm told that at the age of two I was trying to reach down women's necks. They used to say I was attracted by the necklaces. No sir; it was tits. Always loved tits. Not sure why; hell, they're just lumps of fat, aren't they?'

'I guess so,' said Vaughan.

'There's nothing,' said Przeczek, 'quite like that moment when you encounter a brand-new female and you talk and you feel that chemistry begin to work and you know damn well that she's after your bones just as you're after hers. Is there anything in the entire world to equal that feeling?'

'No,' Vaughan admitted.

'Wrong!' Walt Przeczek shook his head as if reproving a slow pupil. 'What beats it is when you *do* get to her bones and she gets to yours!'

'OK. So?'

'So isn't it a shame, a crime, even, that our system is carefully designed to *prevent* that feeling? Countless children experience it but once. Then, thinking quite wrongly that it is some way connected with love and permanence, they marry. In other words, they never let it happen again. Christ, it's unhealthy! Unnatural! Wouldn't you think that men and women—thinking, caring, feeling human beings—would have the common sense, not to mention the basic charity, to arrange things a little better? What is it about man that the stupid slob can't wait to legislate all the fun out of being alive?'

Vaughan smiled. 'Do you think everyone should be hopping into bed with everyone else?'

'Why not? If they want to, why shouldn't they? It'd be a hell of a lot less hypocritical, if nothing else. I'm not saying it should be *compulsory*; hell, it's a free country. If you don't want to, you don't have to.'

Vaughan drained his coffee cup. 'What's your current opinion of guys who have extra-marital affairs?'

Walt Przeczek shrugged. 'I guess some of them screw around because their happy home isn't; some do it because they have to keep convincing themselves they're still virile and irresistible to women; and some do it simply because they find women delicious and enticing and altogether yummy! But a lot of guys deceive themselves as much as their wives.'

'How?'

'They think what's happening is significant, important. They lose their sense of proportion. Biggest affair since Dick and Liz, Jackie and Aristotle. This it *It*! Guaranteed to last for ever! Balls!'

'Why do you say that?'

'Because, with rare exceptions, such affairs have little to do with the whole man, just his private parts.'

Suddenly Vaughan was saying, 'I met a girl in Toronto. She's young, only twenty-four.'

'Nice age.'

'Yes,' said Vaughan, wondering why he had mentioned Lee's age.

'What do you want me to say? "Congratulations"? Or "You rotten son-of-a-bitch"?'

'I don't know ... it's just that I have a ... problem; I guess that was the reason I mentioned it.'

'What's the problem? You've knocked her up?'

'What? Christ, no, of course not.'

'It's been known to happen,' said Przeczek.

'Well, it hasn't, not with ... er, us.'

'Good. Then you've got no problem.'

'But I have, Walt. Look, I know it's crazy. I'm far too old for her. And, hell, I'm married—*happily*, that's the crazy thing about it. But, still, I can't get her out of my mind.'

'Is she a good lay?'

'What?'

'I asked you if she's a good lay.'

'For God's sake——'

'No need to get sore, buddy. I'm just trying to get the picture. She's built, eh? Nice legs, breasts?'

'Walt——'

'I figured. Would you feel the same way about her if she was flat-chested?'

Vaughan stared, feeling the heat of anger in his cheeks. 'What the hell sort of a question is that?'

'A perfectly valid question,' said Przeczek mildly. 'I've been through this, you know. And, yes, you do know because that was why you told me about this chick in the first place, right? And I want to help you, Chuck, I honestly do. Tell me, when you think of her, what do you remember?'

'Remember?'

'Sure. Do you remember all those deep, philosophical discussions the two of you had, all those learned yaks about books and life and the finer things. Or do you remember scrambling around in the sack with her for hour after hour?'

'Christ, Walt, I——'

'No need to tell me. I know. Bet you found you were quite a swordsman with her, right? Surprised even yourself, didn't you? You had no idea you could swing that long, did you? Suddenly you found you were nineteen again with a pencil full of lead. Believe me, buddy, it's because of the change of scenery——'

'I'm going,' snapped Vaughan.

Walt Przeczek grasped his arm. His voice was low, harsh and sincere. 'I'm telling you the truth, Chuck. I'm giving you the benefit of a hell of a lot of experience—painful experience. I'm as ashamed as hell about most of it. Truly. Deceive Sue if you have to, Chuck. But for Christ's sake don't deceive yourself. Get laid. Enjoy it. But don't rate it as any more important than it really is ...'

The anger boiled over.

'You bastard, go to hell!'

'Chuck, I'm telling you the *truth*!'

'You couldn't see the truth if you fell over it, you cynical son-of-a-bitch!'

Heads turned as Vaughan strode angrily out of the coffee shop, his shoes beating a brisk tattoo on the tiled floor.

Alone at the table, Walt Przeczek sighed. It was impossible to be honest with some guys. Poor old Chuck. Such a sweet guy. Why was it that it was always the sweet guys who got hurt the most? Why was that?

10

T. Roydon Goodall, M.D., F.R.C.P., D.P.M., M.R.C., Psych., positioned his note-pad in the centre of his desk, equidistant between his onyx ashtray and his electric digital clock. He then arranged his pen, calendar and appointment book in a perfectly straight line along the far edge of the desk. He liked tidy appurtenances. It often amused him to reflect that this passion for tidiness was in all probability a subconscious reaction to the extreme untidiness of most of his patients' lives.

Dr Goodall's person, although short and distinctly overweight, was as neat as his desk. His white shirt was crisp, the starched collar-points standing rigidly on either side of a grey tie boasting a superbly symmetrical gully immediately below the knot. His suit was a black pin-stripe. Dr Goodall's kind, round face was clean-shaven; he wore the remnants of his dark hair brushed smoothly across his skull in a gallant, if not totally successful attempt to cover it.

Mrs Latham buzzed.

'Mr Carter,' she announced in her somewhat strident tones.

Carter. New patient. Telephoned last Friday for the first appointment. A private patient, therefore unquestionably an admirable fellow, Dr Goodall thought with a smile.

He rose and crossed to the door. Through the refracted glass panel he was able to have a leisurely look at Mr Carter without Mr Carter's knowledge. Such looks were often helpful; patients could sometimes undergo veritable metamorphoses between the waiting room and the office. Carter seemed a well set-up fellow, head firmly placed on shoulders, nothing apparently lolling or drooping. Dr Goodall frowned. There was something familiar about Mr Carter. Where had he seen him before? The golf club?

The bank? He concentrated for a moment; but it was no use; he couldn't recall. No matter. He opened the door and asked Mr Carter to enter.

They exchanged good mornings. Carter spoke well, distinctly, firmly, but he seemed ill at ease. He glanced around the room as if expecting to find someone hidden behind the coat-rack. He wore a good-quality blazer and striped tie—silk by the look of it. His hair was well-trimmed. One might take him for a military type in mufti, Dr Goodall reflected. And, by George, there *was* something familiar about him.

'You are aware that I'm a psychiatrist, Mr Carter?'

'Yes, of course.'

'I mention it only because people have been known to come and see me in regard to everything from gallstones to gout.'

Mr Carter's smile was brief. 'I know you're a psychiatrist. I looked you up in the medical directory.'

'I see.'

'You don't remember me, do you?'

Dr Goodall shrugged, smiling vaguely. 'To be perfectly honest, it did cross my mind that our paths might have crossed at some time or other.'

'I had a little trouble recognizing you too.'

'Me?'

'At school I used to call you Hoke—but I can't remember why.'

'Good lord!' Suddenly Dr Goodall knew. 'Frank Beatty! Of course, I should have known you at once. How extraordinarily nice to see you.'

'Thank you, Hoke. It's good to see you too. You're looking well.'

'I rather think the years have been kinder to you,' smiled Dr Goodall, touching his slightly protruding stomach and thinning hair. Then he frowned to himself, alarmed. Why was Frank calling himself James Carter? Were the police after him? Was he a criminal? A murderer? A spy? The awful possibilities were numberless. A slight squeakiness affected Dr Goodall's voice as he asked Frank about the name Carter.

'I'll explain it in a minute, Hoke. It's quite simple.'

'I'm sure it is.' Dr Goodall smiled in what he hoped was a

casual way. But apprehension had formed a doughy-like lump in his stomach. And it was obvious that Frank was no more relaxed; he kept entangling his fingers as he said:

'I'm delighted to see that you've done so well, Hoke. Harley Street and everything. Most impressive. I read about your success in the Old Boys' Newsletter some time ago. Imagine that old rag actually being of some real value!'

'Imagine,' said Dr Goodall.

'It's been ... a long time. Years and years.'

'Thirty or more.'

'Hardly seems possible, does it?'

'Hardly,' said Dr Goodall. Most probably a loan, he thought with distaste. Or he's selling some beastly rotten mining stock.

'And, Hoke, have no fear. I'm not here to sell you anything or touch you for a loan.'

'I didn't think for a moment ...'

'You probably did and I don't blame you. But the fact of the matter is, I'm here solely because I need your professional services—or, rather, I think I need them.'

'I see.' Dr Goodall felt the doughy lump begin to dissolve. Good chap, Frank, always was. 'Perhaps we ought to start out with a spot of personal background. Often very helpful. Helps one get the full picture. You went into the RAF, didn't you? You were jolly keen on aeroplanes.'

'You remember, do you? Yes, I was in the RAF for a few years.'

'And what do you do now?'

'Now? I'm ... a commercial traveller.'

'A salesman.'

'What? Oh yes. That's right, a salesman.'

'What do you sell?'

'Aircraft parts ... and systems ... electronics, that sort of thing.'

'Interesting. Are you married, Frank—sorry, Mr Carter?'

'Yes, and I have a son of twelve. And you, Hoke?'

'Regretfully, no. I still live with Mother. You recall her, I imagine.'

'Yes, rather. She's well, I hope.'

'Very, for her age.'

'I'm glad. Hoke, will you be a friend and put me down on your records as James Carter?'

Dr Goodall had been considering the question for several minutes. No law stated that a chap had to demand proof of identity from private patients. Presumably then, such a patient could call himself Attila the Hun if the fancy took him. On the other hand, in a Court of Law, a chap could hardly claim that he didn't know the true identity of a patient who had been a close chum at school ...

Frank said, 'The reason I want to use a pseudonym, Hoke, is my employers. They're rather a sticky lot, if you know what I mean. Now, if there's nothing wrong with me, I'd much rather they never knew that I had ever been to see you. If there is something wrong with me, it really won't matter much because I probably won't be able to continue working for them. You see the pickle I'm in, don't you?'

'Of course,' said Dr Goodall, relieved that Frank had provided a good reason, a reason that a chap could stoutly defend for an old school chum.

He placed the fingertips of one hand against those of the other hand and then spread his fingers as if attempting to describe a blossoming flower. 'Perhaps you should tell me about your ... problem.'

Frank nodded. 'I'll try, Hoke. It's a bit difficult because I don't quite know what I'm talking about, but I'm afraid I may be heading for some sort of mental breakdown.'

'What makes you say that?'

'A couple of times I seem to have ... well, faded away. I've woken up to find that I've been *out*.'

'Asleep?'

'In a way. Once I was jogging. I found that I had fallen down.'

'Perhaps you slipped and knocked yourself out.'

'Perhaps I did.'

'But you don't think so.'

'I don't *know*, that's the trouble.'

'Has it happened more than once?'

'Yes, yesterday. I was sitting on a bench in Leicester Square. A policeman thought I was drunk. I had almost fallen off the bench.'

'Well, one does tend to doze more, Frank, the older one gets. I do it myself, quite frequently. Mother has spoken to me about it several times.'

'It's more than a doze, Hoke. It's a sort of ... *cutting off.*'

'Have you consulted your family doctor?'

'No.'

'Your wife?'

'No. She knows nothing about it.'

'Why is that?'

'I don't want to worry her needlessly. If it's nothing, I'd much rather she didn't know about it.'

'I understand.' Dr Goodall nodded thoughtfully. 'Naturally, I'll be most happy to do whatever I can, Frank. First, it might be as well if I quickly checked your heart, lungs, blood pressure, that sort of thing. Odd, how frequently a problem in one location is associated with a symptom in another....'

Amory answered the telephone with a characteristic 'Yup?'

'It's Frank Beatty, Mr Amory.'

'Sure. How are you?'

'Fine, sir. And you?'

'Never better. Well, what's the good word?'

'I would, er, like to take you up on your offer ... if you still want me, that is.'

Amory's heavy chuckle sounded metallic over the telephone. 'You decided in our favour, eh?'

'Yes, you might say that, sir.'

'Good show.' The ancient RAFism sounded odd with a Canadian accent. 'When can you start?'

'Whenever you want me, sir.'

'How about tomorrow morning?'

'First-rate.'

'OK. Gatwick. Nine a.m. I've got an office up on the second floor—only you call it the first floor. Just ask. You'll find it.'

'Yes sir, I will. Thanks very much.'

'See you,' was the breezy farewell.

Beatty hung up the telephone. He grinned. So that was settled. He had a job. Of sorts. Good old Amory. Three cheers for Amory. He was a dirty old man of his word. He hadn't suddenly changed his mind about the whole thing and buzzed off back to Canada. No doubt working for him would bear only the most fleeting resemblances to working for Anglo-World. So what? It was time for a change. And, he thought wryly, time to slide down a few professional ladders. No matter. He would soon be flying again. That was what mattered. And, dash it all, if the Amory thing didn't work out, there was no law compelling him to stay. Wasn't it always far easier to get a job when you had a job? I'm not *marrying* Amory, he thought with a smile.

But there was no point in thinking about the next job before getting started on this one. And succeeding brilliantly at it.

He hailed a taxi.

'Sloane Square, please.'

'Ri', guv'nor.'

He settled himself. What made everything splendid was that Hoke had failed utterly to find anything wrong with him. Indeed he had remarked upon his apparent normality and good health. 'I do wish,' Hoke had said, 'that I possessed your figure and wind. But then,' he had added, 'I always wished that.' My guess, Beatty told himself as if considering a malfunctioning aircraft component, is that the whole thing will turn out to be some idiotic virus and that it's already gone for ever. Already it's something to chuckle about in retrospect. Admittedly, Hoke didn't have time to delve very deeply. Another appointment had been set for the following week; and there was talk of some tests; Hoke hadn't gone into details. He had merely said that there were still a number of questions that had to be answered. But Beatty was convinced that all was well; he had never felt better. Good old Hoke. Had to have him over to the house for dinner some time. His mother too; although, Good Lord, she had to be about one hundred and ten by now. Good old Hoke. Good old Amory.

He met Diane at the entrance to Peter Jones. She wore a bright green coat that she had just bought. It suited her admirably.

'Do you like it?' she asked. 'Really?'

'You look gorgeous,' he told her. 'And no more than nineteen. And, by the way, in case I haven't mentioned it for a while, I love you.'

She glowed. 'You haven't mentioned it for about ten years,' she said. 'Your business must have gone well.'

'Very well indeed.'

'Are you going with Amory?'

'I start tomorrow morning.'

'I'm so glad, Frank.'

'I know you are. So tonight we celebrate. The old man's working again. It's dinner at the Café Royal for us!'

'Frank, that's terribly extravagant!'

'I know; that's why we must go there. It's essential.'

'Essential for what?'

'For our morale.'

'What on earth are you talking about?'

'I have no idea.'

She laughed, drawing close to him as they walked. It was a moment of happiness without reservation after three bleak months. Frank was an entire person again because he would be flying again, revelling in the responsibilities, the decisions, the challenges, fretting over check-rides and medicals, management and seniority lists; and she would again be embroiled in a life of partings, of coping alone with blown fuses and plugged drains, of being the odd girl out at neighbourhood gatherings, of worrying about weather and about the fact that stewardesses were continually becoming younger, prettier and more spectacularly shaped.

Beatty spent three hours at the controls of one of Amory's Boeing 707s. A pilot named Williams flew with him, first in the left-hand seat then in the copilot's position. Williams was an Australian, a taciturn individual who had been working in Asia; an excellent pilot, he was Amory's senior man.

'You seem to remember the thing pretty good,' Williams observed as Beatty performed a faultless engine-failure procedure.

Beatty nodded, smiling. He had done more than three thousand hours in 707s. He had a high regard for the aircraft. She was superbly designed and had no faults except for a tendency to weakness in the travel bars of the main landing-gear. They were constantly being replaced. Beatty had graduated to 707s from the Tudor. He had been flabbergasted by the awesome power of the jet engines—and by their phenomenal reliability and quite remarkable cleanness. After only an hour or two of jet flying he had relegated piston engines to the limbo of hopelessly outdated aeronautical devices—there to join bracing-wires and open cockpits, wicker seats, goggles and tailskids.

This particular 707 had seen a good deal of service. According to Williams, Amory had purchased it from a French company that had fallen on hard times. Since then, the aircraft had been repainted in pale grey with maroon trim. The legend AMORY INTERNATIONAL adorned the fuselage over the passengers' windows. The main cabin had been redecorated; the seats were almost new, having been acquired from a Danish operator. Only on the flight deck did the machine's age reveal itself. The crew's seats were worn; there were splits in the upholstery that had been mended. The metal of the control column was dented and dulled. Paint had been rubbed from switches and levers by years of contact with busy hands. The glass over the ILS indicator was cracked, although the instrument functioned satisfactorily. The aircraft had been flying almost continuously for thirteen years; its log books were shabby relics held together with tape and clips. An American line had bought her new and had subsequently sold her to a carrier in South America; the French company obtained her in the late 'sixties.

'Did Mr Amory buy all three aircraft from the same company?'

Williams shook his head. 'This is the only one from France. The other two came straight from the States. They're good aircraft, all of them. Amory knows what he's doing when he's buying aeroplanes.'

Beatty agreed. The 707 handled well. And what if it was older than Vincent? Clearly it had been expertly maintained; indeed there was probably little left of the original aircraft, parts having been replaced one by one during countless inspections and overhauls. She would do her stuff admirably for years to come. Perhaps she might find her way to yet another owner after Amory had replaced her. Aeroplanes were capable of astonishing longevity. Old Ford Trimotors still flew; DC-3 N21728 of North Central Airlines in America flew more than eighty thousand hours before being retired to make way for jets.

Beatty had spent most of his adult life around aeroplanes. Still they fascinated him. They were as individual as people. Some aircraft plodded through the sky like old, dour men. Some were unpredictable, some were gentle and forgiving. Some cockpits seem to have been designed by individuals who had never flown and who thus had never experienced the nerve-jangling strain of being forced to search for an awkwardly located switch during a landing approach. Undercarriage levers were oft-times placed beside flap levers, fuel-tank switches beside pitot-head heat switches. Under pressure, in the darkness, it was easy to use the wrong one. Many British cockpits tended to favour large, no-nonsense handles and levers as if naval architects had had a hand in the design. American cockpits were generally more comfortable but seemed to favour banks of switches in odd places. No aircraft in the world had a thoroughly good cockpit layout, in most pilots' opinion. There was no attempt at standardization among manufacturers; the result was that important levers might operate forward in one machine, backward in another; two of the same models of an aircraft type might differ in many respects on the flight deck if different airlines had ordered them. Each line had its own ideas of what constituted the correct arrangement of instruments and switches. And no flight deck had sufficient room to stow the crew's collection of bags, hats, tunics, manuals, check-lists, approach plates and signal books.

Amory was waiting on the ramp.

'How do you like her?'

'She's no chicken,' Beatty said, 'but she seems sound in wind and body.'

Amory grinned. 'Good to be flying again?'

'Marvellous,' said Beatty.

'Good. You'll be flying copilot with Mr Williams here for your first few trips. It's Athens for you on Saturday. OK?'

'OK sir,' said Beatty with enthusiasm.

11

It was indeed a surprise party. 'Honestly,' Vaughan assured his guests, 'around eight I was starting to doze and Sue made me get up and put on a clean shirt and pants. I thought she wanted me to take her to a movie! And suddenly the place is full of people! A surprise birthday party for me!'

'For your fortieth birthday!' someone yelled. 'Don't forget that, old-timer. It's not just a run-of-the-mill birthday!'

Everyone chuckled. The ploy had succeeded. The catering firm had delivered the food on time to the Arlens; the extra liquor and mixes had arrived as planned at the Gregorys.

'It's absolutely adorable of Sue to arrange all this,' said Maureen Biggin between nibbles at a bacon, chicken liver and water chestnut hors d'oeuvre. Her jaw worked energetically; she put Vaughan in mind of a brightly painted squirrel. 'You're a lucky bastard, Chuck. There's a hell of a lot of work arranging one of these things. You men never realize just how much.'

Vaughan assured her that he did know. But she shook her head; he might think he knew but he really didn't.

Lloyd Foreman, who sold a spectacular volume of insurance but gambled inexpertly, clapped a hot hand on Vaughan's shoulder and babbled on about life beginning at forty, spluttering with laughter as if he had just created the remark.

Peter McIlvray, who did something at Universal, said, 'When I got to be forty I didn't have a party. I had a goddam *wake* in honour of the sudden and untimely death of my goddam youth!'

Soon the guests stopped talking about Charles Vaughan and his birthday; they drifted naturally to the familiar topics of the prices of food and property, relatives, sewers, garbage pickup, local, State and Federal politicians. As the bottles emptied, the guests became louder and, apparently, wittier. George Phipps fell down the three steps leading to the sunken section of the living-room, he laughed so hard at a remark of Dan Ericcson's. Marsha Wein seemed anxious that Joe Merton look down the neck of her dangerously low-cut dress; she was affronted when Joe told her in a confidential whisper that he was a leg man. Marty Laisch told an involved story about three Chicago prostitutes and a homosexual rabbi. Sheila Dryden had several gins too many and had to be restrained by her husband Carl from unzipping her yellow and black striped dress. Phil Beane suggested to Beulah Fyshe that she meet him at 1.00 a.m. at the Sunset Motel. She agreed; but he didn't know whether to take her seriously.

The last guests finally departed. The last car doors slammed; the last tyres squealed. Mellow and pleasantly tired, Vaughan latched the front door. He went back into the living-room to find Susan sitting beside the window that overlooked the lake. He yawned.

'Care for a nightcap?'

She held up her glass; it was almost full.

'A wonderful party,' he told her. 'And you were a doll to go to all the trouble to fix it. It must have been a hell of a lot of work.' He leant down and kissed her cheek.

'A party seemed a good idea,' she said, looking out at the black water of the lake.

'Damn right it was a good idea. Did you see Sheila? I thought for sure she was going to peel.'

'I wanted to arrange the party,' said Susan, still gazing at the lake, 'because I thought you would be grateful.'

'I am grateful. Of course, I'm grateful ...'

'And I thought you would think kindly of me.'

'Kindly of you?'

'It's really rather funny,' she said, turning to him. 'It's funny because I went to all this trouble for a reason. And the reason was that I felt frightened and insecure. So I thought if I did all this it might solve my problem. And now, because of what I did, I've consumed enough alcohol—and therefore I've acquired sufficient courage—to face the thing that was bothering me in the first place. That's funny, isn't it, Chuck?'

'Very,' said Vaughan but he felt the heat rising in his face.

'I *know*,' she said.

'Know? Know what?'

'Please don't insult my intelligence by denying it. You're seeing another woman. You have been for some time. I know it, so there's no point in trying to deny it.'

'Susan ...'

'Yes?'

He looked at her. The glow from the coffee-table lamp slanted upward to highlight the set of her cheekbones. Only a slight fullness beneath the chin suggested that this wasn't the profile of a girl in her early twenties.

Vaughan groped for the words, but there weren't any. He wanted to apologize but he couldn't.

She said, 'Who is she? No, on second thoughts I don't want to know her name. Just tell me where it's been happening.'

'Toronto,' he said.

'For how long?'

He shrugged. 'I don't know.... Why?'

'It's nice to get one's facts straightened out, I feel.'

'A few weeks.'

'Longer than that, I fancy,' she said. 'I know it's been much longer than that.'

'What the hell difference does it make?'

'Late summer, I believe,' she said as if he hadn't spoken. 'Did you really think I was unaware that anything was going on?'

'I don't know what I thought.'

'You're quite transparent,' she said. 'You gave yourself away a thousand times.'

'Then why didn't you say something sooner?'

She drank deeply of the whisky. 'I guess it was for the same reason that someone with a suspicious pain doesn't go to the doctor right away. You hope the trouble will go away by itself. And I thought I could maybe help make it go away by doing things for you, like arranging this goddamn stupid party.'

'It was a good party.'

'I don't know how long I might have gone on saying nothing. Months, maybe years. I guess some women never say anything. Probably half the women at this party have had the same problem some time or another. But you know, somehow, I never thought I'd have it.'

'I'm sorry,' he said. 'I didn't mean it to happen.'

'Bullshit!'

'It's true.'

'Bullshit!'

'Please, Susan, don't say that ...'

'Bullshit, bullshit, bullshit!'

A powerboat streaked across the lake, its light probing the darkness ahead like some great antenna. Numbly, Vaughan watched it. The air would be cold out there at this time of night at this altitude. Christ, Jesus Christ.

'Do you love her?'

'What do you mean?'

'You know perfectly well what I mean.' Susan reached for the Scotch bottle. With a slightly unsteady hand she poured another drink. She banged the bottle on the table as if demanding his response. 'Well?'

'No, I don't love her ... not the way you mean.'

'The way I mean? What way do I mean, for God's sake?'

Vaughan said, 'I don't love her the way I love you.'

She turned and laughed in his face. 'That's for sure, you bastard!'

It was a nightmare. He rubbed the flesh above his eyebrows. His fingers seemed to burn into his skull. With a start he realized that he was pressing his fingers hard against his forehead. What was he doing, performing some kind of instinctive penance? He clasped his hands in his lap, interlocking the fingers as if afraid they might escape.

'I was telling the truth,' he said, 'when I told you I didn't mean it to happen.'

'Helpless in the storm of flaming passion.'

'For Christ's sake, Susan, I told you ...'

'You told me you didn't mean it to happen. But it goddam well did happen, didn't it?'

'Yes, it did.'

'So what are you going to do about it?'

'I'll ... I'll give her up.'

'That's as big as hell of you, Charlie boy ...'

'Susan, you're getting drunk. Let's talk about this in the morning.'

'Why didn't you give her up months ago?'

'I tried.'

'Bullshit.'

'I honestly tried, Susan.'

'But you couldn't quite make it.'

'No ...'

'She must be some dish. Tell me about her.'

'Don't be silly ...'

'I want to know, Charlie. Is she built? Big boobs? Blonde? Brunette? Nice legs? Does she do a lot of fun things in bed? Tell me what she does. Always willing to learn. I mean, Christ, when you won't take the trouble to learn you deserve to lose, right? So let's hear all about it, Charlie. How does she get you going?'

'Please, Susan ...' He leant towards her—but she shrank away.

'No, I don't want you near me,' she said. 'It sounds like a goddamn cliché but I don't want you to touch me. Matter of fact, I find you quite repulsive at this precise moment. Strange that, isn't it, after all these crummy years....'

'I'm sincerely sorry.'

'You keep saying that. I'm sincerely sorry too. Sorry as hell. But I haven't had any fun out of it, not like you. So I'm a hell of a lot sorrier than you, you son-of-a-bitch!'

The telephone rang.

Vaughan took it. 'Yes?'

'Captain Vaughan?'

'Speaking.'

'It's Mangione, Captain.'

'Who?'

'Mangione; from the office.'

'Yes, of course. Sorry.'

'Captain. I'm sorry to have to tell you, but there's been an accident.'

'Accident ...'

'It was Captain Przeczek.'

God. 'Is he ... ?'

'Yeah. I don't think there were any survivors.'

'Have you told his wife?'

'No. We thought, maybe, as you and he were friends, like ...'

'All right,' said Vaughan, icily calm now. 'I'll tell her.'

'Thanks, Captain.' Mangione sounded grateful.

Vaughan hung up. He turned to Susan. 'It's Walt Przeczek,' he said. 'He crashed. He's dead.'

'Sweet Jesus,' she said softly.

'I've got to tell May.'

'I understand,' she said, nodding in an almost mechanical way. Her eyes were bright with tears. 'Poor Walt ... and May, oh Christ.'

The unreal hours began. Hours of anger and agony. Hours of sheer disbelief. Hours in which tiny worlds were smashed for ever. May wanted to know precisely what had happened. At first Vaughan couldn't tell her. Later, however, shortly before dawn, the official word came from the company that the aircraft had been taking off from Runway 32 of a mid-Western city. After an apparently normal lift-off the aircraft had suddenly plunged vertically into the median strip of the highway leading into the city.

'Those bastards have killed him,' May declared, shaking her head helplessly. 'They killed him.'

Vaughan knew the airport well. If an aircraft flew straight out after taking off from Runway 32 it would find itself over the city's swankiest sub-division—which had been developed some years after the siting of the municipal airport. The residents of the sub-division had pull at City Hall. They objected to the noise of aircraft using the airport. They organized committees; they obtained forty thousand signatures; they cornered the mayor; their complaints snared headlines in the local press, top-of-the-news placing on television and radio. Soon the Federal word was transmitted to all pilots using the runway that pointed towards 320 degrees magnetic: Turn left to 290 degrees as soon as practicable after lift-off; intercept Brewer Beacon, then make another left turn at 2,500 feet to intercept Markton Beacon. The manoeuvres guided the aircraft around the sub-division; they were not particularly difficult manoeuvres provided everything was working properly, and provided the weather was reasonable. But something had gone wrong with Walt Przeczek's aircraft in foggy, wet conditions.

'They don't seem to know why its happened, not yet,' he told May.

'He would have been all right if they had let him fly straight out, wouldn't he?'

'It's impossible to say.'

'He told me about that stinking runway, Chuck, and how you had to turn in case you disturbed some rich bastard's peace and quiet. He knew he was going to run into trouble one day....'

She began to sob silently. Susan tried to comfort her but May seemed hardly conscious of her presence.

Vaughan watched the pale light creeping along the walls of the neighbouring houses. Soon it would be the new day, the day that Walt and his passengers would never see. God, but it was hard to believe him dead. Hard? It was impossible, inconceivable. Walt, so full of life, now just a pulp, one of the objects that the company staff would be trying to identify by means of fingerprints, hair, shirt size, undergarments, necktie, jewellery, anything to decide who the object was.

Sick at heart, Vaughan shook his head. It ached; his eyes were sticky from lack of sleep. What went wrong? Why couldn't Walt handle the problem? Was it that damned field and its Runway 32? Every pilot had his own pet fears. For some it was turbulence, for others fog, for still others cross-wind landings and take-offs. Was Walt Przeczek's fear a certain runway facing 320 degrees magnetic? If so, he might have reacted with far less than his customary efficiency when a problem occurred there. Psychologists talked of 'regression': reverting to sub-standard or immature behaviour as a kind of unconscious defence mechanism. Something of the sort might have happened to Walt, superb pilot though he was. He feared that particular runway—the fact that he had mentioned it to May was revealing; therefore he was probably more than normally tense when using it. When something went wrong did he regress; did he suddenly shed the years of experience and skill and react to the emergency as he might have acted as a student pilot?

But there was no instructor to get him out of the mess.

It could only have been a matter of instants; Walt would undoubtedly have straightened himself out and would have been doing the correct thing in no time at all. But in this case, no time at all wasn't time enough. He hit the ground vertically, according to eye-witnesses. What did the poor bastard think in those last horrific mini-seconds? Did he think of May? Did his life hurtle past his eyes like a movie in a runaway projector? Or did he believe to the very last fragment of a scintilla of a moment that he was going to get out of this near thing just as he had gotten out of all the other near things in the past? There was, it seemed, a useful device attached to the brains of pilots that refused to permit the acceptance of inevitable death. Did it stem from professional conceit? Was it that they simply couldn't believe that anyone with their skill could possibly end up dead and smashed and burnt just as God knows how many other skilled pilots had ended up for decade after decade after decade? Vaughan had heard tapes from flight recorders recovered from wrecks; the voices were calm and confident right up to the moment of impact. No screams. No prayers. Only an occasional apology, in mild tones, for having done something inexcusably stupid.

Susan was beside him. 'I'm going in the kitchen and make some more coffee,' she said softly.

Vaughan nodded. He looked at May. She sat motionless, a handkerchief balled in her hand. She stared at the pattern in the rug.

'Hi.'

Vaughan turned. It was John. Six-year-old John, tousled from sleeping, eager for the day. Delighted to see Uncle Chuck and Auntie Sue. Wanting to know why his mother was up and about before him; such a thing was entirely new in his experience. Before either adult could respond, he pattered into the kitchen and opened the refrigerator.

'I'm not going to tell him,' May said.

'You have to,' Vaughan told her.

'No; I can't.'

'It's not right to keep it from him, May. Do you want me to ... ?'

'No,' May said. 'Christ, why, Chuck? Why?'

'God knows.'

'He was a bastard at times. He hurt me often. But he was a good and gentle man the rest of the time. And I loved him very much. And I'm going to miss him like hell.'

'I'm going to miss him too,' Vaughan said. 'I know how you feel.'

She looked at him. She shook her head. 'No, you don't, Chuck,' she said, 'you don't know at all.'

12

Take-offs weren't too hard, in Henry Peel's limited experience; landings, however, were quite another matter. While the aircraft would float good-naturedly into the air given sufficient power and enough runway, it seemed positively cantankerous when the time came to return to *terra firma*.

Joe Machin was patient.

'People get up-tight about landings,' he said, 'but all you're doing is flying her back to earth and then slowing her up until she can't stay in the air any more. You flare out and fly straight and level down the runway two or three feet up. Then what?'

'You want her to settle down,' said Henry.

'Right. But you can't. Why?'

'Because she's going too fast. She'll sort of bounce and keep on flying.' Henry remembered only too vividly.

'So what do you have to do?'

'Lose speed.'

'And how do you do that?'

'Cut the power.'

'And?'

'And keep on pulling up the nose when she starts to settle. This slows her progressively so she won't be able to stay up any more. She'll stall on to the ground.'

'Right on.'

Henry nodded soberly. He had no difficulty in answering his instructor's questions; he could have answered them when he was ten years old. He knew the theory inside out. The problem lay in converting theory into action. Since taking up flying, he had discovered that air is seldom still, rarely reliable. Trees, buildings and hills create treacherous currents close to the ground, lying in wait for the unwary, like icy patches on city streets. And, he had learned, aircraft could be wilful, like spirited animals. They loved to wander off to the left or right when they thought you weren't paying attention. And then, when you corrected them, they delighted in sliding off in the opposite direction. Machin said Henry had a 'leanin' for over-correctin''; he should relax and nudge the ship into doing what he wanted her to do: coax her, not kick her. In Machin's hands the Cherokee was docile and obedient, settling on to the runway with an obsequious little sigh from her two main wheels. When Henry landed, the very same machine wallowed into the ground in a semi-drunken manner; from the bounding cockpit it sounded as if the landing-gear consisted of a thousand metal components tied together by iron chains.

'You're getting the hang of it,' said Machin, chewing his gum with determination after a particularly bumpy arrival.

'I don't think I am.'

'Sure. Just practice. Let's go round again. I'll look after the flaps and trim. Away you go.'

Henry eased the throttle forward with his right hand. The propeller dissolved. The aircraft rolled; the broad runway began to unwind. It was a moment that never ceased to thrill. He, Henry Peel, was at the controls, was indeed entirely responsible for the safety of an aircraft that was rushing at breakneck speed and was about to take to the air. Right foot on the rudder pedal to keep her heading straight. Controls angled slightly to the left to compensate for the few knots of wind coming across the runway from that direction. Centre line continuous. Gentle heave back on the yoke.

At once the Cherokee soared, as if relieved to be free of the tiresome earth. Her left wing dropped a few degrees. Henry applied right aileron control. But too much. Now the right wing was too low. Up; down; it was as if he was trying to signal. At last she was level. Three hundred feet. Flaps up: lever to the floor. Fuel pump to Off; check fuel pressure still OK.

A glance over the side. Two kids standing outside the variety store in the shopping plaza, ignoring the Piper. What was the matter with them? Why weren't they staring up, envying him?

'Always keep an eye out for other traffic,' said Machin. 'Old pilots are pilots who've spent a lot of time looking around for other traffic. I'll bet Lindbergh looked for other traffic all the way across the Atlantic.'

'Right,' said Henry as if to say that that was his opinion too. He eased the Cherokee's nose down and looked from left to right. Nothing to be seen but flat land dotted with patches of snow. The sun was bright. Henry pulled the blue-tinted anti-glare mask into position.

Machin pointed.

'Two o'clock,' he said.

Henry looked at his watch. Automatically. Idiotically. He cursed himself. Holy cow, he chided himself, you're a bloody *groundling* through and through! Two o'clock meant off the right beam a bit. You had to imagine the nose as the hand of a clock pointing to twelve.

'See her?'

'Well ...' Henry stared.

Machin transferred his gum from port to starboard. 'OK,' he said, 'she's turned off. A One-Fifty.'

'Right,' said Henry. He had caught not even a glimpse of other aircraft. Until he had started flying he had no idea how difficult it was to see other machines in the sky. Now he wondered about all those stories he had read about sharp-eyed heroes in Spads and Camels spotting enemy Albatrosses five miles away and ten thousand feet below. Wonder-men indeed; they must have had infra-red eyesight.

Machin raised a languid hand and indicated the left. Henry nodded. It was time to turn into the cross-wind leg of the circuit. Check speed. Damn! Too fast! Over a hundred! Nose up a spot more. He felt the nervous sweat sticking his shirt to his body. Co-ordinate, he told himself. Rudder and aileron. Keep the ball in the middle of the turn and bank indicator at all times. Trim the aircraft to take the weight off the controls. Please behave, he begged the Cherokee. You're getting irritable with me again.

'Watch your height,' Machin murmured.

Jeepers! Two hundred feet too high! Throttle lever back. Slowly, reluctantly it seemed, the altimeter needle jogged down to indicate a height of one thousand feet above the ground: the official circuit height. But now one wing had mysteriously drooped. Correcting,

Henry gained a hundred feet again. He was flying the downwind leg of his circuit, parallel to the runway on which he would land. In a moment it would be time to turn on to the base leg.

'Landing checks,' said Machin with a yawn.

'Oh, I forgot.'

'Don't forget again.'

'I won't,' Henry promised fervently.

Landing checks. What were they? For a moment his brain seemed to have seized solid. He was conscious only of the fact that he had reached the end of the runway and it was almost time to turn. But he still had his checks to do. Ah yes. Fuel. Left tank. Almost full. Fuel pump on. Carburettor heat on. Reduction in revs? Yes, thank God. No ice. Count to five but keep looking out for traffic. And listen to Machin suggesting, in a slightly bored voice, that it might be nice to let the tower know his intentions.

God, yes. So many things to do. So little time—or room—to do them in. He grabbed for the mike fastened to the window post, dropped it, had to fumble for it. And simultaneously he was attempting to make a smooth turn to the left and keep an eye open for other traffic.

He gabbled the message to the tower: turning left base for a touch-and-go on Runway Zero Six.

Now he was too close. He would have to turn on to final at once. But he was still travelling at well over one hundred miles per hour. Christ, if only the bloody airplane would stop still for a moment and let a guy catch his breath and sort things out. Power down to twelve hundred revs. Nose up. Speed dropping off. Trim nose up. No—wind it clockwise, you dumb jerk ...

Beside him, Machin sat, arms folded, apparently bored with the proceedings.

At last Henry got the nose of the Cherokee pointed at the runway. One notch of flap. Two. Trim nose up some more. Speed: ninety-five. Too fast. Nose up some more. But now where was the runway? Vanished behind the nose. Was this the time to abandon the landing attempt and do an overshoot?

Ah, the runway reappeared in more or less the right position. The speed had now dropped to eighty-five. Not bad. Bit on the fast side but it was, according to Machin, fount of all aeronautical knowledge, better to have too much speed on final than too goddamn little.

The end of the runway sped towards him, its large white number 06 dirtied and scarred by umpteen little black streaks, mementos of countless descents, some superb, some horrendous. Important-looking lights poked their heads a few inches above the ground like pertly interested spectators. Control column back now to stop the descent. Power off. Easily, no chopping. Nose up.

The runway unrolled beneath him, a mile-long carpet of grey concrete. Keep your eyes on a spot forty or fifty yards ahead during the flare-out, Machin had said again and again. The speed began to drop; but simultaneously the Cherokee developed an inclination to wander off to the left. Machin muttered something about making her stick to the middle of the road.

Rudder, thought Henry desperately. Use some rudder.

But the Cherokee had already landed. On one main wheel. It bounced to the other. Then on to the nose wheel. At last, shaking herself, she ran along on all three wheels.

'Oh God,' said Henry.

'I've seen worse,' said Machin.

'Honestly?'

'Sure,' said Machin, ' 'though not without some blood.'

13

Beatty discovered that charter flying had a character all its own. For one thing, it was maximum capacity business all the time; every seat was occupied; there were no easy trips for the cabin crews. As for charter passengers themselves, they were a breed apart. Consistently good-natured and noisy, they were wont to carol greetings from 4B to 22E; once airborne, they seemed compelled to visit and make friends throughout the aircraft. (Sometimes it was necessary to discourage them by dipping the aircraft a few times, announcing over the PA that turbulence was being encountered and instructing all passengers to return to their seats and fasten their safety belts.) Inevitably they organized boisterous bingo games which were a major trial for stews trying to serve meals and collect empty trays. But it must be said that charter passengers were, as a rule, far more philosophical about delays than their scheduled brethren. The reason was simple: charter flights were holiday flights. Ulcerous executives didn't take charter flights to make life-or-death meetings in New York at 11.00 a.m. To the majority of charter passengers an hour or two or three made little difference. Heck, the booze was plentiful. And free. Cocktails before supper; a nice spot of wine with your meal; a Drambuie or brandy afterwards. Couldn't complain about that, could you? What if the flight was going to land at twelve instead of ten? What if the seats were jammed so close together that six-footers had to travel in semi-foetal postures? What if every other seat seemed to be occupied by females nursing six-month-old infants with acute cases of diarrhoea? Day after day they trooped aboard Amory's aircraft: members of social clubs, athletic clubs, glee clubs, international friendship clubs, church clubs, servicemen's clubs. Noisy and congenial, they wore union lapel badges and read the *Mirror*; they joked with the stewardesses about each other's capacity for free airline alcohol and warned darkly to watch out for Bert and George for both were widely known to be terrors with the girls once they got outside a couple of healthy snorts. Every planeload produced at least a dozen wits who, after the first drink, announced loudly and with a genuine pride of authorship, that after two more of the same they would be able to fly to the destination without the assistance of the aeroplane.

And, almost without fail, charter passengers burst into apparently spontaneous applause the moment the jets touched down at journeys' end.

Because Amory's 707s usually flew to airfields where the company had no service facilities, they carried a substantial inventory of spare parts, from main landing-wheels to electric light-bulbs. They also carried a fourth crew member, a flight engineer who, unlike the majority of flight engineers, was a qualified aviation mechanic who could tackle major repair jobs successfully and sign for them afterwards. Amory's machines often found themselves heading for places on the Adriatic and Aegean, to towns in Czechoslovakia, Jugoslavia and the Middle East. There were times when not one member of the crew had even seen the destination before; often, when briefed, they were unsure just where it was. If Amory had been running scheduled services, such flights would have been illegal for, before taking command on unfamiliar routes, pilots on scheduled lines are required to do familiarization trips as copilot and learn about the terrain and the airports and the facilities.

Like most organizations, the Amory company seemed to take on some of the characteristics of the head man. There was a brash, pioneering air about everything. Things were done, but often crudely. Amory kept promising to get stationery printed but, in the meantime, reams of business letters went out with the company name typed in capitals at the top of the page. ('I give people goddam good deals, not fancy letterheads,' Amory commented.) Supplies of company cheques ran out one week; Amory paid the staff with his own cheques and in cash. Schedules had a habit of becoming badly scrambled; shortly before Christmas Beatty found that he was supposed to fly to Nice, France, and Montreal, Canada, the same morning. More than once, Amory himself flew as second officer; no one had the nerve to ask him if his licence was still valid.

When Diane asked her husband how he enjoyed his new job, he said, truthfully, that he never enjoyed flying more.

Hoke seemed a little testy.

'Frank, I do wish you'd try not to cancel appointments at half an hour's notice. It's really not playing the game. This is the third one in a row.'

Beatty couldn't help smiling into the telephone, Hoke's tone was so plaintive. 'I apologize, old man. I'm really most awfully sorry, but it's this job of mine. I ... travel a lot, you see. I have to go out of the country unexpectedly at times.'

'I see.'

'Besides, I've been feeling much better, Hoke.'

'No more spells?'

'None at all.'

'I'm glad to hear it, but ...'

'I think just coming along and talking things over with you did the trick.'

'I don't really think we talked long enough, Frank ...'

'Mr Carter, please.'

'What? Oh yes; Carter, of course. Those tests we talked about ...'

'But I've been feeling so much better, Hoke.'

'Quite so. But I do think they are advisable. They won't take too long, and they could be important.'

'You really think I should have them, do you, Hoke?'

'Most definitely. I'm going to make an appointment with a hospital lab. It won't take long. Now, do you wish me to make the appointment for you in the name of Carter?'

'Yes, I suppose so.'

'When will you be back in this country?'

'Next week. Thursday.'

'I'll make the appointment for Friday. Now do be a good fellow and keep it. It could be important.'

Two hours after the take-off from Gatwick, the intercom signal buzzed. A stewardess with a Welsh accent reported a problem. One of her passengers had gone berserk; he was convinced the aircraft would crash.

Beatty told Hallman, the captain, who sighed long-sufferingly.

'Shall I go back and see what I can do?' Beatty offered.

Hallman nodded, relieved. 'Good show.'

Beatty unbuckled his belt and eased himself out of the right-hand seat. The floor beneath him drummed with a pleasant insistence. He put on his tunic and cap. Full uniform often seemed to help in this sort of situation. Symbol of authority, law and order, and all that.

He opened the flight-deck door.

The trouble-maker stood at the rear of the cabin. He was about twenty-five, thin and sallow-faced. He stood with his legs apart, his arms folded tightly over his narrow chest. His long hair fell untidily to his shoulders.

His eyes bulged with terror. He was screaming.

Any moment now, he yelled, the plane would crash. Its flimsy structure would fail; passengers would be tossed into the freezing air to tumble to lonely deaths.

Sourly, Beatty noted a certain poetical quality in the way he described things.

The rows of seats at the rear of the aircraft were empty, abandoned by their occupants who now stood jammed in the centre aisle, frightened and confused.

'I can't do a thing with him,' the stew told Beatty. 'He just suddenly went potty.'

'What's his name?'

'Birdlett.'

'Is his wife on board?'

'No; he's travelling alone.'

'Damn.' He drew a deep breath, conscious of the scores of eyes upon him. 'All right, I think I'd better have a word with Mr Birdlett.'

He made his way along the packed aisle. Nodding. Smiling confidently. Assuring one and all that everything was under control, or shortly would be.

At last he stood a few feet from passenger Birdlett.

The man was trembling. Sweat poured down his grey-toned face. The strands of his hair quivered as if frightened too. He looked at Beatty and shook his head repeatedly.

'It's hopeless ... we're going to crash ... we'll all die.'

'Everything's all right, old man,' said Beatty in what he hoped was a conversational tone. One of the hirsute gang, he thought. Trust them.

'We're all doomed!'

Beatty smiled. 'I can assure you we're not.' He took a pace forward. Birdlett's mouth opened as if to utter a cry of pain but he made no sound. 'It's quite safe here,' said Beatty. 'Safe as houses. Safer, in fact, I'd say....'

'We're going to die!'

'How do you know that?'

'I know it, I know it.'

'But how?'

Was this specimen a suicidal bomber?

Beatty took another step forward. This time Birdlett swung wildly. Beatty ducked, but the blow caught him on the shoulder. He heard the shocked inhalations of the spectators. He plunged forward, trying to pin Birdlett's arms. A thin, bony fist thudded into his cheek. Angered, he hit back. He clutched at Birdlett; the man's body seemed light and insubstantial. Both men went down, Birdlett's head cracking against the toilet door. Clumsily they scuffled in the confined space.

Now there were dozens of hands, eagerly helping.

'Sit on him!'

'Knock 'im out!'

'Throw 'im out more like!'

Beatty rescued his cap from among excited feet.

'Are you all right, Mr Beatty?'

Beatty nodded at the stew.

'He hit you.'

'Not too seriously.'

They tied Birdlett down on a crew seat, using the belt extensions normally reserved for exceptionally corpulent passengers. A man named Forbes said he was a policeman; he was given the duty of keeping guard over Birdlett until the aircraft landed.

Beatty returned to the flight deck. He closed the door behind him. Then he passed out.

It was easily explained. A nasty scuffle: vicious blows from a deranged passenger: a thoroughly upsetting business all round. A shock to the system. Passing out wasn't all that surprising when you thought about it. So said the crew. So said the doctor at the airport.

Brisk fingers cleansed and purified the skin with alcohol and saline jelly. A solution of pyroxylin in acetone formed tiny transparent patches of secondary skin which secured the electrodes in position. Each electrode was the terminal for a slender wire leading to a control panel. 'Not nearly as complicated as the aeroplane systems you deal with, Mr Carter, but quite interesting. The object of the exercise, you see, is to detect and record rhythmic changes in the electrical potential of the brain. We can learn quite a lot about the brain if we can study its electrical discharges. So we attach the electrodes to various areas of the scalp. When you are fully plugged in, so to speak, we can measure the impulses. They are recorded in waves which assume a certain form. Rate, height and lengths of the waves vary in different parts of the cerebrum.' The hospital technician chattered in a bright way about the equipment having eight channels, each with pre-amp, input circuit feeds, recording-pen amps, dual-triodes, differential amps. . . .

'Please sit down, Frank.'

'You mean Carter, don't you, old man?'

'What? Oh yes, of course. Carter.' Hoke didn't smile. He cupped his chin in his hand and rubbed it as if it ached. He used to do the same thing when a master asked him whether Charles the First was the son of James the First or vice versa. 'How have you been feeling?'

'On top line, except for a silly little incident.'

'Incident?'

'I got into a bit of a scuffle. A chap hit me. See the bruise? I sort of flaked out afterwards, but I don't really think that counts as a *spell*, do you?'

'Possibly not. But you feel quite well now?'

'Perfectly. Don't look so disappointed, Hoke. Surely you have other patients.'

Hoke appeared not to have heard the remark. He said, 'I have the results of your EEG, Frank.'

'EEG? Is that what it was called?'

'Yes, mind you, these results are not absolutely conclusive but they do appear to indicate most strongly—' Hoke cleared his throat —'an abnormality.'

Beatty watched the numbers patiently parading past the face of Hoke's desk clock. He cleared his throat, feeling his insides chill and contract.

'An abnormality? What sort of abnormality?'

Hoke said, 'This really isn't my field, Frank. All I can tell you is that it's a sort of ... well, electrical problem. The brain discharges electricity ...'

'I heard all about that from your colleague.'

'Quite so.'

'What happens now?'

'Again I must emphasize that this is a neurological problem rather than psychiatric. It's my understanding, however, that this type of condition can frequently be treated very successfully.'

'How? Surgery?'

'It depends, Frank.'

'On what?'

'On what is causing the problem. It could be a tumour.'

'Christ.'

'In which case neurosurgery or radiotherapy would be required. On the other hand it might be caused by a scar on the brain. Such scars are often caused during birth ...'

'Birth? Hell, I'm nearly fifty.'

'I know. But sometimes people have such scars and they cause no ill effects until adult life. Sometimes indeed they remain dormant for ever. There's a great deal that isn't yet known about this, er, condition, Frank. A lot of research is going on ...'

Beatty said, 'What is the condition called?'

The chubby little man looked haggard.

'You'll have to tell me sooner or later, Hoke.'

'It's a form of epilepsy, Frank.'

'God.'

'You see, the disease comes in many forms.' Hoke began to talk rapidly, tumbling over the words in his anxiety to get them out. 'People hear the word epilepsy and they jump to the conclusion that it means frightful, uncontrollable fits. But it isn't always like that. And it's not in your case, Frank, not at all. I believe you have a form of what is known as psychomotor or temporal lobe epilepsy ... and quite a mild case at that, I'd guess. It's characterized by short losses of consciousness such as you have been experiencing ...'

'You're sure, Hoke? There's no doubt at all?'

'I don't think so, Frank. But I do want you to see a neurologist, a good man; you see, it's his field ...'

'Bloody incredible.' Beatty shook his head as if still unable to comprehend the truth.

Hoke said, 'I'm awfully sorry to be the one to tell you. But you must believe that it isn't the end of everything. Lots of people have some form of epilepsy, probably a far greater number than you can imagine. I believe the statistics state that between two and five persons per thousand are ... er, affected. Most of these people manage to lead productive lives, Frank.'

'I've always loathed that expression. It puts me in mind of sad little people standing at factory assembly lines producing things.'

'Perhaps I should have said *normal* lives.'

'Normal? Epileptics? Come on, Hoke, don't insult my bloody intelligence.'

Why me, for Christ's sake?

'I'm going to make an appointment for you.'

'An appointment?'

'Yes, with the man I was telling you about. The neurologist.'

'No; I'm not going to anyone else.'

'But you must, Frank. This is outside my field, really. It's impossible for me to treat you.'

'If I do nothing will the attacks continue much as they have done so far?'

'I have no way of knowing.'

'Or will I suddenly go round the bend, frothy mouth and all?'

'Frank, please ...'

'Don't look so pained, Hoke. I'm merely asking you a simple medical question.'

'And I can't answer it. I'm a psychiatrist.'

'Yes, but you're a doctor too. I bet you got jolly good marks in Epilepsy classes, didn't you?'

'Frank ...'

'Tell me all about it, Hoke. I'm really interested. It's nice to know what's happening to one's brain, I always say.'

Hoke frowned unhappily. 'Well, the medical term is cerebral dysrhythmia. It's the result of disturbances in the electrical discharges from the brain.'

'Go on,' said Beatty.

'As to the attacks themselves, they are usually triggered by such things as changes in the chemical balance of the blood, by hypoglycaemia—which is a very low glucose level in the blood; by exhaustion, sometimes, or psychological stresses; sometimes by something as innocent as a stroboscopically flashing light.'

'Which,' Beatty said, 'might be caused by running under a long line of trees on a sunny day; the sun streaming through the branches.'

'What? Yes, I suppose so.'

Jesus Christ.

Hoke said, 'Children tend to be afflicted more than adults.'

'Do they really?'

Why the hell did he say that?

'Yes. Treatment varies, Frank. Phenobarbitone and phenytoin is often used successfully, I believe. Mind you, there can be side effects if the dosage is heavy: drowsiness, lethargy, that sort of thing.'

A minor inconvenience for an airline pilot.

'But, Frank,' said Hoke earnestly, 'you must believe me when I say that people under this sort of treatment do usually manage to get along awfully well. Often their friends and neighbours have no idea that there's anything wrong with them at all.'

'Except when they do odd things such as cutting off ears and posting them to girl-friends.'

'Pardon?'

'Isn't that what Van Gogh did? And wasn't he an epileptic?'

'I have no idea.'

'I read it in a paperback book sitting in Logan Airport at Boston, waiting for the weather to clear. Funny, I never thought for a moment ...'

Funny as hell.

He walked for three hours. Along Oxford Street and through Hyde Park, along Piccadilly, down to Trafalgar Square, along the Strand. He took Hoke's prescription ('For Mr J. Carter') into a chemist's shop and waited for it to be filled. It turned out to be pills. 'To be taken four times a day or as required.' He paid the chemist and walked on. At last he found himself somewhere east of the City. There were cheap clothing shops and windows full of second-hand musical instruments and electrical parts. It was raining now in a sullen and insistent manner. He had a cup of tea in a grubby little café with a dozen customers who talked rapidly and excitedly and looked like Arabs. He drank from the lip of the cup directly opposite the handle. It was a habit his mother had inculcated upon him. 'Always drink like that in restaurants, Frank. There is a frightful risk of germs in public eating-places. They don't wash things thoroughly; they merely rinse them in half-cold water of questionable content. So always try to avoid placing your lips where other people have placed theirs.'

Warn the next user of this cup, he thought. An epileptic used this last!

Epileptic.

God, how he hated the sound of the word.

He swallowed one of Hoke's pills.

'Anything to eat, mister?' A doleful black man.

'No thanks.' The black man shrugged.

Don't look so glum, Beatty told him silently. You're not an epileptic. How much would you charge to exchange healths? I'll make you a generous offer, I promise.

He rested his fingertips against his forehead. Inside, he thought, the electricity is hard at work and operating properly, according to the manual. But for how long? If it goes awry I will probably experience short periods of semi-consciousness. I suppose I might in fact continue to sit at this table, my fingertips resting against my forehead, and none of these Arabian gentlemen might observe anything untoward. On the other hand, I might be wracked by delusions and hallucinations, according to Hoke; there's no telling precisely what form an attack might take.

Perhaps, he thought, I'll hack off an ear and post it to Diane. A little token of my devotion.

Must be frightfully brave about this. Must look the problem squarely in the eyes. It's something that can't be ignored. But it isn't the end of the world. So said Hoke. Who doesn't happen to have the problem. Odd to think that the thing might have been lurking in one's head, waiting for the right moment to strike. Nice of it to pick the moment when one was bringing in a jet to land ...

The fact of the matter is, he thought, you have to find another line of work. But the choice of employment must be a bit limited for forty-nine-year-old epileptics who have never done anything but fly aeroplanes.

I wonder if it's a tumour. I might die during brain surgery. Nasty, shuddery thought, someone slashing and slicing in one's brain.

Oh damn the bloody brain's electrics!

A few rotten sparks.

Anger surged within him. But it was impotent anger. There was nothing to strike; the enemy was invisible, a cullion who lurked deep within the—what had Hoke called it?—ah yes, the cerebrum.

It was as unfair as hell. But then, so was practically everything else in life. A realist, Beatty rarely wasted energy on matters over which he could have no influence; he could not influence the unfairness of the present situation therefore he thought no more of that aspect.

The truth was that his licence would be revoked the instant the authorities knew of his condition. There wasn't the slightest fragment of a hope of ever having it reinstated. Perhaps, under the most favourable of circumstances, assuming a platoon of doctors furnished glowing reports on his present and future health, he might at some remote point in the impossibly distant future be issued with a private pilot's licence. But a senior commercial ticket? Never.

Therefore, he told himself, you no longer have a profession. You can claim insurance against the loss of your licence on medical grounds. But you can't live on it for ever. You have to do something else. Think positively: there are thousands of ways for a chap to make a living.

He ordered more tea.

Selling in a shop? Pushing a pen? Leading a productive life in a factory? Whenever he thought of employment on the ground he seemed to see herds of people streaming out of Underground stations, waiting at bus stops, piling into office buildings that looked like colossal coffins on their ends. Always masses of grey-faced, cheerless people. Always hurrying and pushing. Worrying about being late. Fretting their lives away.

I want to keep on flying, he said, as if he had only himself to persuade.

You can't, you clot. You've had it. Anyway, it's time you had a change. Think of the number of times you've cursed flying. Think of all those times you had to fly on Christmas days and on family birthdays. And all those times you were scared, really paralytically scared, and you wanted nothing more out of life than to get down in one piece. So at long last you have the opportunity of getting down in one piece permanently. There are, after all, other things in life besides flying aeroplanes.

It was a futile exercise. He tried sincerely and gallantly but he failed. There was nothing in the world he wanted to do but fly. It was his life; he had known no other.

It's a bloody shame when you think about it, he told himself as he poured another cup of the sour tea. He recalled how extraordinarily hard he had worked during his career in aviation. The flying had been the easiest part of it; the real battles had been fought in the classrooms: countless hours over learned tomes coaxing his reluctant brain to accept and retain the fact that one horsepower represents the amount of work done when 33,000 pounds are raised one foot in one minute, that pressure expressed as 29.92 inches of mercury is equal to a pressure of 14.69 pounds per square foot at a density of .077 pounds per square foot at sea level, that the balance moment of an aeroplane is calculated by multiplying its weight by the moment arm in inches from the balance datum to the centre of gravity. Information by the notebookful on pressure altitude and field-level pressure, on the coriolis force and the pressure gradient, on depressions and occlusions, on isogonic lines and compass deviations. Hard, unrelenting work all the way. And never a chance to relax because there were always checks and more checks: route inspectors who expected you to know every telegraph pole from London to Madrid and medical examiners who prodded and poked and peered at you every few months. It was a hell of a life when you came to think of it. You flew to God knows where and found yourself trying to get a night's sleep at eleven o'clock on a sunny morning with the hotel full of maids screeching at each other in some grating tongue. 'Diurnal disturbance' was the official term; to groggy airline pilots it meant stupefying fatigue, constipation or diarrhoea (rarely the happy in-between), irritability, sometimes impotence, sometimes a savagely heightened sexuality. Wives' jabs about the morals of stews, Thirty-Thousand-Foot clubs, gossip about that captain and this navigator's wife, about 'switchy parties'. The intolerable but seemingly irreplaceable seniority system. A life of levers and dials, of strange voices crackling through the ether, of winds and fronts and load factors and route weather and alternates.

A hell of a life when you came to think of it. But Beatty wanted no other.

Blast his brain's fuses for robbing him of it!

Rain dribbled disconsolately down the café window.

Beatty recalled that he was due for his next medical in three weeks.

Three weeks. Twenty-one days. During that time he was scheduled to fly about a dozen trips. He would be flying them as copilot, therefore any landings and take-offs he performed would be under the supervision of the captain in command. Hell, there really wasn't any danger, was there? His particular brand of the complaint (he preferred not to use the word epilepsy) was mild, according to Hoke; therefore even in the unlikely event that he began to feel whoozy in the air, chances were good that he wouldn't be actually flying—and, damn it all, even if he was flying, there would be someone to take over from him at once. That was one of the reasons for having two pilots, wasn't it?

Just a few more trips.

It wasn't much to ask.

Then he would go to his medical. The doctor would discover that all was not on top line. Beatty would express surprise and shock. No need to mention having gone to see old Hoke. No need to admit to any symptoms. No need to do a bloody thing except stand still to be stamped UNFIT.

He drained the tea cup.

God, how he would enjoy those last trips.

14

Mr Cox disappeared into the attic. Below, balanced on the steps on the top landing, his wife could hear him moving about in his heavy, puffing way. She asked him how he was getting on. In reply, there was a crash of some falling object. For an anxious moment Mrs Cox thought the object was Mr Cox. Then she heard his voice. Triumphantly he announced that he had found them. 'Gawd, but they're dusty,' he added.

A moment later he reappeared, his blue serge waistcoat sporting patches as grey as his moustache. He passed the suitcases down to her, one at a time. They were indeed dusty—but, Mrs Cox reckoned, since they had been up in the attic since the summer of 'forty-eight, the year before Joycie went off to live in Canada, it would be more than a little surprising if they weren't dusty.

When he had successfully negotiated the steps and had recovered his breath, Mr Cox examined the cases. He was relieved to find them sound; at his time of life, he didn't want to be buying expensive new luggage—mind you, a couple of stout straps would be a good insurance policy, just in case.

'They'll do, old girl,' he affirmed. 'They'll see us to Toronto and back all right.'

His wife giggled in a surprisingly girlish fashion. 'I can't hardly believe we're really going, I really can't.'

' 'Course we're going,' said Mr Cox, gruffly reassuring, as if it was the most usual thing in the world to have a Transatlantic trip in prospect.

They agreed that there was little point in putting the cases back in the attic now; in fact, there would be no harm at all in starting to pack the odd thing or two. No point in leaving everything to the last moment.

Mr and Mrs Cox were due to fly to Toronto via Amory International in four months and two days.

Vaughan watched her as she slid the crab meat out of the tube-like legs. She tackled the job in the total way she did everything. For the moment all her energies and abilities were concentrated on this one task. Earnestly she searched and scraped the interiors of the legs. Not a scrap would be allowed to escape. With Lee it was all or nothing. If she listened to music, her attention was directed without reservation. But if the performer failed to deliver, he was condemned without mercy. Recently she had purchased a guitar; now she practised assiduously as much as five hours a day. Lee hurled herself headlong into the business of being alive. And damn the torpedoes.

She dipped the last morsel into the drawn butter.

'Heavenly.'

'Glad you enjoyed it,' Vaughan said.

'Adored it.' She wiped her fingers on the warm damp cloth supplied. 'Is it on my face? I feel as if I've been wallowing in the stuff.'

'A smidgin right there.' He touched the corner of her mouth.

She thanked him; he said she was welcome.

She looked at him for a moment, steadily. 'I think this is the time to tell me what's on your mind, Chuck.'

'How's that?'

'My antenna tells me you have something to say to me.'

'Your antenna could be wrong.'

'Could be. But isn't.'

The waiter materialized. Dessert? Coffee? Liqueurs? Vaughan ordered coffee and Hennessy.

'Nothing's wrong,' he said.

'I didn't say anything was wrong. I just said you have something on your mind.'

'I haven't.'

'OK.' A gentle little shrug.

God, she couldn't have been fairer, couldn't have made it easier for him to tell her. But he had shaken his head; he had said no, nothing was wrong; nothing untoward had occurred; everything on the adultery scene was still hunky-dory.

He turned the cognac in his glass. Why the hell didn't he say what he had to say? It was simple enough. And it wouldn't be any surprise. Secret revealed: Wife irked: Decision in her favour: The kids: The end. Deep regrets, but that's life. In his imagination he had seen her, nodding bravely but flinching, absorbing the harsh truths like a boxer taking uppercut after uppercut. But uttering the words had become as unthinkable as reaching across the table and thrusting a knife into her heart.

He seemed to be suspended in a kind of maddening limbo, wanting to be with her yet wishing he had the courage to break with her.

The conversation became politely automatic.

She said that Clark Terry would shortly be coming to Toronto for a week's stay.

He said he hoped he would be in town at that time.

She said she was now working on a new account, writing ads for a feminine hygiene spray in aerosol cans. She said her headline SPRAY THEN PLAY had been turned down.

He smiled, remarking that fate seemed to conspire to keep her writing about subjects that vanished.

She asked him what was new in the airline world.

Bigger and bigger aircraft, he replied, requiring smaller and smaller flight crews per passenger.

She asked him if he thought his job was in jeopardy.

No, he told her, it was a question of fewer pilots coming into the profession.

She said, 'Never were so many flown by so few.' Her eyes roamed his face as if examining every feature and committing them to memory. 'I wish,' she said, 'we could go back to the beginning of this evening and start all over. Or would it end up just the same?' She looked down as the waiter appeared with more coffee. When he had gone she said, 'Your wife knows, doesn't she?'

He stared at the card promoting French pastries for dessert. Delectable. Mouth-melting flavours.

He nodded.

'Why didn't you say so?'

'I couldn't. I don't know why. It was impossible.'

Her lips tightened. '*Shit,*' she said. Her eyes glistened 'I knew it had to happen. Sometime. I mean, it was inevitable, wasn't it? I wasn't kidding myself. I just hoped it might last a bit longer.'

'I'm sorry,' he said inadequately.

'Poor Chuck.' She smiled, her lips trembling. 'He has to apologize to two women. It must have been rough for you. I guess she was bloody sore about it.'

'Yes, she was sore.'

Her eyes searched his face again. 'I don't blame her,' she said. 'I'd be bloody sore too if I was in her position. You're a nice man. And there aren't that many nice men around. It's a hell of a job replacing them when they go.'

He touched her hand. 'You sound as if you're talking about spark plugs.'

'What happens now?' Lee's tone became falsely bright and businesslike. 'Is this it? Finis? End of the line? Jesus, it sounds like a song title, doesn't it? I just want to know where I stand, Chuck. The next move is up to you. Hell, more song titles. I can't stop it. Why the hell does one always sound so trite and platitudinous when one wants to sound serious?' She poured too much cream into her coffee. 'We both knew it wasn't going to last for ever. You know, that would make a pretty good title too. How the hell does a girl turn herself off? Maybe this is the beginning of a new career for me. Lyricist. Sad song specialist.'

Vaughan heard himself saying: 'I don't want it to end, Lee. You matter too much. You're important to me. Somehow I just can't imagine life without you.'

'You're not playing fair, Chuck.'

'Why?'

'You're saying dangerous things. The sort of things that build up a girl's hopes. Makes her think there's a future when there isn't.'

'I'm being honest,' he said. 'I'm telling you how I feel.'

'It would be a hell of a lot simpler if you were Felix.'

'Felix?'

'The public relations man. If you were Felix I would tell you to please get lost so that I could get my life back in some sort of sensible order.' She rubbed her forehead as if she had a headache. 'But you're not Felix the public relations man and I want every damned moment I can get with you, because ...'

'I won't let you go.'

'Please don't say things you don't mean.'

'I'm not.' He took her hand. 'I don't know what the hell I'm going to do. I don't know what's going to happen. But I do know I love you and I'm not going to give you up.'

A few hundred yards away a grey-haired, innocuous-looking couple named Hardcastle walked out of the Queen-Richmond Street exit of Simpson's department store. Mr Hardcastle carried a paper bag in which nestled two large cans of paint. He planned to start painting the spare bedroom the very next morning. It was only a little while—a matter of weeks, really—until his sister would be occupying the room; she was booked on a charter flight from Gatwick to Toronto. Mr Hardcastle eagerly awaited his sister's arrival; he hadn't seen her for more than twenty years. He hoped she would like the room. He and his wife, after more than an hour of wondering, had selected a pale, rather beautifully fragile shade of pink. It didn't strike either of them as strange that they should take so much trouble to select a colour for someone who had been blind since birth.

As the DC-8 sped towards California, Vaughan found himself entangled in a maddening game called What Walt Przeczek Would Have Said About It All. It was an easy game to play. You simply spoke and then shuffled a lot of old memories and sat back and listened.

'I'm in love with two women.'

'Like hell. You're getting love and lust all mixed up.'

'How do I separate them?'

'Easy. Lust is the honest one.'

'I don't buy that. My feelings for Lee go much deeper. I can't bear the thought of letting her go.'

'Letting her go? Christ, man, you'll have to pry her free with a crow-bar. Be realistic. You're a good catch.'

'What? I'm forty years old and I've got a wife and two kids.'

'Makes no difference. Airline captains are high on the list of success symbols for ambitious young broads. Sure, it's better if they

can find one who's single but your average ambitious broad is realistic. She knows that single airline captains are as rare as virgin stewardesses, so she'll take on a married model; he's still one hell of a good status symbol. He's kind of like a diploma. "The presence of this Airline Captain (married or unmarried) hereby certifies that the undersigned Ambitious Young Broad can take on the thirty-thousand-a-year-and-up traffic." Don't kid yourself. If you were a seventy-five-hundred-a-year shipping clerk she'd find she didn't have all that much interest after all.'

'I don't believe that.'

'Of course you don't. You can't.'

'Why didn't I tell her we were through.'

'You know why? You were scared of how she might react. Frightened of the unknown. You thought she might throw a fit. Or a knife. Women can be unpredictable at such times.'

'I couldn't bear the thought of hurting her.'

'You couldn't bear? Who are you looking out for? I thought it was her feelings you were so all-fired concerned about.'

'I was.'

'Why? Because she seemed vulnerable?'

'Yes! That's it exactly!'

'My friend, it's time you realized that your average broad is about as vulnerable as a Sherman tank. It's an appalling indictment of the educational system in this country that a fully-grown man could still be under that impression. Don't you understand: it's part of the plot. Tits and legs and vulnerability! It's the formula; it's been working for millions of years and still the male of the species falls for it! It's the greatest con-game in the history of the world.'

'I don't want to hurt her.'

'That's very sweet of you, Chuck. Would you rather hurt Sue? And the kids?'

'Of course not.'

'So take your choice. And think of it this way: If you'd stood up and gorged up a lot of poetic crap about it being a decision that would shatter your life for ever but your devotion to your wife and howling brood was unshakeable and you'd always love her and all that ... If you'd really made a production of it, it would have been something she could have remembered for the rest of her days.

Her big moment, something to savour over and over again, like a scene out of Gone With The Wind *with her as Scarlett O'Hara. Jesus, she'd probably have been grateful to you.'*

'I can't imagine life without her.'

'A guy I know couldn't imagine life without his legs. He lost them in a T-33 crack-up. He made out. He adjusted. People do. It's one of their more admirable characteristics.'

'Losing a person can't be compared with losing a leg.'

'You're right. It's nowhere near as rough. I sympathize with you nonetheless. It's always rugged, saying goodbye to a great lay, especially if she's got great legs and breasts and ...'

'God man, she's more to me than a collection of components!'

'Yes? How much more?'

'I don't know how *much*. You can't measure ...'

'She can. In amazing detail. Women have minds like IBM computers. In a flash they can punch a card that rates you down to the size of your big toe. Age, job, prospects, height, weight, manners, virility, marital status, religion, ethnic background, the works. And in a matter of some three-tenths of a second they can come up with a rating for you. If you get a number one rating, you are pursued with all vigour and wiles. Number two rating: pursue with interest until something better comes along. Number three rating: drop like hot brick. My guess is, you've been honoured with a number one rating, so, brother, you've got your work cut out if you want to escape.'

'I don't want to escape. I love her.'

'Lust conquers all.'

'But I love Susan too. And the kids.'

'You'd miss them?'

'No you don't. I'm not falling into your crummy trap again. I'm thinking of *them*; not me. They need me.'

'Modest of you to say so.'

'I told Susan it was all over with Lee. Finished. Kaput.'

'That was clever of you.'

'But I meant it when I said it. I wasn't lying to her. I'd decided. I knew I really had no choice. I had looked at the situation and I knew this was the right move. After all, it's not as if I *hate* Susan ...'

'Hell no, you have a great capacity for love, Chuck.'

'So I had resolved to call Lee and tell her.'

'But you hadn't done so when you told Susan it was all over.'

'No, but you see, telling Lee was a sort of a technicality at that point. I had made up my mind. I knew what I had to do. As far as I was concerned, the thing with Lee was over and done with.'

'But you neglected to tell Lee that.'

'I was going to call her.'

'Why didn't you?'

'It seemed the coward's way.'

'So you chose to tell her face to face.'

'Yes.'

'You made a hell of a mess of the mission.'

'I know.'

'Now she's planning whether to have Contemporary or Traditional.'

'I tried, sincerely.'

'Hitler was a sincere guy too.'

'I'm in love with two women. I feel as if I'm being torn apart.'

'It's likely you will be.'

15

According to flight-deck etiquette it was an unforgivable *faux
pas*. Captains bestowed the privilege of landings and take-offs upon
their copilots; the decision, positive or negative, was theirs alone.
Some captains were notoriously reluctant to relinquish control;
their argument (and it was a reasonable one in many ways) was that
they weren't instructors and that passenger-carrying flights should
not be practice flights for copilots. Other captains were wont to
let their first officers handle more of the landings and take-offs, no
matter what the conditions. In any event, a copilot was never
expected to ask for a landing or take-off. But Beatty did. As the
English coast came into view, he turned to Williams and asked
for the landing.

Williams smiled, puzzled.

'Any particular reason?'

'I'm due for my medical tomorrow,' Beatty told him. 'This
may be my last chance.'

'Do you think you'll fail your medical?'

'I hope not. But there's always the chance.'

A bloody enormous chance, he thought.

Had Beatty been a run-of-the-mill junior copilot and not a former
747 captain, he would unquestionably have been ticked off for being
cheeky and not knowing his place. Instead, Williams nodded.

'She's all yours.'

'Thanks very much. Good of you.'

Auto-pilot off. He wanted to fly her, feel the life of her through
the controls: the tremor of her wings as they forced air to speed
over ingeniously shaped surfaces, bestowing Herculean strength
upon it, the swaying of her sleek body as her jets thrust her through
the waves and swells of the ocean of air. She was a creature of metal

but she had life. She breathed; she possessed identity and individuality; she was subtly different from every other aeroplane ever manufactured. She was capable of incredible feats but to the uninitiated she was touchy and dangerous. Only a privileged number were permitted to understand her; they knew when to be firm with her and when to be gentle; they knew her strengths and her weaknesses. They adored her because she was superlatively beautiful.

Beatty settled himself, adjusting his posture slightly until he was nicely balanced. Time to concentrate completely. No matter how skilled and experienced, a pilot could never permit himself to relax during a landing; too much could happen too rapidly.

The ether was full of chattering voices: voices from other aircraft identifying themselves, reporting positions, intentions; voices from the ground accepting the intelligence, requesting descents to certain heights, turns to certain headings. The nearer the airport, the more complex the patterns, the more risk of misinterpretations, of lost transmissions leading to heavily loaded aircraft straying blindly into the paths of others. Somewhere in the grey sky were Lord knows how many jets, arriving, departing, climbing, descending. *Hurtling.* The men on the ground had to keep them in their proper places, safely apart. Down to the next aerial storey, recently vacated by another 500-m.p.h. occupant. Turn. Circle. Descend.

'Clear to descend. Advise established inbound on ILS.'

Checks of seat-belt and no-smoking signs, altimeters, speed brakes, pneumatic pressures, ADF, VOR.

Beatty glanced at the ILS dial to ensure that the tiny failure-flag hadn't appeared. It was easy to miss when one was busy and pilots had been known to fly to their deaths faithfully following the directions of an instrument that had failed and was trying desperately to tell them so.

'Established on localizer. Ready to call glide-slope.'

'Flaps fourteen. Flaps twenty-five.'

'Undercarriage down.'

'Three greens.'

'Anti-skid?'

'On. Four releases.'

'Flaps forty.'

'Hydraulic pressure.'

'Three at three thousand. No lights.'

'Flaps fifty. Runway in sight.'

She was docile in his hands as she descended smoothly towards the concrete strip ahead. The ground rolled beneath him: damp, shiny fields, a road packed with Dinky-toy traffic, tiny houses, ant-like people. A bang-on approach, a steady, progressive settling down of 100 tons of machinery and humanity at 700 feet per minute. In 120 seconds the 707 would be whooshing over the threshold of the runway, her bunches of main wheels reaching for the ground. Runway number clearly visible. Brisk cross-wind to be handled with aplomb.

My farewell performance, ladies and gentlemen. No encores, I regret, due to technical difficulties.

The skill in landing lay in knowing just when to apply elevator to bring the machine out of its descent and send it skimming along the runway, at an altitude of an inch or two. Some people were physically incapable of landing an aeroplane smoothly because their depth perception would have them flaring out fifty feet above the ground—or ploughing straight into it. If there was an art to landing it lay in making the machine behave as it neared the moment of touchdown. As its speed dropped off an aeroplane became increasingly vulnerable to wobbles and wanderings brought on by errant wind gusts and eddies. It had to be persuaded, firmly but never crudely, to keep going straight down the runway. Jets were trickier to land than their piston-engine predecessors because they lacked the propeller slipstream which produces extra lift at low speeds and improves an aircraft's power-on stall characteristics and because their swept-back wings were designed for high-speed, high-altitude flight. Batteries of slots, fences, flaps and spoilers were required to make them perform satisfactorily at low speeds.

Beatty relished the challenge of every landing. This one, he decided, would be a greaser, a triumph with which to terminate his career. The passengers would never know the precise moment they ceased to fly. One moment airborne, the next trundling sweetly along the strip. The time for round-out was near. Beatty frowned slightly as he became totally absorbed in his task. His eyes were busy, scanning the runway ahead, mentally computing height, distance and speed.

Now the ground was rushing at him. The runway lights stared blindly at the 707 as it roared overhead. This was the moment. Ease back on the yoke. The runway levelled. Power down. He felt the aircraft's tendency to stray. He understood. He knew she wanted to wander to the left because a strong wind was pressing on her flank. He made her resist by angling her nose and lowering one wing a degree or two. Her speed fell off. Irresistibly the forces of gravity worked on her; her wheels could no longer resist the speeding runway. They touched. Barely a bump. The nose plopped down, the wheel smack on the centre line.

'Reverse thrust, please.'

Reverse lever to detent. Within the four jets, the exhaust stream was deflected; cascades angled the flow at forty-five degrees to the line of path.

Almost time to relax. The 707 slowed. She was behaving like a lady, accepting the reverse thrust without pitching and bouncing as was her occasional habit. Although the cross-wind was brisk, she refused to slide sideways.

Her speed slackened more. Beatty reached for the nose-wheel steering. At this point in every landing there was a temptation to cancel the reverse thrust too soon. An aircraft that has been travelling at 125 knots seems to be moving quite slowly when its speed is down to 85. Beatty waited until the speed was down to 50 knots before cancelling the reverse thrust. The brakes and tyres weren't unduly worked.

He parked the aircraft at the terminal, applying the brakes as the parking pointer touched the windshield, signifying that the main exit was in line with the ramp.

Williams said: 'Good luck with your medical.'

'Thanks very much. Thanks for the landing too.'

'Don't mention it. It was a dandy.'

As he collected his cap, tunic and flight bag, Beatty reflected that this would almost certainly be the last time he stood on a flight deck. He looked around. It was cramped and ugly. But there was nothing quite like it and he would miss it dreadfully.

So long, he said silently.

Thirty-six hours and twenty-one minutes later, Frank Beatty sat in his car at a parking meter near Baker Street. He had started the Rover's engine but he had not put the car into gear. He was just sitting, smiling gently, looking directly at the speedometer without seeing it. An impatient Hillman disturbed his reverie. The driver gesticulated. Did Beatty intend to move or was he going to sit and think about it all day? It wasn't hard to comprehend the man. With an apologetic nod, Beatty backed up a couple of feet and swung the Rover out of the space in a single movement. He waved to the Hillman as he drove off, still smiling.

He felt like a prisoner who has been granted a reprieve on the morning of his execution. Glee bubbled within him. He found himself humming 'I'm Getting Married in the Morning'. He chuckled; even he could tell that it sounded absolutely hideous.

You have a tin ear, he told himself, but, no matter, *you passed your medical*! I'm not dreaming this, am I? It really did happen, didn't it. I'm officially fit to fly.

No doubt about it. He had a slip of paper to prove it.

Admittedly, he had lied to the doctor. When asked the routine questions about his general state of health, he had reported no problems of any type. *(If they're going to ground me, let them find it out for themselves.)* The doctor had accepted the statement without demur. Heart, lungs, hearing, vision: all had been tested and found satisfactory. Nothing had led the doctor to question the working of Beatty's brain. Not given a clue to make him think otherwise, he had passed Beatty as fit.

Lots of chaps lie at medicals.

He felt the flat box of pills in his jacket pocket. They would keep him out of trouble. Good old Hoke.

The sun broke through the overcast as he drove along Oxford Street. He beamed up at it. Life had the funniest habit of plunging him into the depths and then, just as rapidly, hurling him to the heights. He had telephoned the Amory office to report and had been put through to Mr Amory himself.

'Passed your medical OK?'

'Yes sir.'

'Glad to hear it. I just bought a couple more aircraft. Need captains. Seems to me you have done the first officer bit long enough. Interested in stepping up in the world?'

'Christ yes! Er, that is ...'

Amory had chuckled in his throaty way. 'That's OK, feller. I know how you feel. I got to be made captain myself once. A long time ago. I goofed. Did a perfect landing at Toronto. It was a hazy day, though, hazy as hell, and for some goddam reason or other I came down on the runway at Downsview instead of Malton. The two fields are pretty close, you know. Anyway, my employers came to the conclusion they could get along just fine without my services. And I'm sorry to say, they have.'

'I didn't know you'd ever flown for an airline, sir.'

'I don't advertise the fact.'

'I won't advertise it either.'

'Figured you wouldn't, otherwise I wouldn't have mentioned it. Well, so much for ancient history. You're hereby promoted to the dizzy rank of captain in Amory International Airways. Which isn't saying a hell of a lot right now, but it may be one day, eh? We'll talk about dough the next time you're in the office.'

'Right, sir. And thank you very much indeed.'

'Don't thank me. Need another captain. You're it.'

The whole conversation had taken but a couple of minutes. Briskly, as if scared of hearing more words of gratitude, Amory had rung off.

Beatty had telephoned Diane—loyal, long-suffering Diane, on whom he had vented his anxiety and angry frustration that very morning.

'You sound better,' she had said.

'Really?'

'I gather you passed your medical.'

'Yes.' He cleared his throat. 'Er, sorry I was a bit of a bear this morning first thing.'

'Don't mention it,' she replied. 'I'm used to it by now, just like any well-behaved airline pilot's wife.'

He grinned. 'But you're not married to just any airline pilot. And I would appreciate it, madam,' he added with a rapidly assumed tone of pomposity, 'if you would have a modicum of respect for my rank. Be so good as to address me as "captain" from this moment on.'

Diane had shrieked with delight. And he had glowed with the

warmth that is know only to the male who can report a triumph to his mate.

He felt marvellous. Never better. And intensely grateful to Amory and Hoke.

16

On the morning of April 19, after ten hours and twelve minutes of dual instruction, Henry Peel flew solo. It was a brief flight: take-off, turn to the left, downwind leg, another left turn to bring him on to his base leg, then one more left turn on to final.

Henry's instructor, Joe Machin, stood beside the runway chewing gum. He looked bored but he was nervous. You could never tell what a kid might do the first time he got up in an aircraft by himself. Strange things could happen to people when they suddenly realized the father-figure who could solve all problems was no longer sitting in the right-hand seat.

He popped a fresh stick of gum into his mouth as the little Cherokee made its last turn. You're kind of low, Machin thought. As if acknowledging the observation, he heard Henry increase his power. The wings rocked. OK, kid, start bleeding off your power. Henry did as he was silently told.

Thump.

Henry was down. And if his first solo landing was something slightly less than perfection, it had at least deposited him on the runway the right way up and facing in the right direction. And that, in Joe Machin's experience, was considerably better than the way many a first solo had ended up. He sent Henry off to do more circuits.

Fourteen minutes after Henry Peel touched down on his first solo landing, a man in Santa Ana, California, named Earl Gasparac told his wife about the trip he had arranged.

'We fly to New York by TranState,' he announced. 'Spend three days there at the Americana—not bad, uh? Then we grab one of Mr Hertz's autos and it's off for a little exploring. I've got the route all planned. Providence the first night. Then on to Boston. Portland, Maine, the next day. Nice, easy stages; lots of time to look around. After Portland we make a sharp left and head over towards New Hampshire and Vermont—and then New York State and a little joint called ...'

'Utica!' she cried, delighted.

'Right on! How did you guess?'

'Just a wild shot in the dark.'

They laughed. Mrs Gasparac had been born in Utica, New York, thirty-one years before, but it was almost ten years since she had been back east. The Gasparacs had considered such a trip for their honeymoon; at the time, however, they had just made the down payment on the split-level. Earl Gasparac's salary as a Class One Repairman for the Pacific Telephone Company, while adequate, had its limitations.

For this trip he would have to draw heavily upon the resources of the Credit Union. The repayment was going to hurt. But the trip couldn't be delayed. Dr Malcolm had made it horribly clear: if Mrs Gasparac didn't make the trip before the end of summer, she would never make it at all.

A woman in Des Moines, Iowa, counted the money she had been stealing from her husband and from her employer, Associated Security Services, Incorporated, Manufacturers of Ever-Watchful Television Equipment for Stores and Offices. It amounted to nearly seventeen thousand dollars. Amazing, thought the woman, how little bits out of Petty Cash, Housekeeping and the Savings Account can mount up.

'Visiting widows must be a bastard,' said May Przeczek with a brittle smile.

'It's always good to see you,' said Vaughan.

'Of course it is,' said Susan.

'I'm glad you came.'

'How's John?'

'As usual. A ball of fire.' May lit a filter cigarette with a hand that wasn't quite steady. 'Sometimes he cries; he misses Walt like hell. And then sometimes it's as if he's forgotten all about Walt. He goes off and plays and laughs as if nothing had ever happened. I want to grab him and tell him to stop. But he doesn't mean to be cruel and thoughtless. I think he really does forget about it for a day here, an hour there. After all, Walt was always away so much. It's no great change as far as John's concerned.' She drew on her cigarette. 'So how have you two kids been?'

Fine, they said, just fine. May suggested a drink. That would be fine too, they said. Scotch? Fine. But May discovered that she had no Scotch, only bourbon and hardly enough of that.

'Walt used to look after the booze supply,' she said, grinning uncertainly. 'I never had to give it a thought.'

They assured her it didn't matter; coffee would be fine, just fine.

'Walt would kill me, not having enough liquor to serve his friends,' said May. 'I bet he's looking down at me right now, shaking his fist and telling me to get with it. He was very particular about having the proper supplies in his house at all times. It mattered a lot to him. Yet, you know, he hardly drank anything himself. I never once saw him drunk.'

'Is that a fact,' Susan murmured.

'Not once,' said May, 'not in all the years I knew him. He was the tiniest bit mellow on our wedding day—all that champagne and those crazy toasts—but you certainly would never have called him drunk. I already said that, didn't I? How about you, Chuck, did you ever see him drunk?'

Vaughan said he had never seen Walt Przeczek drunk.

'Were you at our wedding? Isn't that awful; I can't remember now.'

'We didn't know you when you were married, May. I met Walt a couple of years after when he joined TranState.'

'That's right, he was instructing when we were married.' She spoke with a kind of false enthusiasm as if trying to add importance to the subject under discussion.

The visit was an ordeal. May was still in semi-shock. There was so much to say and yet there were no words. Talk became little more than a respite from silence. May and Susan made tentative plans for shopping expeditions, bridge parties and picnics for the kids, knowing that none of them would take place.

When it was time to leave, May thanked them for coming. They said they would come again soon, guilty with the relief they felt at parting.

'I think old Walt was laughing like hell at us,' said Vaughan as he accelerated away from the house.

'Why?'

'Because we were such phonies. We weren't honest with each other. Walt respected honesty above all things.'

Susan said, 'He didn't deserve May.'

'Why do you say that?'

'He had other women.'

'How do you know that?'

Susan shrugged. 'May told me. I think he boasted to her about them.'

'I doubt that.'

'I suppose you would,' she snapped.

'Walt couldn't resist women,' Vaughan said. 'He loved to be in their company. And when he was in their company he couldn't resist making passes at them. It was a kind of compulsion. With Walt, flirting was as natural as breathing.'

'I know,' said Susan.

'You do?'

'Yes, he made a pass at me. In fact he made several. What do you say about that?'

'What do you want me to say?'

'Aren't you going to ask what happened?'

'No, I don't think so.'

'Why not?'

Vaughan steered past a parked truck. A man stood beside it, hands in pockets, jaws moving rhythmically.

'I think it would be in kind of poor taste,' he said, 'under the circumstances.'

'You don't give a damn any more.'

'It's not that.'

'What the hell is it then?' Her voice crackled with anger.

Vaughan shrugged. 'It just seems kind of pointless,' he said. 'The man's dead. And if you'd had an affair with him, I don't think you'd want to talk about it now. It isn't something you'd do.'

'You sound damned sure of yourself.'

'No,' said Vaughan, 'I'm not sure at all. But I think it might be better if we dropped the subject.'

Susan was silent for a couple of miles. Vaughan waited in leaden expectation for what he knew she would say next.

'You're still seeing that bitch in Canada.'

He lied. Too easily. 'No, it's all over. I told you.'

'I don't believe you, you bastard.'

'It's true.'

She turned away from him and huddled against the passenger door. Her shoulders jerked spasmodically. Vaughan pictured her eyes full of bitter tears, her mouth trembling. She hated him. And he didn't blame her. He drove faster. The substance of his world, the order, the stability of it, was disintegrating about him. And it was all his fault. He made no attempt to deny it. But he was powerless to change things. He wanted to take Susan in his arms and tell her, convince her, that everything was going to be all right. She *deserved* to hear it. His hands tightened on the steering-wheel. God, was he becoming a kind of sexual schizophrenic, loving two women equally: a conventional family man with his family, a swinger, a swordsman when he was away? The lousy truth of the matter was, in Lee's company, he had no family; conveniently, without fuss or muss, they evaporated—and they never crossed his mind until he was away from her. You are a despicable son-of-a-bitch. How did you ever get yourself into this mess? More important, how the hell are you going to get yourself out? All this, this ... *situation* was the kind of thing that happened to kinky actors and writers, not dull, conventional guys.

Vaughan found himself cursing Lee for plunging into his life like some missile, destroying its balance and its direction. What a goddamn idiot he had been! Was there still time to salvage the wreck of his marriage and make amends? Was there still time to be forgiven? All he had to do was call Lee and tell her goodbye. That was all. He swallowed, remembering the time he had stopped at the phone booth on Wilshire Boulevard, determined to end it all there and then. But even as he had lifted the receiver he seemed to hear her voice and see her face. Hopelessly, as if bereft of his power of decision, he had let the receiver drop back on to its cradle.

You're not content with making one woman unhappy. You have

to do it to two! You're no damned good at this. Your wife is broken up because she knows you're being unfaithful and you may leave her. Lee is no better off because she thinks you won't.

Why in God's name, he wondered, did I have to tell Lee there might be some sort of permanent relationship? What right did I have to say that? None! Zero!

'Stop at the grocery store,' said Susan, 'if you don't mind. I have to get a loaf.'

Vaughan nodded. No matter what the crisis, the domestic machinery still had to function.

It was a strange part of the Vaughans' lives, full of silences, full of television, magazines and books. When he was off duty, Vaughan tended to take long walks alone, gazing for hours at the lake and wondering how to put his life back in order. Inevitably the situation touched Janet and Lynn. They sensed the tension between their parents and they reacted, taking their mother's side, with the sure instinct of the young. They looked at Vaughan and wondered. Why wasn't he playing his part properly? Why couldn't he stop whatever it was he was doing wrong? And yet, through it all, the family still somehow functioned as a unit. As if from sheer habit, the annual trip to Disneyland at Anaheim took place and Lynn's birthday was celebrated as usual by dinner at the Fox and Hounds. There was even brave talk of a summer vacation. Sometimes there was laughter—but it tended to stop in mid-flight as if reality had cut it short.

In early May they drove to Carmel to visit Susan's parents. ('We've got to,' she said. 'It's been more than three months. They'll think something's wrong.' Vaughan was of the opinion that a visit would remove all doubt but he kept silent.) The Jearards' house overlooked the Pacific; there was the smell of salt in the air and the gulls and the bass accompaniment of the ocean thudding against the rocks a hundred feet below. It was a pleasant, tranquil spot. Harold Jearard was a retired, steel-mill vice-president, a slim, stooped man with tired eyes and a wry sense of humour. Susan's mother was plump and warm and a superb cook. The visit turned out to be remarkably successful. In the company of her parents Susan seemed to soften; it was as if she was calling a silent truce, a temporary shunning of the immediate past. There were strolls along the cliffs, visits to boutiques, a movie. When Sunday came, Vaughan prepared for the return drive in a relaxed mood, glad that the visit had been made. He was due to fly to Houston and Miami the following morning. Soon after breakfast he asked Susan what time she wanted to leave.

'I'm not leaving,' she said.

He looked up from his packing. 'What?'

'I'm not leaving,' she said. 'Is that clear?' Her voice sounded brittle; she avoided his eyes. 'I suppose I'm leaving you, although you're the one who's leaving, aren't you? I'm staying here. So are Janet and Lynn. You know why. There's really no need for me to say it.'

He shrugged helplessly. 'What about their school?'

'There are schools in Carmel. If necessary they can transfer here. Besides, they're due for vacations soon.'

Vaughan shook his head. Why was his first reaction to wonder about the girls' school? He accused Susan of arranging everything with her parents behind his back.

'Naturally,' she said.

'It's a hell of a thing to do.'

'You should talk.'

He looked at her. There was an assurance, a confidence about her. Home territory. Allies galore.

'What do you want from me?'

'You know.'

'I told you: it's all over.'

'Please don't lie to me.'

'I mean it, Susan ...'

'Yes, I know you do, Chuck, when you're with me.' There was the hint of a sad smile on her lips. 'I think you're sincere when you say such things to me. But you haven't been able to make them happen, have you? I'm sorry for you. I guess it must be a hell of a burden for you. But it's up to you to work it out. It's your problem.' She turned and crossed to the door. 'You'd better come up,' she called to her parents. 'We may as well get this over with. Where are the girls?'

'On the patio,' came her mother's voice.

And then her parents were in the room. They shuffled as they stood, as if they didn't belong there. For ghastly moments there was silence. No one looked directly at anyone else.

At last, Susan said, 'I've told Charles that I'm staying here.' She clenched her fists then released them. 'He's driving back to Blue Jay now. The girls will stay here with me. They'll lose a bit of school but I really don't give a damn.'

Suddenly all eyes were upon him. He felt like an actor who has missed his cue. He looked at them. Susan, her face flushed, her head held high. Her father, wearing an expression of mild regret, the fair man who wanted neither adversary to win or lose. Her mother, bewildered, apparently close to tears.

'I'm sorry,' he said. 'It's as embarrassing as hell for you and for me. I don't know why Susan had to bring you into this. It's something between her and me.'

Mrs Jearard said something which became sobs.

'You really shouldn't have done this,' Vaughan said to Susan. 'Shut up.'

Mr Jearard said, 'Susan, why don't you take your mother into her room and give her a glass of water or something.'

Vaughan swallowed. He felt slightly sick. What was to follow? A beating-up by a seventy-year-old outraged father? Jesus, was this nightmare really happening?

When the door had closed, Mr Jearard said, 'I agree with you.'

'About what?'

'Susan should not have brought us into this room. It simply made a painful situation rather more painful. There are times when it is much the best course to sidestep the truth and pretend with all your vigour. All of us, I think, would have felt better if we had pretended that you had to return for business reasons.'

'I suppose she knew why she did it,' said Vaughan. He tossed socks into his bag. The sooner he left the better.

'I just want to tell you,' said Mr Jearard, 'that I think I understand something of the ordeal you're going through. Of course, I deplore what it is doing to my daughter's happiness, but I find it hard to condemn you out of hand. I don't believe you are the sort of man who purposely plunges into a situation like that. In other words, I doubt that you went looking for the problem you found.'

'But maybe if I was the sort who looked, I'd be able to get out a hell of a lot easier.'

'I think you're absolutely right, Chuck. Your handicap is that you're an honourable man. You try to avoid hurting. And by so doing, you hurt more. It's one of the more confusing aspects of being a human being that one so often seems to get further away from one's goal the more one strives to reach it. In any event, it makes things terribly hard for a man with a conscience. Yours is a strong, vigorous conscience, I believe. But now, I suggest, is the time to be dishonourable. To hurt. Because I truly am convinced that you are far better to stay with Susan than go with ... let's say anyone else. There are also the children to consider. And me. I'm very fond of you. I would be most upset to lose you as a son-in-law.'

Vaughan smiled. 'Nice of you to say so.'

'I mean it. And you mustn't think for a moment that Susan or her mother will fail to forgive you. Of course they will. Indeed, they will probably think the higher of you.'

'Higher?'

'Certainly. The prodigal son syndrome.'

'I doubt it applies in this sort of situation.'

'Oh, but it does,' said Mr Jearard. 'I can assure you it does. And I can assure you of something else. I can assure you that—and please don't think me presumptuous although I suppose that is precisely what I'm being—but I can assure you that you will recover from the blow of giving up ... *her*. Indeed, you will relish her memory the more keenly for it. A morsel or two of memory is good for a man as he approaches middle age. Believe me, I know.'

Dr Goodall munched a lunchtime sandwich as he listened to Sibelius on the FM radio. The telephone rang. He sighed long-sufferingly. Was a chap to be granted no peace, no respite? Would Mrs Latham never learn that lunch-time was sacred? Then he remembered: Mrs Latham was on holiday Mrs Whateverhername-was had taken her place.

'It's Mr Carter,' said Mrs Whateverhernamewas. 'I told him you were having your dinner—' Dr Goodall winced—'but he said it was very important.'

'Carter, you say?'

'That's right.'

Oh Lord. Frank Beatty. 'All right, put him on, will you.'

Frank's voice had a jovial quality that was oddly mechanical. 'Hullo, old man, awfully sorry to disturb your lunch.'

'It doesn't matter,' said Hoke.

'The fact of the matter is, I need a few more of those pills, Hoke, so be a good chap and reach for your pad, will you?'

'Pills?'

'The ones you prescribed. They're just the job. I've been on top line ever since I started taking them. Not a hint of a spell.' Frank spoke rather rapidly; it sounded as if he was reading the sentences or had learnt them by heart before calling.

'You mustn't think those pills are a cure,' Hoke cautioned. 'All they do is tend to nullify the symptoms; you see ...'

'I understand that, old man. But I need some more. And to get them, I need a prescription from you.'

Hoke sighed. 'Frank, as I explained to you at some length, your condition is really outside my field of competence. I recommended a man ...'

'I know you did, Hoke.' A chuckle—a trifle hollow and forced. Frank wasn't good at this sort of thing. 'But I'd much rather give you the business. Old school tie and all that.'

'You haven't been to see him, as I recommended.'

'I will, Hoke, I will. I promise. But I've been most frightfully busy; you've no idea; travelling all over the place.'

'Your employer still knows nothing of your condition?'

'No, I haven't passed on the good news, yet, Hoke. I have a few details, sales and contracts and that sort of thing, to wrap up before I do so. You can understand that, can't you? You see, they'll remove me from the scene the moment they know what's wrong with me, and I want to do as much as I can while I can. Now be a good chap ...'

As he hung up the telephone, Frank Beatty grimaced. Rotten business, deceiving Hoke, quite rotten. Nothing to be proud of. But what the hell could one do? Give up without a struggle?

Glumly he wondered which would give out first: the pills or Hoke's patience.

17

Mrs Latham felt better the instant the jet's wheels touched the runway. At last her stomach settled back in her abdominal cavity where it belonged. She sighed with relief. She could cease eyeing the neatly folded paper bag in the seat pocket before her; she could stop her calculations of how long it would take to snatch it and open it and use it. She wouldn't need the bag now; the steak and kidney pie was safe.

She gazed through the small window at her side. Everything looked grey and drab after the dazzling sunshine of Bermuda. A light drizzle was falling. A typical English Spring day. She started to click her tongue in vexation, then she decided she was rather pleased by the weather after all. It would have been irksome in the extreme to have returned from a distinctly costly two-week package holiday only to be told that it had been just as sunny and hot at home. She looked at the ground staff ambling towards the aircraft. They all looked nice and pale. Good. Her studiously acquired tan would not have been in vain.

She disembarked and passed through Customs without delay. Her purchases had been modest: a silver charm depicting the policeman directing traffic from the 'birdcage' at the corner of Front and Queen Streets in Hamilton, a reproduction of a seventeenth-century map of the islands and a small bottle of locally manufactured perfume. What a shame, she thought, that poor Albert never saw Bermuda. He would have adored it. (Or would he? No, come to think of it, Albert was never particularly fond of going anywhere, even Southend.) What a shame also, she thought, that the widower from Cleveland, Ohio, hadn't invited her to occupy his motor-cycle pillion seat to St George; he had apparently been on the point of making such a suggestion when those wretched people from Saskatchewan had burst into the lounge playing guitars and beating dust-bin lids. A singularly unamusing incident, but for some reason it had steered the widower's conversation into other channels; regretfully he had never returned to the matter of driving to St George.

She walked through the terminal building and headed for the railway ticket office. Then she stopped dead.

'Why, Mr Carter!'

'No, you're mistaken. My name's not Carter.'

'And with that he dashed off,' Mrs Latham told Dr Goodall the following morning.

'Possibly you were mistaken.'

'No. It was definitely Mr Carter.'

Dr Goodall shrugged. 'Perhaps it was him, then. I understand he travels a great deal.' He glanced at his watch and his appointment book. He faced a busy day.

Mrs Latham smiled. 'Travel a great deal?' She paused a moment for dramatic effect. 'I imagine he does. He's an airline pilot.'

'No; he's a salesman. He sells aeroplane parts.'

'I know that's what it says on our records. And for all I know it might have been true when he first came in. But he's a pilot now.'

Dr Goodall stared. 'He can't be.'

'He had the uniform, the cap, everything. He was walking along with two other men. They were pilots too. It was definitely Mr Carter. I'd recognize him anywhere. Distinctive face, you know.'

'Good God,' said Dr Goodall softly as if something had just occurred to him. 'Some commercial traveller!' He looked at Mrs Latham and rubbed his chin, frowning. 'You're absolutely sure about this, are you? There's no question that you mistook him for someone else?'

'Oh no, it was definitely him.' She wagged a professional finger at the doctor. 'He knew me too. He recognized me. You know how you can tell when someone recognizes you. The eyes sort of flicker and light up, you know. It was Mr Carter all right.'

'What airline, did you notice? BEA? BOAC?'

'It was a blue uniform with a peaked cap.'

'I think they all wear that.'

'Oh, do they?'

Dr Goodall leant back in his chair. 'He never intimated for a moment that he was ... flying.'

'He deceived you,' said Mrs Latham.

'True,' said Dr Goodall. 'But one can hardly demand proof of every statement a patient makes.'

'What would you have said if he'd told you he was an airline pilot?'

'I would have urged him to resign immediately.'

'Criminal, that's what it is, taking people up in the sky in his condition. He might have flown me to Bermuda and back.'

'True.'

'He could have an attack any time.'

'The last time I spoke to him—when you were on holiday, actually—he assured me that he had experienced no recurrence as yet. The phenobarbitone and phenytoin seem to be effective, but only up to a point of course.'

'Of course,' said Mrs Latham.

'I think,' said Dr Goodall, 'that we must contact Mr, er, Carter and tell him in the most forcible manner than we have discovered his secret and that he must, er, I think the expression is "ground" himself.'

'You're right there,' said Mrs Latham, 'but the crafty beggar hasn't given us an address or a phone number. There's nothing in your file. I can't think where you planned to send the bill.'

Dr Goodall shrugged apologetically. 'He told me he was ... mobile.'

T. Roydon Goodall understood Frank Beatty's actions—although of course he did not condone them. Poor Frank, he had been head over heels in love with aeroplanes at school. Used to chatter endlessly about them. Babbling on about the differences between Mark Ones and Twos. Rushing outside if one happened to buzz by. Audibly longing for the day when he could be up there too. Hoke had never shared Frank's passion for the air—indeed, the very thought of flying was quite terrifying—but he had a keen appreciation of its intensity. How sad that Frank could fly no more.

Hoke had been tempted to reveal the true identity of 'Mr Carter' so that Mrs Latham could tackle the tedious business of trying to find out which airline Frank Beatty worked for. But, upon reflection, it seemed prudent to keep that morsel of information to himself. He telephoned BOAC, introduced himself as Dr Goodall and said that he had a most important message for one of their pilots, a Frank N. Beatty. Someone said he was very sorry, Doctor, but BOAC did not have a pilot by that name. Perhaps the doctor should try BEA. The doctor did. It was a wearisome business; the world seemed to be full of airlines; it was more than an hour before Hoke reached Amory International—to be told that Frank was in Rome.

'When will he be back in London?'

'On Wednesday.'

'Please ask him to telephone Dr Goodall. It's rather important.'

'Certainly, Doctor,' said a most agreeable girl.

But Frank didn't call on Wednesday. Or Thursday. Or Friday.

Hoke rang Amory International once more. The same young lady assured him that she had personally given Captain Beatty the doctor's message. She would, however, remind him when he returned from Boston.

Frank telephoned a week later.

'Hullo, Hoke. I understand you've been calling me.'

His offhand tone wasn't convincing. Hoke felt the warmth of righteous anger in his plump cheeks. Dash it all, one's patience did have limits. Couldn't Frank realize what a wretchedly invidious position he was putting a chum in? Didn't he care?

'So it was your nurse at the airport.'

'Yes. Good God, Frank ... you're a *pilot*, of all things.'

'I told you I was a commercial traveller.'

'A deceit.'

'If you wish to take it that way.'

'In what other way can I possibly take it?'

Frank said: 'As far as your files are concerned, I'm a commercial traveller named Carter. You're not involved, Hoke. That was the whole idea. I used a false name for that very reason.'

'You haven't followed my instructions and seen Hesketh.'

'Who?'

'The neurologist.'

'I will, Hoke, I promise.'

'That's what you said before. Frank, it's absolutely out of the question for you to keep flying. It's most frightfully dangerous.'

'Not really.'

'But it is. Suppose you had an attack ...'

'Hoke, listen to me.' Now Frank sounded patient and good-humoured. 'There's no danger at all because I'm not doing any landings or take-offs. I'm giving them all to my first officers.'

'Giving them? I don't think I quite follow.'

'You see, Hoke, an airliner has two pilots, a captain and a first officer. How much flying the first officer does depends entirely on the captain. Some captains make the poor chap nothing more than a very junior assistant. Others let him do a lot of the flying and perhaps half the landings and take-offs. But I'm giving my first officers *all* the landings and take-offs. I can tell you, it's making me remarkably popular among the first officers. And the amusing thing is, I've told each of them to keep quiet about it because he's the only one getting such privileged treatment. So you see, there's really no danger.'

'But if your employers knew ...'

'They will soon enough, Hoke. Airline pilots have to take regular medicals. I don't think it will be very long before my little secret is discovered, do you?'

'Possibly not, but ...'

'I just want to keep on flying as long as possible. I happen to enjoy it enormously.'

'I know you do, Frank, but ...'

'I've been flying commercially ever since I left the air force. It's been a long time. I'm reluctant to give it all up.'

'But you must,' Hoke said fervently. 'I consider it my duty, Frank, to instruct you to ... er, ground yourself immediately.'

'Are you going to tell Amory about me?'

'No. It's up to you, Frank.'

'OK.'

'When will you tell them?'

'Soon, Hoke, soon.'

The man from the Medical Defence Union said, 'I take it you have advised your patient to resign his position.'

'In the strongest possible terms,' Hoke said.

'And he has refused?'

'Not exactly ... but he's reluctant. Do you think I should tell his employers?'

'Under the circumstances, yes, quite definitely yes.'

Unhappily, Hoke said, 'I was taught that information given one during treatment was privileged. To disclose any of it for any non-medical reason was to commit a blatant breach of ethics. They told me the only aim was to help the patient—"to benefit the patient or protect his interests" was the way they put it, if I remember correctly.'

'True,' said the MDU man, 'but it's a complex world we live in these days, Doctor, and from time to time we are faced with situations such as yours in which physicians have a moral right—or even moral duty or *legal* duty—to break secrecy in order to prevent reasonable, foreseeable harm to others. My advice to you, Doctor, is to inform your patient that if he fails to tell his employers the truth, you will be obliged to do so.'

Hoke thanked the man—resenting his cheerful 'Good afternoon!' Blast him. He looked at his clock. Ten minutes before the next patient. Time enough. It had to be done. He reached for the telephone; but he didn't lift it. He stared at his fingers as if they belonged to someone else. Damnation! It was easy enough for the MDU man to talk. Not so easy to do what he said, though, not when you've known a chap thirty years ...

He rubbed his chin. Then stopped. He knew. He would write Frank a letter. Put the whole thing to him in a straightforward manner; tell him that he had a week or so (possibly two) to advise Amory; a deadline; if by that time, etcetera, etcetera ...

Yes, a letter was the answer, a personal, handwritten letter. He would get on it first thing in the morning. In the meantime he would think about it. Such a letter had to be couched in just the right terms.

Beatty flew, delivering planeload after planeload of holiday-makers to Nice, to Rome, to Montreal, to Lisbon, to Acapulco, to Miami. He worked hard, often exceeding the legal monthly maximums of on-duty hours. He welcomed the extra work for he was revelling in his craft as never before. The knowledge that his flying days were strictly numbered added a singular keenness. He knew he had been incredibly lucky to pass his last medical. Such luck couldn't hold. Those doctors weren't fools. Eventually one of them would spot his problem. Then there would be batteries of questions. Puzzled, bewildered, he would declare that he had never felt better. But the game would unquestionably be up. And it would almost certainly happen at his very next medical. Everyone would be full of regrets and be most awfully sorry. He wouldn't mention having been to see Hoke. As far as anyone would be concerned officially, James Carter would simply vanish. Case closed.

In a curious way he had never been happier.

Henry Peel taxied to the ramp, keeping the engine revs bang on eight hundred. He parked with care, lining up his wingtip with that of the next aircraft on the line, ensuring that his nosewheel was pointing dead ahead. Brake on. Radio off. Mixture to Lean. The propeller slowed and gurgled to a halt. Ignition to Off. Master Switch to Off.

Henry mopped his dripping brow.

The man in the right-hand seat scribbled something on his clipboard, then he sniffed and unlatched the door. He was halfway out of the aircraft before he turned and looked back at Henry Peel.

'I guess you passed,' he said.

Henry felt an absurd, shameful tear spring to his eye. He had done it; he had actually done it. He was a licensed pilot, approved by the *government* to fly All Types of Aeroplanes: Single Engine: Land: Up to 4,000 lb gross allowable weight for take-off.

Within the hour he was on the telephone to a man in St Catharines who had a dainty little blue and white Aeronca for sale.

18

Lee arrived at Brockton shortly before noon on a bright Sunday morning. The club's two Piper tugs were busy hauling the students' Schweizers up for their thousand-foot tows, descending, dropping the nylon line at the end of the strip, then landing, turning and taxiing back for another customer. Lee turned her green MG on to the gravel path leading to the members' parking-lot. There she exchanged a few words with an instructor named Fletcher, an ex-RCAF fighter pilot. For the umpteenth time he offered her the hospitality of the trailer parked a couple of hundred yards from the hangar; he lived in it every weekend during the soaring season. She reminded him—also for the umpteenth time—that his wife and daughter resided in the trailer too. He snapped his fingers in mock annoyance and said that that detail had quite slipped his mind. Smiling, Lee strolled past the club house and the hangar on her way to the flight line. She liked Fletcher; he could make an improper proposition in the pleasantest of ways: the way that made a girl feel better for it, rather than worse. The day promised good soaring, according to the sky watchers, but it was still too early; the cumulus clouds which provided the essential up-currents of air would not be 'popping' until afternoon.

She sat in the long grass beyond the landing-strip. It was good to be alone; the sun was warm and the flying was a non-stop show for her benefit.

It was time for rumination. To do or not to do. To cut free or become more and more entangled.

Larry, the Air Canada second officer who doubled as a club tow-pilot, interrupted her thoughts. He wanted to know what she was doing all by herself. She told him it was none of his business.

'That's true,' he admitted. 'But I still want to know what you're doing over here by yourself.'

'Thinking,' she said. 'Wondering why we don't spend all our lives soaring. It's only when we come down to earth that they get nasty.'

'Very philosophical today, aren't we?'

'I may write a poem about it.'

He smiled. 'Are you flying today?'

'I will when the thermals pick up.'

'The cu are beginning. Look.'

Tiny white clouds were indeed appearing against the blue, like balls of cotton. She asked him if he was towing.

He nodded. 'Duty tow-pilot. Just having a break for a sandwich. I've been here since eight for my sins. Kay was mad as hell; I woke her getting up.'

'How is she?'

'Fine. And ...?'

'Chuck's fine too,' Lee said. 'He said he might be coming to town next week.'

'Say hullo for me.'

'Will do. Larry?'

'Yes?'

'Take me up to five thousand, will you?'

'Five? It's above club's limits.'

'I don't care. Will you take me?'

'Sure.'

The wind had freshened. It nudged the slender sailplanes as they sat waiting in their lopsided way; ailerons and elevators sighed lazily, moving against safety locks, signalling that they wanted to be free.

Someone held the Blanik's nose down while Lee clambered into the cockpit, bulky in her parachute which was mandatory for solo flights. She sorted out the harness straps: two for the shoulders, two lap-straps, all meeting in a buckle at the waist. It felt good when the straps were snugly adjusted; you became part of the aircraft, a comrade of all the other components. She tested the controls: elevator, ailerons, rudder, spoilers. Release lever OK. Altimeter, ASI, variometer, compass, all OK. The canopy closed over her. The world tilted as a ground handler raised the grounded wing. On the instrument panel, the turn and bank indicator obediently registered level flight.

Minutes later she was in the air, her eyes fixed on the tug's ailerons and rudder, anticipating his turns, like the Red Baron on a victim's tail. It had seemed an impossible task when she had first tried her hand at gliding; she kept straying and swaying, to be jerked back to reality by abruptly taut lines. Now it was second nature; her movements of the stick and rudder were smooth and instinctive. Up, up. The fabric on the Cub's wing rippled daintily in the blast of the propeller. The machine seemed stationary; it dangled in the air while the grass and trees moved around it like some colossal verdant roundabout.

At 5,000 feet Larry explored the air for a minute, seeking the elusive up-current of warm air. His wing waggled. Success! Time to release. Lee leant forward and tugged on the lever. The line went wriggling away. She was on her own. She turned quickly. Now the noise of the Cub receded. A gentle wind enfolded the Blanik, pressing on the canopy, shouldering the broad wings. The structure creaked as the stresses were absorbed and apportioned from stringer to longeron to former to bulkhead.

More bumps. Lee smiled. The world was a long way below.

She turned. A strong thermal surrounded her. Good signs from the variometer and the altimeter. Five hundred feet, a thousand, won from Mother Nature. Fine strong lift. Lots of guts. There was no feeling quite like that of defying the laws of gravity.

The field was a mere spot, a dot, a postage stamp. Down there, all eyes would be on her. She was the first to attempt any serious soaring that day. Her success would be only too evident. Now there would be a flurry of activity on the flight line; everything with wings would be dragged aloft in the search for thermals. But for the moment she had the sky to herself. She was the queen, soaring, turning, the metal of her slim craft sparkling in the sun. Still she climbed: six thousand, seven, eight, almost nine. But at last the vigour of the lift began to wane. The forces cancelled one another out: the strength of the up-current no longer exceeded the drag of the sailplane. The variometer registered zero. Time to look elsewhere.

Lee turned as if suspended on wires. It was delightful. Utterly peaceful. Her mind wandered. A sailplane was a good vantage point from which to study your life. You saw it in perspective.

She thought about Charles Vaughan.

There was a chance—a real chance—that he might leave his wife and children for her. Would that solve all problems? Or would it simply create a whole batch of new problems? Runaway husbands sometimes came to regret leaving their original partners. And hating their new partners. It had happened. It could happen again. What would Ann Landers have to say on the subject? 'Stick to boys your own age'? Yes, there was the age thing. It didn't matter now, but how about later on? She shook her head as her brain became entangled yet again in the torment of When-he's-fifty-how-old-will-I-be? and When-I'm-as-old-as-he-is-now-how-old-will-he-be?

But, she thought, if there is such a thing as love, I think this has to be it.

He's a wonderful guy, the nicest, gentlest man in the whole crummy world. But I have to give him up.

It wasn't a noble decision. She acknowledged the fact. Indeed it was selfish. She refused to settle for a future that was jeopardized even before it began. She shook her head. No, it wouldn't work. The odds were stacked too high. She had been leading up to the decision for weeks. Now it was definite. She would write him a letter, explaining everything ...

Suddenly she noticed the altimeter. She had descended almost three thousand feet. Her thermal had long since abandoned her. She looked around. Where the devil was the field? She frowned. The terrain looked unfamiliar. Damn! She hadn't paid attention to the wind. It had been brisk on take-off; since then it had been busily pushing the thermal along—and her with it. She had allowed herself to drift God knows how many miles from the field. OK, no need to panic. Think. There's the lake to the north. Now, the wind was blowing from the west, so she had strayed to the east. OK, so steer approximately 270 degrees and see what there is to see. Still a good deal of height, thank God.

She peered ahead, lifting her sunglasses and propping them on her forehead. No sign of other gliders. But that didn't mean a thing. They were practically impossible to see until you were almost on top of them. Just keep heading west, she told herself, you're bound to find the field sooner or later. Make it sooner, please, she thought.

'Anyway,' she said aloud, her voice assuming an odd tonal quality in the enclosed cockpit, 'even if I don't find the field, I can always put her down in a field. No sweat, girl.'

The Blanik descended gently but steadily as it carved a silent passage through the wind. Now the sky seemed devoid of cumulus or eagles. No welcoming signs of lift for lonely girl glider pilots.

Her stomach was knotted. She forced herself to breathe slowly and evenly. Nothing to be gained by getting all a-twitter. She told herself again that putting the Blanik down in a field would be no big deal. All she had to do was look out for power lines and barbed-wire fences. The sailplane could alight in a few yards.

Now the altimeter indicated 2,000 feet.

Below were fields of every size and shape, but none that looked familiar. A road—but going to and coming from where?

She eased back on the stick. The airspeed dropped a few knots. She pulled the nose up more, the instinctive action of the glider pilot 'stretching the glide'. The Blanik's speed hovered around the stall mark; the wings wobbled, uncomfortable and ill at ease in the slowly moving air.

Then Lee smiled. Two gliders at ten o'clock! Mere specks, but definitely gliders—and presumably right over the field. She turned to the left a few degrees.

Now she was down to 1,500 feet.

The ground became identifiable. That highway and that restaurant were familiar friends—and the field was only a hop, skip and a jump away. She could see the orange hangar and the windsock.

'I'm coming straight in!' she chortled. 'So anyone else had better get out of the way!'

But her progress was painfully slow. God, how the wind must have picked up. The field was tantalizingly close—but it hardly seemed to move. 'Like an arthritic snail,' she said without being aware of it. 'A sleepy arthritic snail. A disinterested, sleepy, arthritic snail ...'

And then, as if she had drawn a diagram of the distance and had measured the speed and the rate of sink and the strength of the wind, she knew without a doubt that she wouldn't make it.

'OK,' she said, swallowing, 'then I must put her down. Now.'

But below, it was all fences and sheds. Biting her lip, Lee turned. No; power lines. Could she get under them?

'Make your dumb mind up,' she said loudly. 'You haven't got all day.'

There it was—a little strip of ploughed land, just beyond the road. The wind was blowing across her path, but this was no time to be choosy about wind direction.

With her hand on the spoiler lever, she angled the nose to the left. She felt the Blanik's side sway as the wind pressed against her.

'That's it,' she said. 'Between the trees, over the road and you've got it made.'

Her approach was good. There was no reason why she shouldn't have made a safe landing—except for the wires stretching between the tall elms. She couldn't see them; but they caught her wing as she banked, her spoilers jutting into the slipstream. There was a snapping, a screeching, a crumpling. The Blanik swerved, shuddering. Lee saw the white lines of the road rushing up at her. Her hands and feet still moved the controls in a perfectly futile attempt to straighten out in time. But there was no more time. As the wing thudded into the road, she heard the squeal of brakes.

Thirty-seven miles away, Henry Peel touched down on his private landing field: eight hundred feet of the family farm that had been carefully levelled and rolled. The blue-and-white Aeronca bounced gently then settled down. With a burst of throttle, Henry turned and taxied to his hangar, formerly an implement barn.

His parents were waiting for him there, shaking their heads and saying they never thought they'd see the day when a member of the family would be flying his own airplane.

He took them both for a flight. But one at a time, for the little aircraft could not manage more.

19

It had drizzled all day. On the way to Gatwick, Diane said she hoped the weather would improve for Vincent's holidays—he was due home from school in two days. Beatty said he wished he could be there.

'Gosh no,' said Diane, 'it would be too much of a shock for the poor lad if he came home and found his father there.'

Beatty smiled. 'Actually I don't think he was too keen on it when I was at home more or less permanently. I was too much competition for your attention.'

'Flatterer.'

'I suppose he'll be another inch taller.'

'If not two.'

'He'll need new suits and flannels and Lord knows what else.'

'Almost certainly, I'd say,' said Diane, apparently savouring the thought of spending countless hours in the West End, shopping for her son.

'I think I'll have to start the kid on cigarettes,' said Beatty.

'Why?'

'To stunt his growth.'

She grinned. 'Will you be spending any time in Toronto?'

'Six hours to be precise.'

'Will you have time to ring the Baxters?'

'I'll see.'

'That means you won't. Mrs Baxter is always asking when you're going to see them. She says Bobby would love to see you.'

'Yes, but would I love to see Bobby? We weren't particularly compatible when they lived next door. God knows why his mother thinks we'll be great chums simply because he's moved to Canada.

In England I found him an opinionated little twerp. I can't imagine why he should be any different now.'

'But Mrs Baxter keeps asking.'

Beatty patted her hand. 'Just tell her I keep hoping against hope that I have to go to Toronto, but never seem to.'

'I'm not a very good liar,' Diane said.

I am, he thought. I've become an expert. But the question is: how long can I keep it up? Until the next medical? Until the one after that? For six months? A year? Two? There was an airline pilot in America who managed to keep the truth of his serious heart condition from doctors for more than ten years. But, because his condition was not treated, the pilot had a seizure during a flight. He died almost instantly. Fortunately, the copilot was able to take over and land without any of the passengers being aware that there was a problem up front.

Diane had slipped her reading glasses on. Her private log book was open and her pen poised.

'What time will you be leaving Toronto?'

'Twenty-two-forty local.'

'What's that in English time?'

'Twenty to four in the morning.'

'I may miss your take-off.'

'I'll forgive you.'

'When do you get to Belfast?'

'Eight in the morning your time.'

'All right. And you're off to Lisbon that afternoon?'

'Correct. At two-thirty your time.'

'Then where? Lisbon to Rome to pick up a planeload of insurance men?'

'Correct.'

'When will you be home?'

'Thursday evening. About ten, with luck.'

Diane made the last entry in the book and nodded, satisfied that she had put her affairs in order. Over the years she had filled several small notebooks with particulars of her husband's journeyings. Strictly speaking it wasn't necessary for her to keep track; his whereabouts could always be known by telephoning the line. But Diane preferred to keep her own records—and woe betide him if he neglected to inform her of a change of itinerary. She would have felt cheated if she had mentally flown with him from Nassau to London, only to be told that due to maintenance problems someone else had taken the flight and he had returned via New York.

At the terminal building, he stopped the Rover and took his bag from the back seat. Diane took the wheel.

'Drive carefully,' he told her. 'It's a bit slippery in spots.'

She nodded. 'You drive carefully too.'

He gave her a five-pound note. 'Vincent will need a spot of pocket-money when he gets home.'

'A bit! Five pounds!'

'The cost of living is up, you know.'

'You're spoiling him. Two pounds would be ample.'

'I feel like spoiling him today.'

'Why today?'

'I'm hoping that generosity of this calibre will earn me high marks wherever the score is being kept.'

She laughed. 'All right, darling, I'll give it to him. But I'm going to tell him it must last a month.'

'God, you're a hard-hearted wench. I can't think what I ever saw in you.'

He stooped and kissed her through the car's open window. She touched his cheek; her fingertips were cool and soft.

'Have a nice trip. Don't forget to put your wheels down.'

It was her stock farewell; she had been telling him about his wheels for a long time.

Beatty gripped her hand for a moment, then he let go and waved. He watched her as she put the Rover in gear and drove away.

Jordan, the flight engineer, met him in Dispatch.

'Sorry, number four's U/S. Temperature.'

'Damn,' said Beatty. 'How long?'

'Don't know yet. Could be the thermostat spring. We're looking into it.'

'OK. Keep me posted, will you?'

'Roger.'

He headed for the ramp, a stocky, vaguely untidy figure, his cap set at a jaunty angle. A good engineer, Jordan; he would get the recalcitrant engine working if anyone could.

Lewis, the chief purser, asked if there would be a delay in departure. Beatty said he didn't know yet. Lewis nodded, indicating the proper degree of professional interest in the news. A sallow-faced man of forty-five, he had served on airlines all his adult life. He considered himself as much an airman as any pilot.

'We have five girls for this trip, sir.'

'Good,' said Beatty who was not very interested—and who had never found the cabin-crew briefing to be of the slightest value.

'One brand new one, the rest pretty experienced.'

'Good,' said Beatty again.

'Nice spot of filet mignon for dinner, sir.'

'Splendid.'

'And a very tasty bit of apple pie afterwards.'

'I shall look forward to it.'

Corfield appeared, beaming as usual. He was Beatty's first officer for this trip. An uncommonly cheerful individual, Corfield.

The Fixed Time Prognostic Chart afforded a God-like view of the wind and weather patterns over the North Atlantic. Lines described gracefully erratic paths across the chart; they were identified by innocent-looking series of digits. 'FL320 110Kts 57' told the airmen that there was a jet-stream, a screaming, blinding hurricane at 32,000 feet, a wedge of air hurtling along at 110 nautical miles per hour at a paralysing temperature of 57 degrees Fahrenheit below zero. The question was: could the jet-stream assist the flight or was it simply something to be avoided en route?

Beatty joined Webb, the navigator; together they examined the charts and checked on the available levels and routes. Each trip was a matter of planning the best route and height, considering the load and the distance and the amount of fuel aboard, then finding out whether that route and height was free. Often it was found that another aircraft had claimed it moments before. The North Atlantic was heavily travelled; thus each aircraft was allotted a block of airspace and, in theory, it should never be less than 120 miles from the next aircraft. In practice it occasionally worked out to be rather less.

On Beatty fell the responsibility for a number of crucial decisions at this point. How much fuel should the aircraft carry? What alternate airports should be selected? What runway should be used on take-off?

Mr and Mrs Frederick Cox had found themselves a window seat in the cafeteria. Over a nice cup of tea they could watch the aeroplanes landing and taking off. It was deliciously exciting to think that in a little while they would be inside one of those glistening monsters high over the Atlantic; it was indeed a marvellous age in which to live. Mr Cox (who had never been inside an aeroplane) said he had seen the whole air age in his lifetime. He told his wife how well he remembered the news of the Wright Brothers' first flight. He was wrong. What he was actually recalling was the excitement over Bleriot's first flight across the Channel in 1909. It didn't matter. Mrs Cox nodded happily just the same.

A thin, almost emaciated young man sat down a dozen feet away. His name was Len Sparrow. He wore cowboy boots and jeans that had faded to a watery blue; they matched his eyes perfectly. Len Sparrow was twenty and was on his way to spend three weeks with a married brother who lived in a place called Oakville, Ontario. What a ruddy relief to kiss J. L. Pratt & Son, Printers and Bookbinders, goodbye for a bit. Len Sparrow was looking forward to seeing America—well, it was almost America; not far from The Border, according to George's letters. (It never crossed Len Sparrow's mind to confirm these facts for himself by means of the atlas in the local lending library.) As he lit a Camel he caught a hazy reflection of himself in the glass of the door. It pleased him. The lean, lone stranger. The silent man with a secret. Cold, steely eyes missing nothing. Wiry frame rippling beneath the stylish denim. He would have been deeply hurt to know that the few people who noticed him saw him as an undernourished, nervous-looking nonentity in desperate need of a haircut and a shampoo.

The baggage checkers received their instructions: a delay on Amory Flight 1010; tell the passengers an hour and that an announcement would be made in due course over the PA. The checkers sighed. Passengers seemed to think that they, the checkers, were responsible for delays. If it was to be a long delay, the custom was to let the passengers have the good news a morsel at a time. An hour or ninety minutes was irritating but not usually enough to make anyone hostile.

'And remember,' the senior dispatcher told a new girl on the job, 'if one of them starts getting obstreperous, just tell him it's a technical problem with the aircraft and the safety of the passengers is our only thought.'

As a rule Miss Hardcastle was a patient individual—you learn patience when you have been blind since birth. But on this day, waiting in the Gatwick terminal for the Amory flight to Toronto, she found it difficult to contain her impatience. She had a quite absurd desire to stand up and shout, 'Oh, do hurry up, will you!' at the top of her voice. She had looked forward to this day too long. This would be her first trip abroad, her first opportunity to experience *foreignness* and she wasn't at all sure just what was in store for her. She was certain, however, that in a score of ways Canada would identify itself. Places had that ability. After all, if the air in Scotland could be so totally different from the air in the southern counties, it stood to reason that the air in Canada would be that much more different again, the distance being that much greater. She felt the wallet in her handbag; the passport, ticket and folder of travellers' cheques were safe. A most amiable young lady from the airline had found this seat and had assured Miss Hardcastle that she would return the moment the flight was called to guide her through the official formalities and to her seat on the aircraft. It was like being a celebrity. VIP service, no less. Miss Hardcastle amused herself by listening to the airport noises. They struck her as essentially happy noises. People sounded as if they were pleased to be going wherever they happened to be going. Such was not the case at railway and bus stations, in Miss Hardcastle's experience. There, a great many negative sounds could usually be heard, suggesting that a major proportion of railways and bus passengers would prefer to stay put, if given the choice.

Miss Hardcastle heard someone sit down on the bench beside her. Someone light-sounding. And smelling rather delightful. A most pleasant perfume. Obviously the someone had commendable taste. Was she as pretty as her presence suggested?

Had Miss Hardcastle asked Len Sparrow, she would have received an enthusiastically affirmative reply. Seated a dozen feet away, he watched as the girl sat down beside the biddy with the dark glasses. The girl was unquestionably a bit of all right. In fact, Len Sparrow was prepared to take it further; she was a smashing bit of crackling. He studied her profile. Just the job. All her parts looked as if they were *meant* to go together. That nose seemed just right for that mouth; the eyes were exactly the right size and shape and colour for the hair and the cheeks and everything. Everything belonged, whereas most people's faces looked as if they had been assembled from parts just grabbed out of a box and stuck on without a second thought. Len Sparrow lit another Camel. Our paths have crossed, girl. No use fightin' fate. This thing is bigger than both of us.

Beatty told Amory that the No. 4 temperature problem had been solved, but now trouble was being experienced with the transponder, the 'secondary radar' system which enables ground controllers to identify individual aircraft on their radar screens.

'This isn't my goddam day,' said Amory.

Beatty followed him out into the drizzle.

Slattery, the Chief Mechanic, said the transponder was working satisfactorily when they had tested it earlier in the day.

'I don't care about earlier in the day,' said Amory. 'I care about right bloody now. What the hell's wrong with the transponder?'

'The problem right now with it,' said Slattery, 'is that it won't work.'

'That's helpful. What about the back-up unit?'

'They're both U/S.' Slattery had a flat, measured way of talking. 'We're checking back through the circuit as fast as we can, Mr Amory. And the longer you talk to me, the less I'm getting done.'

'You insolent bastard, you're fired,' said Amory.

'OK,' said Slattery with a lazy grin. 'I'll get it going as soon as I can.'

'Thanks,' said Amory.

Back in his office, he slumped in his chair, still wearing his damp raincoat. 'Sit down, Frank; take the weight off.' He scowled at the rain through the office window. 'We've got to get that flight off the ground, Frank. You've got a tight schedule and it's important you stick to it. I've got a lot of money riding on you, my friend.' He punched the palm of his left hand. 'That transponder could just as well have gone U/S in the air as on the ground.'

Beatty agreed, knowing what was coming.

'You wouldn't have turned back if your transponder went U/S, would you? I mean, it wouldn't make any difference, landing here or there; you'd be in exactly the same situation.'

'Depending on conditions.'

'Let's assume the conditions are the same here as there.'

'OK, sir.'

'If your transponder went out, you'd be OK. You'd simply advise ground control, right?'

'Right.' Beatty nodded. 'And that's what you'd like me to do.'

'Correct.'

'I'm the one who stands to lose my licence for taking off in an aircraft I know to be improperly equipped.'

'I know that,' said Amory. 'But it's important that this flight goes. Damned important. If you hold it up any longer, you'll just compound the problem. Belfast, then Lisbon. I can't afford to let that happen, Frank. I mean that. Literally.'

'Is a few hours going to make that much difference?'

Amory rubbed his eyes. 'I'm afraid so.' He sounded tired and dispirited. 'To tell you the truth, Frank, I'm out on a financial limb. Just bought the new aircraft. New crews to fly them. Bigger payroll. I'm extended, Frank, over-extended, in fact. It's going to be all right in a little while. The heat will be off. There's a hell of a lot of business lined up and the new aircraft will more than pay for themselves, in time. In time. You see, time's the bloody problem. Right now, to be precise. This goddam week; this month. I'm a juggler, Frank. I'm going to wind up catching all the parts in the end, but right now they're all flying around and I'm trying to grab them. So what I'm saying to you is, I can't afford to have any more problems, not now, not until the heat's off and I can grab some of those parts.'

Beatty felt embarrassed. It was as if his father had confessed to sexual indiscretions. 'I'm very sorry to hear you have problems, sir.'

162

Amory shrugged. 'Jesus, don't apologize. It's business, Frank. It's the way things are. Christ knows why I don't keep out of it; I know what it's like. Balancing jobs and payrolls and bills and contracts and interest payments. The juggling act. It's a dumb way to live. The trouble is, it's a goddam triumph when you win! You feel like Napoleon!' He laughed. 'And I always win! Always, in the end! It all works out somehow or other. And instead of being dragged off to the clink as a crook, I'm a big business leader, a bulwark of the good old capitalistic system. It's a crazy world. But we've got to live in it. No choice, eh?'

Beatty agreed that there was indeed no choice.

'So what I'd like you to do,' said Amory with a smile, 'is to load your airplane up with passengers and get the hell over to Toronto.'

'I'd be less than honest if I didn't tell you that I'm reluctant to fly without a transponder.'

Amory nodded. 'I know.'

'There is an element of risk.'

'Sure there is,' said Amory. 'But there's an element of risk every time you get into an airplane. It's a goddamn dangerous way to travel. But it's fast, so people will take the risk. Some of them are going to get killed. But not many, so we gamble that it won't be us.'

'I've never looked at it in quite that way.'

'You should,' said Amory. 'It's the truth. You're a hell of a good pilot, Frank. No; it's no bull; I'm levelling with you. You're a good pilot and you're the reason more people don't get killed. Sure, all the radar and nav.-aids are great. But all they mean in the end is that your job gets tougher because you have to fly in worse conditions. Sure, we cut down the risks as much as possible but a man's a fool if he thinks we're doing the job totally. Equipment fails; machines break down. And so we rely on the pilot to get us out of the mess. Usually he does.'

Beatty smiled, shaking his head. 'After that, how can I refuse? What about Slattery?'

'Don't worry about him,' said Amory.

Does Mr Slattery have a debt to pay too? Beatty wondered.

'We'll load and leave right away.'

'Thanks, Frank,' said Amory. 'You won't regret this.'

I hope not, Beatty thought.

The voice over the PA was bright and cheerful.

'Amory International apologizes for the delay in the departure of its Flight 1010; however, that flight is now ready for boarding ...'

Miss Hardcastle was already on her way through Passport Control, the briskly courteous hand of the Amory official steering her.

Len Sparrow eased himself out of the chair. Got to mosey along. The keep-movin' man. Sorry, girl, he said silently. Then his jaw dropped. The pretty girl was gathering her belongings too. Could it be that she was catching the Amory flight too? Strewth, he thought.

'The transponder is U/S,' Beatty told Corfield, 'but we're going anyway.'

'Roger,' said Corfield cheerfully.

It was the captain's decision, the captain's responsibility. One didn't waste one's breath questioning captains' decisions. Working one's way up the aviation ladder was hard enough without *creating* problems for oneself.

The four-man flight crew sat at their stations on the flight deck while the passengers were boarding. Through the closed compartment door they could be heard shuffling and thumping, cattle-like, on the 707's thin metal floor. The cabin-crew types would be wearing their professional smiles and checking seat numbers on boarding-passes, pointing and persuading the clots who sat down in the first seats that took their fancy to get up and collect their belongings (they always had the most) and shove their ways to the correct seats. An incredibly high percentage of passengers were apparently incapable of reading a seat number on a boarding pass and relating it to a number on a seat.

Corfield was whistling an old Beatles tune. He was an amicable young man in his late twenties, ex-RAF. But, Beatty had discovered, it was a very different RAF to the one he had known. Once, during a lay-over in Madrid, they had discussed the matter and had found that they had distressingly little in common. Corfield had never flown an aircraft with a tail-wheel; he had never been in an open cockpit or worn helmet and goggles; he had seen biplanes only at the Science Museum and at antique aeroplane displays. There was, Beatty reflected wryly, a generation gap among airmen too.

Through the window panel at his left, Beatty could glimpse the passengers as they moved along the walkway to the forward entrance door. Most of them peered inquisitively into the cockpit and marvelled at the maze of instruments, after which they glanced at him. The order was invariably the same: the instruments then the pilot. Did they expect someone looking like a composite of John Wayne, Charlton Heston and Jack Hawkins? Were they disappointed with the features they found?

Beatty ran his eye over the instrument panel. The aircraft was one of Amory's new acquisitions, a 707-320B. He had purchased it from an Italian company; it was in excellent condition but its cockpit layout differed from those of the other aircraft in the Amory fleet. The machmeter, the vertical speed indicator, the altimeter: all were positioned to the left of the panel instead of along the top section as on the other machines. Some of the switches and levers, too, were in unexpected positions. Beatty, like umpteen pilots before him, wondered why there couldn't be a standardization of cockpit layouts. There were occasions when one's hand had to speed unerringly to a button or handle. Seconds spent fumbling about trying to find the thing could mean (and in countless cases had meant) the all-important difference between crashing and not crashing. From aircraft to aircraft all one could rely on was that the control column would almost certainly be in front of one and the rudder pedals would be under the panel.

He rolled up his shirt sleeves and loosened his tie. He liked to be comfortable; modern jet aircraft were well heated and free from draughts. There was no need for special garb or even full uniform. It was only actors in aviation epics and models for airline advertisements who wore tunics and caps on the flight deck.

The light on the interphone glowed.

'Yes?'

'Passengers all loaded, sir.' The girl had a soft Scots accent; it sounded charming. 'Doors and chutes are secured.'

'Thank you.' He turned to Corfield. 'Stand by for engine start.'

Henry Peel was, at that moment, taking off on his first flight of the day. It was 6.00 a.m. The air was calm and cool. He scurried over the diminutive hills and dales of his landing-strip, the Aeronca's engine bellowing in its high-pitched way, the undercarriage clattering self-importantly. And then he was aloft, riding on the gentle morning air, balancing lift and drag and power and gravity with a hand that, until a few months before, had done nothing more subtle than wield a rubber stamp at the Post Office. He swooped into a smart turn over the pond. That maple tree that had once seemed so enormous now looked like a twig sticking out of the ground. Wing down more. Let the world slip by at forty-five degrees on the button. The angle of the world could be adjusted to suit one's whim of the moment.

Henry flew until his fuel gauge cautioned him to return to earth. He filled his tanks and then took off again. This time he simply flew around in circles, landing and taking off. He continued this routine, polishing and refining his skills, until he observed his mother gesticulating. It was time for breakfast.

20

Vaughan walked from room to empty room. The windows were latched and the television and radio sets and electric blankets were unplugged and harmless. The air in the house was utterly motionless.

He wrote notes for the milkman, the paper-man, the man from the dry cleaner's and the man who delivered orange juice. No deliveries until further notice, thanks.

His packed bag sat at the front door like a patient hound. It had been there an hour. Vaughan went down to the basement and disconnected the washer and dryer. The washer still bore a small dent where Lynn had hit it with a toy shovel. A few items of children's clothing lay on the table, folded neatly and forgotten.

Outside, he met the mailman with the leathery face and watery eyes.

'Hi there, Mr Vaughan. Off again?'

'Yes ... off again.'

'Where to this time, Mr Vaughan?'

'New York.'

'Can't say as I envy you.'

'I can't say as I envy myself.'

The mailman chuckled as if something funny had been said. 'Just one for you today. Have a good trip.'

Vaughan thanked him as he took the envelope. The painful, childish scrawl, all round letters and dutiful serifs, was Janet's. She was having a nice vacation in Carmel but she missed him and wished he would finish his work and come and stay with them and Lynn threw up in a store and Grandpa caught a cold.

Vaughan folded the letter and replaced it in its envelope. He blinked; his eyes had suddenly become prickly and irritated. Then he became angry with himself for making his daughter write letters to him as if he was a goddam uncle or something. You're her father, he told himself; you should be with her. So do something about it!

As he backed the Cougar down the driveway, he knew without doubt that he had to end the affair. The whole thing boiled down to a choice—and he was the one who had to make it. And it wasn't as if he hated Susan or wanted to leave her or the kids. Nothing could be further from the truth. He loved them. And he missed them. Alone, he was only half alive.

'Jesus Christ,' he said aloud, 'you're like some French nobleman; you want your family and your mistress too! You just love everyone, don't you. Good old, ever-lovin' Chuck!'

He stopped talking to himself. He saw the lawyer's wife looking curiously at him from her patio. He nodded to her as he put the car into drive and sped away.

A man named Hobbs was also driving to the airport at that moment. The trunk of the rented car contained two leather suitcases of excellent quality in which were neatly packed Grant Hobbs' entire wardrobe of three suits, a dozen shirts, six ties and ten changes of underwear, and, equally neatly packed, the complete files pertaining to his business enterprise. Hobbs had for some years made a prosperous living by sending invoices to selected companies all over the United States and Canada. The invoices covered listings in various business directories—which were never published.

Grant Hobbs was moving—something he found it necessary to do from time to time. The fact of the matter was, he had had the post-office box number in LA too long already. By now it was certain that there would be letters on the way to the postmaster informing him in outraged tones that his post office was being used for fraudulent purposes. It always happened eventually; it was one of the inevitable hazards of the business. But in the meantime a remarkably high percentage of the companies invoiced had sent in their cheques. They always did. And Grant Hobbs always cashed them. The trick lay in knowing when to move on. Hobbs prided himself on knowing. A man couldn't last a dozen years in such an enterprise without knowing. Thin, wearing a perpetual frown, Hobbs was heading east for a vacation. He badly needed one. Later on, perhaps after the turn of the year, he would set up operations in the Hartford area. He liked Connecticut, although he regretted leaving the Coast; the weather agreed with him.

In Santa Ana, Earl Gasparac poured a second cup of coffee for his wife. She had had a bad night; the pain must have been savage; you could see the evidence around her mouth and eyes. Her smile, merry as hell, didn't fool him. Neither did her chatter about the trip and how it would be a ball to see all the old places again. She was suffering the tortures of the damned and yet she kept going on about cousins and neighbours and kids she had been to school with. Would she bump into any of them? Would they remember her?

Earl looked down. He found that he had bent the handle of his coffee spoon at right angles. But no, it wasn't him; it was the anger within him, the impotent, seething anger at a fate that could condemn an innocent to a slow, lingering death without dignity or hope. How could anyone believe in *anything*?

TranState's Flight Planning Department was full of teletype machines that clattered and telephones that jangled. Its product was information; it absorbed information from a score of sources; it disseminated that information to the crews who flew the company's aircraft. Captains called at the Flight Planning Department to ascertain the serviceability of their airplanes, the weather conditions, availability of radar and radio aids, the numbers of passengers his aircraft to be carried, the weight of freight....

'Er, Captain, I'm Garten.'

Vaughan turned. Garten was a young man with a bland, in- genuous face and corn-coloured hair. He had the anxious-to-please look in his eyes.

'I'm your copilot, sir.'

Vaughan nodded. 'Sure. How are you?' He knew he sounded terse and disinterested. 'I haven't seen you around. How long have you been with TranState?'

'Two months, sir. I finished the course last Friday.'

'And this is your first line ride?'

'Yes sir.'

Vaughan nodded again, mechanically. He wanted to welcome the young pilot to the line; it was the nice thing to do; today, however, he seemed incapable of doing anything nice.

Cutshall, the navigator, was already at the Met desk.

'Looks pretty good, Captain, until we get near Detroit. There's some stuff building up around there.'

The airmen studied the Met reports and charts. Weather fronts moved across the continent like tidal waves. The air was never still; it told a constantly changing story and, from the clues provided by temperature, humidity, wind velocity and pressure, the Met man was able to provide a reasonably accurate picture of the weather Flight 738 could expect. For most of the trip, conditions looked good; it was only on the last lap that problems seemed likely to materialize. Thunderstorms were brewing east of the Mississippi but it was hard to predict just how severe they might turn out to be and just where they might form.

'Anything reported en route?'

'A Northwest flight reported some CAT at thirty thousand.'

'OK.' Vaughan decided to stay well away from that altitude; clear air turbulence could be thoroughly unpleasant and exceedingly dangerous. He would request air-traffic control to route him at a minimum of 35,000 feet—flight level 350. He would travel along an invisible highway in the sky, a Jet Route, in a block of air reserved for his aircraft. He would be observed and identified by one air-traffic controller after another as he made his way across the continent.

Garten was making notes of the conditions at Chicago, Toronto and New York: ceiling, visibility, sea-level pressure, temperature, dew point, wind altimeter setting, visual runway range.

Bleakly, Vaughan noted that Garten had a laboured hand, not unlike Janet's.

A captain named Fletcher breezed in from somewhere and said he hadn't seen Vaughan since God knows when and how the hell had he been and how was that doll of a wife of his.

'She's well,' Vaughan said.

'You don't deserve her, you bastard. Tell her that from me.'

'All right,' Vaughan said.

'Promise?'

'I promise.'

'Where're you going?'

'Kennedy.'

'You'll never find it. See you.'

Garten was industriously calculating the amount of fuel required for the trip—an amount that had to include reserves that would enable them to reach alternate airports in the event of emergencies and spend up to two hours circling waiting to land.

It always made sense to carry as much fuel as possible. You never ever knew when you might need it. A famous case in point was the four-engined airliner that took off from a field in Africa bound for the United States with scheduled refuelling stops at the Azores and at Gander, Newfoundland. The first stop was made without a hitch; soon the DC-6's propellers were spinning and she was off on the next leg of the trip. But before reaching the mid-way point between the Azores and Newfoundland, a radio message was received: dense fog had descended upon Newfoundland without warning. The airport was closed. There was nothing for it but to turn around and head back to the Azores. No sweat. The navigator worked out the course and the DC-6 droned over the lonely waters of the Atlantic. But now came another shock. In response to a radio message from the aircraft, a voice from the Azores regretted having to announce that fog now blanketed the Azores also. The nearest fog-free airport was Casablanca. Grimly the crew calculated how much fuel remained in the DC-6's tanks and how far it would take them. The answer: just to Casablanca, with luck, but there might not be enough fuel remaining in the tanks to circle the airport on arrival. The course was set for Casablanca. The hours passed. The fuel gauge needles edged towards Empty. According to them, the tanks were already empty when the aircraft made a safe landing at Casablanca; upon inspection it was found that only a gallon or two still sloshed around. The arrival at Casablanca caused some dismay among the passengers, for Casablanca was the point from which they had embarked so many hours before. The moral was: always pump in as much fuel as you can lift; you can never tell when it may come in handy.

In the Crew Lounge, the cabin crew awaited him: six girls in the pale blue pant suits that were TranState's current uniform for stews. Jane Meade, the chief stew for the trip, had been with

TranState a dozen years. She had flown with Vaughan on many occasions. She greeted him with the easy respect of one veteran for another. Vaughan recognized three of the girls; the others were unfamiliar to him. But unfamiliarity was the norm where stews were concerned. Few stayed on the job more than a year or eighteen months.

'Mr Garten will be the first officer and Mr Cutshall is our navigator,' Vaughan said. 'I think the trip will be pretty smooth for the first leg, to Chicago. After that we might run into some rough stuff.'

As he spoke, he found himself wondering what the girls knew about him and the fact that his wife was living apart from him and that he had a mistress in Toronto. He remembered with a shock that Walt Przeczek's carryings-on had been common gossip at TranState; and everyone had seemed to know about Davison and his black girl friend in San Francisco and Wall's orgy pad in New York. Wasn't it highly likely, then, that they all knew about Lee? And wasn't it probable that they had been giggling about him and making cracks about him moments before he entered the lounge? Anger flared in his cheeks.

Testily, he insisted that the girls demonstrate their knowledge of the DC-8's emergency exits, the escape chutes, oxygen masks, first aid kits and procedures for emergency landings.

Two of the girls became flustered; they made mistakes. Irritably, Vaughan told Jane Meade to ensure that the girls studied their manuals before flight time.

'I don't want amateurs in my crew.'

Jane coloured but said nothing.

Outside the lounge, Vaughan was immediately contrite. For God's sake, he thought, what the hell's the matter with you? Why take it out on those kids? Why make Jane look bad?

It wasn't me, he thought. It was that poor confused son-of-a-bitch who's been inhabiting my body for the last few months. In all probability the stews knew nothing about Lee or about Susan and the kids staying at Carmel or about him living alone boiling eggs and heating TV dinners. At this very moment the new girls were undoubtedly biting back their tears, messing up their make-up and hating him for being a vindictive ogre, which he unquestionably was, at this particular day at this particular hour.

But he couldn't go back into the lounge and apologize. It would only make a bad situation infinitely worse. Better the girls thought of him as a martinet than a mental case.

Garten said, 'Shall I do the external now, sir?'

Vaughan nodded. 'I think I'll come with you. I could use some fresh air.'

Garten smiled nervously. Vaughan thought: now the poor bastard thinks I don't trust him to do the external by himself. I'm doing a great job of instilling confidence and team-spirit in this crew.

The aircraft stood beside the terminal building, connected to it by the umbilical-like tube through which the passengers would shortly enter. The baggage compartment doors were open, waiting.

Inside, the aircraft was empty. It was warm; the sun beamed through a score of ½-inch thick, triple-pane windows. Its 189 passenger seats were unoccupied, the safety belts crossed neatly on the seats as specified in company regulations. The economy-class seats were precisely 34 inches apart—the 'pitch' in airline parlance—and the first-class seats were 42 inches apart. On TranState aircraft, as on those of every airline, first-class accommodation consistently lost money. Thus, ironically, economy-class passengers subsidized their first-class travelling companions. The seat pockets all contained identical items: a map of the United States and Canada showing the routes flown by TranState, a 6-page booklet recounting in some detail how the line was founded in 1931 (by a far-sighted business-man who was dissatisfied with the rail service between Tacoma, Washington, and Eugene, Oregon, and who, due to the vagaries of the Great Depression, found himself the owner of a brace of Buhl Air-Sedans), a grease-paper bag into which queasy passengers could vomit the contents of their stomachs ('snack-sack' was the term used by the TranState cabin crews) and a copy of the company's quarterly magazine TranStatement which contained glowing illustrations of tanned, smiling passengers in several of the cities served by the airline. All articles were written, and separated offset colour film supplied free of charge, by the public relations departments of the cities in question. It was a source of constant vexation to the TranState sales people that the magazine was invariably a month or two behind schedule and a few thousand dollars in the red despite heroic efforts to sell sufficient advertising (principally to suppliers) to make the thing pay for itself.

The aircraft was the result of countless intelligent compromises; its design was a phenomenally complicated business of weighing speed requirements against passenger comfort, cargo capacity against range, ease of maintenance against aerodynamic form, safety against economics. Several hundred thousand decisions shaped the final product, created its character and assured its reputation among passengers and pilots. The aircraft was powered by four JT3D-7 jet engines capable of providing a total of 72,000 pounds of thrust. Their location, in streamlined pods beneath the wings, was one of the designer's major decisions. He might have buried the engines in the wing root, the point at which the wings join the fuselage. By doing so he would have reduced drag and minimized asymmetric yaw in the event of engine failure, and he could have kept the size of his aircraft's tail down because the heavy power units would have been close to the centre of gravity. But he would have paid a price in structural problems, cabin noise and safety. Alternatively he might have positioned the engines on either side of the fuselage close to the tail. By so doing he would have lowered the cabin noise and his wing would have been completely free and thus highly efficient. He would, however, have cut down the amount of space available for passengers and he would have added to the complexities of fuel flow and maintenance; furthermore he would have had to build a larger tail unit because of centre of gravity problems and stronger (therefore heavier) wings and rear fuselage. And so factors, advantages, disadvantages were weighed and measured. And decisions were made and it was hoped that they were the right ones.

It was cool beneath the DC-8's broad, swept-back wings, as if the sun had never penetrated there. Vaughan looked up at the ailerons and flap linkages, the great engine pods that dangled from the wings on the slender mountings. Nothing appeared to be loose; nothing seemed to be leaking more than usual. He inspected the aircraft's tyres, each of which cost TranState roughly $250 and was good for only about seventy-five landings after which it had to be replaced. Plenty of tread on these tyres; no nails or sharp stones embedded in the rubber. Above him, the 200-foot-long fuselage blotted out the sky. It smelt of metal and oil and fuel and a number of other substances which were unidentifiable but which helped to create the smell peculiar to aeroplanes whether they were four-jet airliners or perky little Piper Cubs. He saw Garten peering studiously at the underside of the wing. Was he about to report a larger-than-normal leak? And would the captain delay the flight until the leak was fixed? Vaughan shook his head sadly. You had no business getting yourself killed, he told Walt Przeczek. Dumb Polack, he added with affection.

'Everything looks just fine, Captain,' Garten announced. He looked as if he was about to salute in his eagerness.

'You figure she's safe to fly?'

'Yes *sir*.'

'Captain Vaughan?'

Vaughan turned. Wills, one of the Flight Planning men, was calling him from the office doorway.

'Could you come to the phone, Captain? Air Canada's on the line for you.'

'Air Canada?'

Wills shrugged. 'That's what the gal said.'

Vaughan went inside and took the telephone.

A girl said, 'This is the Air Canada office here at LAX. We've received a telex from Toronto.'

'Toronto?' Vaughan caught his breath.

'Yes, Captain. They asked us to call TranState and pass on the message. I'm glad we found you in. Here's the message.'

Vaughan listened. When it was over he asked the girl to repeat it. This time the words had to mean something different. But they didn't.

'LEE HURT IN GLIDER MISHAP. IN ST MICHAEL'S HOSPITAL, HAMILTON. SORRY. LARRY.'

Larry. The tow-plane pilot.

'That's all?'

'Yes sir, that's it.'

'OK, thank you.'

It seemed to take an hour for the long-distance operator to find the number and put him through.

At last a woman's voice announced, 'St Michael's.'

Vaughan said, 'I'm enquiring about a patient. Her name is Lee
—no, Rosalie Pringle.'

'Pringle. One moment, sir.'

On the other side of the room a pilot named Morrison exploded
in laughter as he recounted his latest dirty story. Morrison always
had a supply of the latest dirty stories.

The voice again. 'Mrs Pringle is in Intensive Care, sir.'

'Intensive Care? You mean ...?'

'I'll put you through to ICU.'

His fingers tightened on the phone. 'Look, ma'am, I'm calling
from Los Angeles, California ...'

'Are you a relative, sir?'

What the hell difference ...? 'No, a friend, a friend of the
family.'

'I'm sorry. The line to ICU is busy at the moment.'

'I'll call back,' said Vaughan. His mouth was dry and bitter.

21

Amory International Flight 1010 was the 23rd aircraft that day to head out across the Atlantic in a westerly direction, the 204th that week, the 6,012th that year. An endless procession of jet airliners belonging to the world's famous lines and dozens of lesser-known companies had captured Atlantic travel from the stately ships. Now the ports of Southampton and New York, Montreal and Le Havre rarely saw a passenger ship. One by one the liners had been reduced to scrap or converted into floating hotels and restaurants. Their days were done. Once the very symbols of modernity, engineering skill and national pride, they had become anachronisms in their own time. To the lovers of ships, the transatlantic jets were evil, noisy things, nasty metallic insects that whooshed through the air without dignity. Unsafe and uncomfortable, all they had to offer was speed. With more than a little justification, the ship buffs pointed out that flying was a thoroughly ghastly way to travel, squashed like sardines into a beastly metal tube, served plastic, pre-heated food and tossed out at your destination dizzy with travel sickness, barely conscious of what time or day it was. Orville and Wilbur Wright had a great deal to answer for.

Transatlantic flight by charter was in some ways the aerial equivalent of a steerage passage. In both cases, the object of the exercise was to squeeze as many paying passengers as possible into the available space. Charter operators felt, since they charged lower fares, that they could take the space-per-passenger down to rock-bottom limits. To this end, the seats in Amory's 707s had a pitch of less than thirty inches. Men of average height sat with their legs hard against the seat in front; taller-than-average men had to angle their legs uncomfortably to the left or right. Space represented revenue. But each trip was relatively brief. And there was usually little difficulty in choosing between double the cost and a few hours of discomfort combined with mild claustrophobia. Muscles and sinews could be made to adapt. Food and drink would find its way down to the right destination eventually. And, astonishingly, contorted bodies found that they could sleep.

Flight 1010 sliced up through the murky clouds. The sun suddenly bounced all over the bright metal of the wing, dazzling many an eager eye. Passengers discovered that their windows had neat little blinds that could be pulled down to keep out the sun. But they didn't stay down long; there was too much danger of not seeing whatever there might be to see. What a shame the ground was invisible; it would have been fun to identify landmarks, thought those who had never flown before. The captain (ever such a calm, dignified voice, he had) said Anglesey was directly below and the Irish Sea was dead ahead.

Mr and Mrs Cox had held hands during the take-off run. It had all seemed rather breakneck and frantic, that enormous, trembling contraption, God knows how many tons of it, hurling itself headlong at the London to Brighton railway line. But, with a great heave, it had gone zooming up—almost vertically, it had seemed. Mr Cox had felt his senses begin to wobble. Then he realized that he had been holding his breath since the beginning of the take-off run. He heard his wife say 'Well, I never' several times, as was her custom when confronted by anything frightening or bewildering. He had patted her hand and smiled at her. She had smiled back. But it wasn't what you'd call a genuine smile of pleasure or contentment. Definitely a bit on the forced side.

The odd thing was, once the rather scary business of the take-off was over, the actual flying-along part turned out to be quite uninteresting. Monotonous, really, with that dull drone from the motors and nothing to see below but a sort of fuzz of grey cloud. Thank goodness for a spot of good reading. Mr Cox had a corker of a book craftily concealed within the generous pages of the Safety Manual For the Information of All Passengers. (It was as well to keep that sort of book away from the Old Woman. Very sheltered, her life had been. Never really had much of an inkling of Real Life.) Thirty new pence, the book had cost. And worth every cent.

178

Jack Meighen had recommended it. Jack should have been ashamed of himself, reading such stuff at his age. The book described in almost surgical detail the life and times of a successful prostitute in Maida Vale. She called herself a 'professional' and, by George, you couldn't argue with her about that. She had set out to learn every trick of her chosen trade. Her aim, she explained, was to give utmost value for money spent. Which seemed to Mr Cox thoroughly commendable. Other members of the business community might well take note. He read on. Strewth! They could print anything these days and get away with it. Nothing was taboo! He glanced at his watch. He had five hours to finish the book. When the plane arrived in Toronto he would leave the book in the seat pocket. He couldn't possibly be carrying it when he met Joycie and her husband Eddie and the grandchildren. Out of the question!

Miss Hardcastle had been led aboard the aircraft ahead of the other passengers. The stewardess—who hailed from somewhere to the southwest of Bristol, unless Miss Hardcastle was very much mistaken—found her a seat beside a window and immediately in front of a toilet. The young lady had then explained the use of the seat belt and the various comfort and convenience controls, after which she had left Miss Hardcastle to await the other passengers. For some minutes it had been eerily quiet, with only a series of odd thumps and bangs beneath the floor to keep her company. But soon the other passengers came clattering along. A young girl's voice said hullo—followed at once by the inevitable intake of air. It was, Miss Hardcastle supposed, a bit of a shock to discover that one is talking to a blind person. She had a lifetime of experience of people's reaction to blindness. Sometimes there was utter silence after the inhalation; there was, it seemed, a fear of talking to a person without sight. Did some people think the condition contagious? But this girl's silence had lasted only moments. Soon she was chuckling about the difficulty of stowing her flight bag. Miss Hardcastle suggested she take the window seat; it was, after all, completely wasted on someone unable to see out. Miss Hardcastle was delighted to find that the girl wasn't one of those people who steadfastly refuse any gesture for fear it might involve some sort of obligation. Julie (for that was the girl's name) was pleased to sit next to the window and much obliged for the offer. This was her first long trip by aeroplane and she wanted to see everything there was to see. No, she really didn't think she was nervous; excited yes, but not nervous. Soon the two of them were chatting thirteen to the dozen, like old friends. Julie was going to Canada to visit an aunt and uncle; she was going to look around and decide whether to emigrate. Miss Hardcastle said she was going to visit her brother in Toronto. She laughed when Julie unthinkingly asked how long it was since she had seen her brother. 'Never!' she said. Julie apologized—but cautioned that she would undoubtedly make the same mistake again within five minutes. Miss Hardcastle didn't care. Smiling, they settled down to enjoy a pleasant trip in congenial company.

They were blissfully unaware of the irritation boiling within the occupant of the aisle seat. In Len Sparrow's opinion, fate had delivered him a particularly low blow. When the flight had been called he had purposely moved smartish and had slipped into the queue right behind the bird with the nice profile. (She smelt nice too, he had discovered.) A bloke with a cap had asked her what seat she wanted. She told him she wanted a window seat but he told her they were all gone. So she chose 8E. Len peeped over her shapely shoulder. He knew the score. When the bloke asked him about his seat preference, he said he wanted 8D. The bloke had said he didn't blame Len, but Len had merely sniffed, disdainful-like. Hopes high, he had followed the mob into the plane—but would you believe it, when he got inside, he found the bird changing places! Now he was stuck next to an old blind bint with dark glasses. What a turn-up for the bleedin' books!

Flying the Atlantic was not particularly demanding. It was largely a matter of guiding the aircraft to the correct altitude and heading, then trimming it and handing it over to the automatic pilot. Thereafter, the job was handled by gyros and accelerometers. As a rule there was little for the pilot to look at during his journey over the ocean—although it was as well to keep an eye open for Russian and Cuban aircraft which were wont to fly north or south across the Europe-America routes without warning.

At 35,000 feet the sky was featureless. The clouds lay far below.

The ocean, when it was visible, looked like a flat, grey motionless pond. In theory a pilot at an altitude of some seven miles can see about two hundred miles. Over Belfast he can see Birmingham; over Copenhagen he can see Berlin. In practice the sky is rarely clear enough to see more than a few score miles, usually not as much as that. It is a problem for jet pilots, for the speed of their aircraft makes their eyes a poor safeguard against mid-air collisions. Before a speck of dirt on the windscreen is identified as an approaching aircraft, it may be too late. Complicating the problem is the fact that heavy jet airliners are not noted for their nimbleness in the air. Speed and weight create colossal momentum. Jets need distance to change direction. Distance means time—and that is precisely what they do not have when another aircraft is dead ahead.

Beatty listened as Corfield sent the latest position report—evidence for the record-keepers that at the correct time Flight 1010 was in the correct position at the correct height and heading in the correct direction.

The roar of the four jets was a mellifluous rumble. It was possible to communicate with the crew without intercom; no need for bellowing in ears as had been the case in the old days. Beatty smiled, thinking of the Dakotas, clattery old workhorses of Transport Command. The windscreens of the Daks were notoriously leaky. A Transport Command pilot was said to have requested weather information by radio; on being told that light rain was falling he replied that the rain may have been light on the ground but in the cockpit it was a deluge. In spite of such minor faults, the Dak was a dear old thing; she would patiently lift just about anything that could be stuffed aboard her. During the Berlin Airlift the RAF and USAAF regularly flew her laden with two or three tons of cargo over her official capacity. Somehow she always tottered into the air, her slender wings bending and flapping but never breaking. The Dak was an infinitely willing but slightly dotty old maiden aunt; the 707 was slick and streamlined and tough as nails.

Would Vincent become an airman? Beatty had often wondered. In a way it would be flattering. But the fact of the matter was, the boy had so far displayed no more interest in flying than in water-skiing. He could handle an Auster in straight and level flight and turns; he was usually willing to come for a flip if there was nothing more promising on tap. (Willing! Ye Gods, Beatty had thought; if only I had had the same opportunities to fly as a kid. I would never have been on the ground!) But flying seemed to Vincent to be just one of a large number of interesting things that living had to offer. It certainly enjoyed no exclusivity in his mind. All his generation seemed to think the same way. It was as if they trusted only themselves; everything adult was to be treated with the utmost caution. If the oldsters like it, it is suspect.

Beatty remembered that when he was Vincent's age his mind had room for little other than aviation. He knew a Sidestrand from an Overstrand, a Gordon from a Wallace. He knew that Whitleys had Tiger engines and Hurricanes had Merlins. He knew also that British aircraft were superior in every conceivable respect to those produced abroad, including those manufactured in America—although he was prepared to categorize them as considerably less foreign than, say, the Capronis of Italy or the Junkers of Germany.

'Captain?'

Beatty turned. Jordan, the engineer stood between the two pilots, his elbows resting on their seat backs.

'Yes?'

'Troubles, I'm afraid. That bloody temperature in No. 4.'

22

The DC-8 streaked upward; the sprawling city of Los Angeles seemed to shrink beneath its trembling wings. Despite the twenty-one square feet of window on three sides of the flight deck, the crew could see little but sky. The shapely nose section blotted out their view and would continue to do so until the aircraft reached cruising altitude and began to travel horizontally. Fortunately the DC-8's path through the sky was reserved; although there were a dozen or more aircraft in the immediate vicinity, none trespassed. Ground controllers, their eyes glued to radar screens, kept the aircraft apart.

'Departure Control, TranState 738, out of five for two two zero.'

'Roger, TranState 738. Contact Los Angeles Centre. One two eight point two.'

'TranState 738, changing to LA Centre.'

At 18,000 feet the pilots reset their altimeters to standard setting: 29.92.

'TranState 738, clear to climb and maintain flight level three five zero.'

Garten acknowledged in curt, text-book fashion.

At 35,000 feet the DC-8 levelled off. Climb-out completed. Thrust levers back after checking outside air temperature and present aircraft weight; the manual provided the answer to the calculation and told the crew precisely how much power was needed to maintain cruising speed. Thrust lever friction locks were tightened.

The DC-8 had consumed nearly 10,000 pounds of fuel. At cruising speed, it would burn kerosene at approximately 12,000 pounds per hour.

Auto-pilot on. Obediently the great aircraft shifted a few degrees as it locked on to the VOR navigational signal. On the panel, the DME digits scurried past the indicator in a frenzy of activity as the computer digested the problem. In a moment it had the answer. The digits stopped. They announced that the aircraft was travelling at a ground speed of 478 knots and would arrive at the next checkpoint in eight minutes. At the navigator's table, Cutshall methodically entered the figures on the company route sheets, Form Number PL807/5M/07.

The sun was brilliant, sparkling on wisps of cloud, like ghostly Spanish moss, bursting and bouncing on the metal of the DC-8, even managing to reflect a fraction of its brilliance against the dull black anti-glare panel painted on the nose immediately before the windshield.

It was superb weather. CAVU—ceiling and visibility unlimited. Far below, the Rockies slid away, the colossal peaks and valleys no more significant to the aircraft's passing than sandcastles on a beach. Ahead lay the gigantic plains of America, the prairies, the endless flatlands that had once seen dogged convoys of covered wagons groaning westward, measuring their progress in miles per day. Hurtling eastward, the DC-8 gobbled up the miles, one every six seconds.

Jane came in, taking orders for coffee. Vaughan shook his head, not looking at her. I'll talk to her later, he thought. She'll understand. He noticed Garten glancing at him from the right-hand seat. He seemed a little apprehensive, which wasn't too surprising. The poor guy had probably been told that Vaughan was all right and that he had been lucky to draw him for his first line flight. Now, thought Vaughan, he's probably wondering how the others can be worse.

After me they'll be a breeze, feller.

What about Lee? What the hell did *hurt* mean? Did she break a leg? A finger? Get a black eye? Was he worrying needlessly? It was often the way things seemed to work out. The things you tore your guts out over always turned out to be nothing. It was the unexpected items that got you.

Chances are she's sitting up in bed drinking beer and reading *Playboy*.

In Intensive Care?

What did that mean? Was it just a department name?

Is this a punishment?

He winced. No, that was absurd, a lot of old superstition handed down by generations of ignorant, frightened ancestors. There was no such thing as the day of reckoning. Lee hadn't sinned, anyway. He was the only sinner. If anyone should be punished it should be him.

Perhaps this was his punishment, he thought.

In Toronto, the revised weather forecast advised that there was a strong possibility of moderate-to-severe thunderstorms developing during the afternoon and evening.

Vaughan glanced at the panel clock which had been set to Chicago time. In an hour and a half they would be landing at O'Hare. He would call the hospital again from there.

Please have good news for me, he thought. Please.

He stared ahead through the $2\frac{1}{2}$-inch-thick windshield. The sky was gradually losing its clarity. The sharp line that was the horizon had become fuzzy, half-blurred. Below, the ground seemed to be slowly sinking, its tones becoming progressively muted as the stratum of moisture particles settled.

He turned to Garten.

'You want to take her in to O'Hare?'

Garten beamed. 'Sure thing, Captain, thanks.'

'OK. I'm your copilot now. You're the skipper. She's all yours.'

'Reducing the power won't help,' said Jordan. 'The oil's cooled by the bloody fuel. Anyway,' he added, 'I'm just about a hundred per cent sure it's the sodding gauge.'

'I see,' said Beatty.

'But the trouble is,' said Jordan, 'I can't be sure until we get on the bloody ground.'

'So we shut down.'

' 'Fraid so, skipper.'

'OK.'

'You'll let her cool a couple of minutes first, won't you?'

'OK, nurse,' said Corfield, grinning.

Ahead was nothing but murky cloud. Beatty asked Webb for a position report, although he had a good idea. A man gets to know an ocean when he has flown it several hundred times.

'Gander's 890 miles, sir.'

Beatty nodded. He told Corfield to call Gander and advise them of the problem. 'But we're not declaring an emergency,' he said. 'Piece of cake getting there on three engines.'

'Roger, sir.'

Thrust lever ... essential power ... start lever cutoff ... nacelle anti-ice off ... ignition off ... generator breaker tripped ... fuel shut-off valve closed ... The check-list dictated the sequence of operations necessary for the shutting-down of engine number four.

The passengers were unaware of any problem. There was no sensation of sudden power loss. And no tell-tale stationary propeller stood guard before the stilled engine.

Shanwick HF radio would already be passing on the news to Amory in London. It was turning out to be a bad day for the line.

Beatty glanced at his watches—the watch on his left wrist told local time, the one on his right told Greenwich Mean Time: 'Zulu time' in airway parlance. Poor old Amory's timetables were becoming properly buggered up. Thank the Lord. Gander was in Canadian territory; the Canadians were usually fairly unemotional about three-engine landings. If the landing was to be made on a British or American field, an emergency would be mandatory and God knows how many fire engines and ambulances and other expensive vehicles would be called out. All very comforting and heart-warming of course, but hardly necessary in this case.

'Overcast at Gander,' Corfield reported. 'No problem, though. Ceiling three thou, visibility five.'

Beatty cleared his throat as he pressed the PA button on his headset. 'This is the captain speaking. I'm sorry to have to tell you that we'll be making an unscheduled stop before we get to Toronto. A minor problem has occurred, a technicality, nothing to get the slightest bit alarmed about, but we want to look into it. So we'll be touching down at Gander, Newfoundland, in slightly more than an hour. No extra charge for letting you have a quick visit to Newfoundland; all part of the Amory service.' He groaned to himself; he really wasn't good at this sort of thing. 'I don't think we shall be on the ground at Gander for more than thirty minutes. Thank you.'

'Got problems, 'ave we?'

Lewis, the purser, came into the cockpit, bearing four cups of tea and biscuits on plastic plates. He smiled knowingly at the crew, seeking inside gen.

Corfield said, 'Don't you believe Captain Beatty?'

'Up to a point,' said Lewis, smiling knowingly, 'but only up to a point.'

'Perspicacious of you, old man,' said Corfield. 'The truth of the matter is that the headwinds have turned out to be far stronger than we anticipated and actually we're going backwards and we're about to land back at Gatwick.'

Lewis flushed. 'Very bloody funny, I must say.' He stalked aft, banging the flight-deck door behind him.

For the majority of the passengers, it was their first glimpse of North America. And a thoroughly dismaying first glance it was. The terrain looked about as hospitable as the far side of the moon. Was there any sign that anyone had ever set foot on the place? Ah yes; a road appeared beneath the 707's swaying wings. And there was a car, a lonely little thing, buzzing along like an eager insect. So people really did live down there.

Len Sparrow was one of the very few aboard the jet who welcomed the unscheduled stop. Perhaps at last he would get an opportunity to work a spot of the old fatal charm on the bird with the profile. Vaguely, he saw himself surrounded by the hostile natives indigenous to this strange region. He was standing his ground, unafraid (and, conveniently, about six feet four inches tall). The natives, scruffy, evil-looking geezers, were keeping a respectful distance from this lean and fearless stranger who gazed at them through slitted eyes. As for the bird, she was staying close, palpitating a bit while he stared them down, broke their will with the sheer power of his presence ...

But the important question was: would the old blind bint stay put in her seat?

'Amory Ten Ten, you are clear for a straight-in approach.'

The 707 touched down, incurring landing fees of approximately $1,000 for Amory International, plus some $300 for such necessities as the provision of steps and ground power.

At that moment, TranState Flight 738 was 2,114 miles away, approaching Des Moines, Iowa.

Jordan cut a shim out of a small piece of aluminium. It was, he pointed out with justifiable pride, worth about two pence, but it would do the trick; it would do the work of the thermostat spring that had been causing all the trouble. The crew ran up the engines; everything checked out.

Beatty found to his relief that Amory's credit was good at Gander. He ordered the aircraft's tanks refilled.

Five minutes later he was clinging to the towel dispenser in the washroom. His limbs were as heavy as lead. He gasped in air. He was conscious of an absurd impulse to protest. He had taken the pills as prescribed. He had done his stuff faithfully. Why, then, wasn't his brain co-operating?

'Everything under control, sir?'

'Under control?' Beatty formed the two words with care; his voice seemed to him to have a distant and curiously mechanical quality. 'Yes.'

'Good show,' said Corfield.

Again, Beatty agonized over the words. 'Be a good chap and do the external, will you?'

'Right-oh, sir.'

'I'll be along in a minute.'

Lord, but it was good to be alone. Good to feel one's senses easing back into place. Good to feel strong enough again to be able to curse the misbehaviour of one's electrical circuits.

Don't come in, he begged of the owner of the footsteps in the corridor, just a couple of yards away. Please don't come in.

The footsteps took themselves elsewhere.

The room began to revolve, then steadied itself like an aircraft coming out of a spin. Everything OK in a minute, Beatty thought.

It was. Strength travelled slowly along every nerve and through every bone. Its progress could be followed. It commenced in the arms and worked inwards to the body, then down to the legs. The head seemed to come last: an afterthought. A clearing, a balancing of unruly forces ...

Beatty stood up. Weak but steady. You're all right now, he said.

But the truth was, he felt sick and wobbly. Why, he wondered, didn't the pills work this time? Why didn't they prevent the attack? Did he need a stronger variety now? Had he outgrown these? He would have to see Hoke about it the moment he got back to London. Perhaps, he thought, I should have that operation Hoke talked about; perhaps that would clear the thing up once and for all. Perhaps I could get a leave of absence or something, and have the operation done under the name of Carter and then go back to work and no one need be the wiser....

He shook his head, pained by his own delusions. He was day-dreaming like some stupid teenager.

You've had it, he told himself. You're through. Grounded. As of this moment.

He drank from the iced-water fountain. Greedily. He was uncommonly thirsty. He soaked his handkerchief and pressed it against his forehead.

Are you going to ground yourself here and now? In Newfoundland?

It was a good question. The fact of the matter was, if he grounded himself the flight would be held up until Amory could organize a replacement captain and get him over to Gander. Which would probably take about twelve hours or longer. Which would mean that the flight would be even more horrendously off schedule and which would also mean that the passengers and crew would have to be fed and probably accommodated too. Altogether, it would represent yet another major slap in the pocket book for old Amory.

Amory, he thought, was the one chap who was willing to offer you another chance. He was the only one.

But I won't be doing him a favour if I take his aeroplane up and smash it and kill all his passengers.

He shook his head. He wouldn't fly. He would take another pill and play at copilot. If he dropped dead it wouldn't make any difference. Corfield was a thoroughly competent chap.

He took a deep breath. He felt better, definitely better. He would telephone Amory from Toronto and explain the situation. Amory could replace him far more readily in Toronto than here in New-foundland.

The passengers for Amory International Flight 1010 filed back across the open, windswept concrete ramp to the aircraft. The Boeing was a familiar old friend now; the passengers felt a certain affection for her; together they had traversed the wide ocean and had ventured into the New World. The passengers were thankful to be on their way. They had found the terminal at Gander to possess few diversions. After waiting in line at the cafeteria for a cup of tea (of sorts) or a Coke and wondering at the curious one-third-Irish-one-third-Scottish-one-third-American accent of the lady at the cash register, they had strolled into the gift shop to study the Eskimo and Indian handicrafts, considering them the ideal gifts for Bert and Thelma and Uncle George and Cousin Myra—until hurried calculations converted dollars into pounds; whereupon their enthusiasm for native handicrafts diminished apace. Some passengers had ventured up to the mezzanine and had spent some minutes with the exhibit honouring all the fliers who had set off from Newfoundland on their lonely—and often fatal—attempts on the Atlantic.

Len Sparrow walked behind the bird with the profile. He was irked. The old blind bint hadn't let go for an instant. So his hands had been tied, figuratively speaking. Poor kid, she hadn't even managed a glance in his direction.

That's life, baby.

You had your chance. But you blew it.

The crew strapped themselves in and reached for their manuals.

Beatty tried to keep his breathing steady and regular. He felt exhausted. Cold sweat embraced him clammily. He wondered if his shirt looked as sodden as it felt.

He turned to Corfield.

'You're the skipper. Take us to Toronto, there's a good fellow.'

23

It was sultry in Chicago, the air still and heavy with moisture—warm, clammy moisture.

Cutshall said, 'This goddam town gives you a choice: dead calm or a typhoon. Freezing or broiling. Nothing in between.'

Vaughan eased himself out of the captain's seat.

'See you back here in twenty minutes.'

The crew acknowledged, glancing at their watches. As Vaughan left the flight deck he heard Cutshall briefing Garten on a night club he happened to know just off State that offered 'special shows' after hours to favoured patrons.

The terminal building was thronged by irritable, shiny-faced people laden with baggage or children. Was it July 4? A holiday? Vaughan couldn't remember the date. He swore as he looked for a telephone that was free. He passed up those being used by blacks —some of them delighted in stretching their conversations to ludicrous lengths if they knew Whitey was waiting. Vaughan had often wondered if he would do the same if he was black. Probably, he thought. He stationed himself behind a stocky man in a crumpled tropical suit who was explaining to someone, presumably his boss, that the business had gone to the competition purely and simply because of nepotism not, as was apparently being intimated, because the account had been poorly serviced.

'The son-of-a-bitch couldn't have done any better himself and he goddam well knows it,' said the man, hanging up the phone. He looked drained and weary. He glanced at Vaughan's uniform. 'Sure wish I could fly airplanes for a living.'

'It's a gas,' said Vaughan automatically.

'I tried for Aviation in the Navy but my eyes screwed me.'

'Tough,' said Vaughan, reaching for the phone.

'Always figured I'd have made a good pilot.'

'It's better than working for a living.'

'I bet to Christ it is,' said the man with feeling.

Vaughan slipped the dime into the slot. The operator answered. Vaughan told her his long-distance credit-card number and the number of the hospital in Hamilton.

'Were you in the service?'

Vaughan nodded. 'Excuse me,' he said, turning to the phone.

But the man wouldn't relinquish the contact, no matter how tenuous. What would Vaughan say to a quick drink in the bar when he was through with his phone call?

'Sorry. I'm flying.'

'A cup of coffee then? Coffee won't spoil your aim.'

'Excuse me,' said Vaughan again as the hospital switchboard answered. He was, he explained to the voice, calling regarding the condition of a patient named Rosalie Pringle.

'One moment, please.'

The salesman stood a few feet away, a rather pathetic-looking figure, swaying very slightly. Vaughan wished he would go away. Why did so many middle-aged men seem compelled to talk to airline pilots? Some wanted to know if it was true what they had heard about airline stewardesses. Others just seemed to want to converse, about anything. There were a lot of lonely people to be found at airports.

The same woman's voice. 'Are you the gentleman who called from California?'

'That's right. Now I'm calling from Chicago, Illinois.'

Pause.

'Did you say you were a relative?'

'Yes. An uncle. From Winnipeg. But I'm calling from Chicago.'

'I see.' Another pause. Then: 'Sir, I'm not supposed to reveal information of ... but as you're calling from so far.... Sir, Mrs Pringle passed away at one-twenty-five.'

'One-twenty-five,' he said.

'Yes sir.'

'Thank you.'

'You're welcome, sir.'

He hung up while the PA crackled something about Memphis

and New Orleans. A man bellowed something about a baggage voucher. The monotonous clatter of rock music combined with the squeaking of a baby carriage. A black woman grinned hugely into the next telephone. The air was heavy with the smell of cigars and popcorn.

'How about that coffee now?'

'What?'

Vaughan looked at the man in the crumpled suit without seeing him. He turned back to the telephone, dazed.

He couldn't find a dime. Pennies, nickels, quarters. For Christ's sake there had to be a dime! He remembered the coin he had already used; the operator would have returned it because he made the call on his credit card. Yes, there it was, in the coin return cup. He inserted it as he searched for the note bearing the Carmel number. Be in, he begged, please be in.

Susan's father answered.

'I have to talk to Susan,' Vaughan said.

Mr Jearard sensed the urgency in his voice and wasted no time on niceties. 'Very well, Chuck. Hold on.'

Somewhere in the house a TV set was playing a rerun of a Beverly Hillbillies episode. Cackles and screeches and canned laughter.

'Yes?' Crisp. Curt.

'She's dead, Susan.'

Silence.

'Susan?'

'Yes, I'm here.'

'Did you hear what I said?'

'Yes, I heard.' Her voice had softened. She sounded uncertain. 'I'm sorry, Chuck ... I don't know what to say. I honestly don't.'

'I had to call you.'

'I'm glad you did. What ... what happened?'

'It was an accident in a glider. I don't know what happened ... she crashed, I guess.'

'I'm sorry.' She added, 'Yes, I am sorry because she was young and ... I mean it, but ...'

'I know you mean it,' he said.

'How are you?'

'I'm ...' He thought, rubbing his forehead with his free hand. 'I'm kind of stunned. I don't know really how I am. Do you understand?'

'Of course I do. Where are you calling from, Chuck?'

'Chicago. O'Hare. I'm due out in a few minutes.'

'Are you flying back to the Coast now?'

'No, I'm going on to ...'

'Where, Chuck?'

'Toronto, then New York.'

'You mustn't fly this trip, Chuck. Tell them to get someone else.'

'I can't, not now.'

'Please. Tell them you're sick or something.'

He said, 'I'm coming back to the Coast tomorrow, Susan. Will you ...?'

'Do you want us to be there?'

'Christ, of course I do.'

'You're sure?'

'I'm sure, Susan. Absolutely. Please come home. I'll be getting in around six, LA time. I can be home around eight, eight-thirty.'

'We'll be there,' she said.

'How are the girls?'

'Fine.'

'Susan.'

'Yes?'

'I know it's ... crazy, my calling you ... to tell you about ... you know what I mean.'

Susan said, 'I don't think it's crazy at all, Chuck, really.' She sounded as if her eyes were full of tears; Vaughan imagined her blinking at them. 'In a way it's ... rather lovely that you called me. At least that's the way I'm reacting. I don't know if I'm supposed to react that way, but I am.'

'I'm glad. Thank you.'

She said, 'Don't fly, Chuck. They can get someone else.'

'Not at such short notice. Besides, I'm OK. Really. Don't worry. Give my love to the girls.'

'I will.'

'See you tomorrow.'

'Yes,' she said. 'Goodbye.'

'Goodbye.'

'Are you through?'

A brassy-voiced woman asked him if he planned to spend the rest of the day standing in front of the phone. He apologized. Snappily, the woman told him not to mention it.

The man in the crumpled tropical suit was still there but Vaughan walked past him, unaware of his presence.

Dead? Was Lee really dead? Had he just had a totally unbelievable conversation with Susan?

He sat down on a bench and stared at the headline of a *Tribune* someone had dropped. No mention of Lee, just a lot of words about the White House and its problems. Unimportant words. Meaningless words.

He shook his head. A marine on the opposite bench glanced at him curiously. He averted his eyes when they encountered Vaughan's.

'Are you a pilot, mister?'

Vaughan turned. A small boy was asking the question. Vaughan nodded. 'Yes, son.'

'D'you fly jumbo jets?'

'No. DC-8s.'

'They're OK too,' said the boy gravely.

'Don't bother the man,' said his mother.

'He's not bothering me,' said Vaughan.

'I've been up in a jumbo,' said the boy. 'I'm goin' to fly one when I grow up.'

'Then you must take care not to call them jumbos.'

'Why?'

'Because jumbos make you think of elephants, don't they? And the Boeing 747 doesn't look like an elephant. Only people who don't know much about airplanes call them jumbos.'

The boy promised to remember that.

'Cap'n Vaughan, sir?'

Vaughan looked up. Garten stood there, perspiring freely.

'It's thirteen forty-five, sir.'

'What?' Vaughan stared at his watch. It was indeed 13:45. 'Sorry,' he said. 'I didn't realize it was so late.' It would be necessary, he thought numbly, to complete a Reason For Delayed Departure form, L908/F2.

'Are you OK, sir?'

'Sure. Why do you ask?'

'Sitting here ... alone.'

The little boy and his mother had gone. So had the marine. 'I'm fine,' he told Garten. 'Dozed off, I guess.'

'I've completed the external, sir.'

Vaughan nodded. 'Good. So let's go.'

Grant Hobbs habitually travelled Economy despite the fact that his income exceeded $100,000 a year (approximately $80,000 of which he studiously neglected to report to the Internal Revenue Service). Hobbs appreciated the anonymity of Economy. In First-Class, people tended to glance at you and wonder if you were Somebody. But, as an Economy passenger, you were just another body, another face. This suited Grant Hobbs; his only desire was to pass among his fellows as uneventfully as possible. To this end, he wore dark grey suits and unadventurous neckties; he buried his small head in large books and avoided communication with his fellow passengers. He disliked flying; it scared him. He preferred to drive, but today some instinct (and he had the greatest respect for his instincts) commanded him to depart the State of California by the most rapid means available. He had purchased the ticket on TranState Flight 738 only minutes before departure time. When he had entered the aircraft, he had asked the stewardess to point out the emergency exits—as was his custom when circumstances compelled him to travel by air. Then Hobbs asked the girl to explain the workings of the exit handles; it was comforting to find out such things; survival was, after all, largely a matter of planning ahead. The stewardess remarked that it was the second time that day she had been obliged to demonstrate her knowledge of the emergency exits.

On re-entering the DC-8 at Chicago, Hobbs had again checked the exit; he then opened his current volume, but before he could start to read, a bright red head appeared over the seat-back and an equally bright voice declared that he didn't need to worry himself about the emergency exits, these airplanes were safe as houses.

'Thank you very much for your information,' mumbled Mr Hobbs, and began to read without delay.

Lillian Dumont turned to the front, a smile on her lips. The quiet little guy had some class. You could always tell class. Perhaps he'd strike up a conversation after take-off. An encounter was needed just about now, to get the Big Adventure off to a swinging start. In a few minutes she would be on her way, out of Chicago, out of the United States. I hope to hell he's getting off at Toronto, she thought. She held her purse tightly. It contained $16,821.37, thanks to Associated Security Services Incorporated's petty cash and, to a considerably smaller extent, the housekeeping. She had left a note for Herman saying it was a shame but she found him a drag and that went for his mother too. (As she had written the note, the din of Herman's mother's TV had reverberated around the house from her room upstairs. She was a little hard of hearing, so the set was on full blast.) It had been fun packing the case. It hadn't taken long because Lillian had known precisely what she was taking. When the cab had arrived, Mother Dumont squealed like an old stuck pig. She wanted to know who was at the door (her hearing was better at some times than others), but Lillian hadn't responded. She had left, slamming the door so hard that the mailbox fell off the wall. She left it and told the cabby to drive her to the airport, where she bought a ticket to Toronto. One-way. She knew no one in Toronto and, indeed, had never been to the city before. But she had heard that it was groovy and there would be no problem at the border if you said you were visiting a cousin for a week or two.

Half a dozen rows farther forward, Earl Gasparac was helping his wife with her seat-belt. She was smiling and chatting, but it was obvious that she was going through hell. There should be a medal, Earl Gasparac thought bitterly, for people who suffer uncomplainingly: For Inconceivable Gallantry Day After Day After Stinking Day.

Briskly the stewardesses in their pale blue TranState uniforms strode down the centre aisle, their well-manicured fingers tapping each seat back in turn, ensuring that it was in the upright position. All passengers appeared to have their seat belts fastened—although it was statistically certain that there were some unconnected buckles beneath casual hands on laps, for there were always passengers who would far rather endanger their own limbs and lives than obey simple and sensible instructions. No one was smoking—but it was likely that at least one passenger would be puffing defiantly before the jet was airborne. The overhead racks contained no brief cases or movie cameras, nothing that could injure or even kill if tossed off the rack during a bumpy flight. The toilets were empty. The emergency chutes were secure. The doors were fastened and latched. TranState Flight 738 was ready for departure. It was twenty-two minutes behind schedule.

24

There were 10,304 aircraft flying in the skies over North America when TranState flight 738 took off from Chicago. One was Amory International Flight 1010 which was crossing the border between Maine and New Brunswick. Another was Henry Peel's tiny Aeronca. He had just made a low pass over the farmhouse; now he was zooming away into the sky at full throttle. He glanced back; the earth was shrinking like a gigantic balloon with a puncture.

There was no feeling to equal that of flying, of outsmarting gravity. He had a God-like view of the world from his Aeronca. It was a view of which he never tired. What struck him as incomprehensible was that his parents failed to share his enthusiasm. The fact of the matter was, they felt a good deal better viewing the world from a base of *terra firma*. After ten minutes of the air they would tap him on the shoulder and suggest it was time to get down once more. What could possibly possess them to prefer being down there rather than up here?

He flew to Niagara Falls.

Utterly content, he circled the huge waterfall, his wingtip slicing the rising mist. Drops of water formed on his windshield and were beaten away by the spinning propeller. Below, the streets were jammed with cars full of hot, uncomfortable, irritable people looking for places to park. Henry Peel looked down at them with the amused pity of a superior being studying the mindless antics of some sub-species.

He felt the urge to wander. Was there any happiness greater in the world than being at the controls of your very own aircraft?

Perhaps, he thought, I should get a bigger aircraft and try to break a record or two.

Why not? LONE EAGLET HENRY PEEL LANDS IN PARIS TO TUMULTUOUS

RECEPTION. 'I JUST WANTED TO SEE IF I COULD DO IT,' SAYS MODEST FLIER-HERO. He grinned. You're nuts, he told himself. But it was rather delicious to think in such terms. Practically speaking, he would have to brush up on his navigation more than just a bit. And learn how to use the ADF and VOR and all those other things. And get a night rating because the trip would take about a day and a half. Obviously the little Aeronca couldn't make it. A Cessna or a Piper was needed. And they were expensive. A partnership, then? Two intrepid aviators instead of one? ATLANTIC HERO HENRY PEEL DENIES ROMANTIC INVOLVEMENT WITH GLAMOROUS COPILOT. 'JUST GOOD FRIENDS,' HE DECLARES.

He laughed out loud at himself as the diminutive Welland airport appeared through the summer haze. He knew Welland well. It was a friendly little place; and it had no control tower and was therefore open to aircraft without radio. He eased back the throttle. Anyone in the circuit? No; it looked quiet. He glanced at his map. Elevation of the Welland field was 580 feet above sea level.

As he drew closer he saw a Cessna taking off. He descended to 1,580 feet and slid in behind the Cessna. Four minutes later he touched down in a thoroughly professional three-pointer.

He refueled the Aeronca, paying for the fuel with his automobile gasoline credit card. Then he taxied out behind a trim white Bonanza.

That, he thought, might be just the job for the transatlantic hop.

He took off and headed north, following the ship canal towards Lake Ontario. The air was bumpy—which was usual at this time of year, Henry Peel had learned. His little machine bounced and swayed as it cut through the up-currents.

Henry Peel hadn't taken the time to check on the weather at Welland. If he had, he might have headed for home.

There was a tightness around the eyes and a feeling of strain in the muscles of the throat. Frank Beatty swallowed. A few minutes earlier he had taken another pill, elaborately pretending to cough and covering his mouth with his hand. But he knew it was pointless. The pills weren't cure-alls.

His consciousness ebbed and flowed like a poor radio signal.

It'll be all right in a minute, he kept telling himself.

He considered speaking to the crew. Awfully sorry, chaps, but your captain is ailing. I hereby report myself officially unable to continue in command.

But that would do nothing but make everyone as jumpy as hell. They would be fussing around him like a lot of bloody hens. And the fussing would be an utter waste of time and effort because they could do nothing for him. Right now Corfield was in command. And he was doing a perfectly competent job. There was absolutely nothing to be gained by adding to his load.

Montreal below.

He glanced at his watch. In less than an hour the trip would be over. And so would his career. Finis. There could be no self-delusion this time. Farewell.

How does one ground oneself? I suppose there's a form for the purpose, he thought bleakly. There's a form for every other bloody milestone in life.

And what of Diane? Dear, loyal Diane. Surprise, surprise, my dear. You'll never guess. She will be the rock of Gibraltar, he thought. Like a champion she will take the shock and absorb it. Then she will brace her shoulders, and prepare herself to tackle something new. Fight on the beaches and in the pubs. Never surrender.

Webb had news of the weather.

'Toronto is reporting thunderstorm activity. Severe in spots, they say. At the moment it's not affecting the field itself but they think it will before we get there.'

'Roger,' said Corfield. 'Let's have another check in fifteen minutes, shall we.'

Beatty loosened his tie. He felt tired and dispirited. Corfield was demonstrating how admirably he could command the aircraft on his own. It was good practice for him. Soon there would be a vacancy for a captain at Amory International. Perhaps Corfield would be the lucky man. Good fortune, Captain Corfield. Keep an eye on your cerebral circuits.

Ahead, ground and sky merged in haze. Typical summer conditions for this part of the world: moisture and heat—with cooler air on the way to stir up trouble. Beatty reflected that from now on the air and its restless movements would merely be of academic interest to him. He would never again have to see and feel it as an airman does: the ever-mobile masses of air roaming over the earth, umpteen billions of tons of it, cold, warm, moist, dry, sometimes tranquil, sometimes angry; molecules of nitrogen, oxygen, argon, neon, krypton, helium, zenon ... always on the move, shunted and shoved by ceaseless winds that stream from the areas of high pressure to those of low pressure.

An airman learns to know and respect the air just as a sailor discovers the vagaries of the sea. The shape of a cloud, the shade and colour on the moon, the cut of the wind: signs and portents, all. The airman discovers, infinitesimally slowly, a miniscule morsel of knowledge at a time, that his instinct is being honed by his *being* in the air. It is the seventh sense: the one that takes over when the instruments fail, the conviction that *that* is the way to head in order to get back to the field, that *now* is the time to slip down through that fog.

All of which, Beatty decided, is of distinctly questionable value in the run-of-the-mill employment office. He came to the dismal conclusion that he had nothing to offer a prospective non-aviation employer that couldn't be supplied—and probably in far larger measure—by any reasonably bright young chap straight out of school. Administrative experience? Would running the flight deck of a jet count?

And what would a prospective employer say about his health?

You poor old bugger, he thought, you can't even get a job as a bus driver. It was true, appallingly true.

Perhaps, he reflected soberly, there are quiet little places where epileptics are given simple jobs to do for a pound or two a week.

He frowned. He didn't like the look of the weather ahead.

TranState Flight 738 was already feeling the turbulence in the air. Invisible fists struck at her as she sped by, jolting her, sending stresses speeding through her $\frac{1}{10}$-inch-thick skin—an alloy of aluminium plus 1.6 per cent copper, 2.5 per cent magnesium, 5.6 per cent zinc and .3 per cent chromium—to be divided and tamed among the 213,000 components that comprised her structure. Her passengers found themselves drawn to the rather disquieting sight of her huge, swept-back wings flexing as they took the loads. None of the passengers knew that the wing was capable of 'flapping' as much as nine feet without damage.

'Seat belt sign, please,' Vaughan told Garten. 'And look after the PA, will you? Tell them we're encountering turbulence and they should put on their belts for their own safety. The usual stuff.'

Garten nodded. 'OK, sir.' He swallowed and paused for a moment, his thumb on the PA button; he looked as if he was practising his little speech.

Vaughan remembered doing the same thing, once, a hundred and fifty years ago.

His eyes scanned the instrument panel. Speed, altitude, course, temperatures, pressures: all OK. But it was getting bumpier by the minute. Behind a score of dials, needles shivered and vibrated.

Christ, Lee, I can't believe you're dead. I can't, I can't.

The ground had almost vanished beneath a blanket of haze.

Cutshall was talking to Garten in his flat Boston accent, telling him to stay away from stewardesses. 'They're marriage freaks, all of 'em. Take one of 'em out more than a couple times and you're liable to read about yourself in the classifieds under "Engagements".'

'I'm going out with a teacher,' Garten said.

'Hell, they're just as bad,' Cutshall said. 'I've tried 'em all. And if you want my advice, do what I do, stick to married women. Unmarried women are a very bad scene, man.'

'Let's knock it off,' said Vaughan curtly. How much did Cutshall know? Was he trying to be smart? Oh, for God's sake, what did it matter, anyway?

Lake Erie was ahead. Detroit lay beneath a layer of brown-tinted air that looked incapable of sustaining any form of life.

'The stuff's building over there,' he said to Garten, pointing.

'It sure is, sir.' Garten wasn't about to disagree on anything.

Before them, the sky was dominated by gigantic, blue-black clouds piling themselves one upon the other as if attempting to build a wall of themselves before Flight 738 reached them.

It had been a sweltering day in the north-eastern United States and the adjoining Canadian Provinces. The air was heavy with heat: saturated heat. Nerves and tempers suffered accordingly. In Cornwall, Ontario, a fifty-year-old woman thrust a bread-knife into her husband's leg when he complained about the quality of the morning coffee. Near Columbus, Ohio, a motorist rammed a freight train because it had, in his opinion, taken an inordinate time to negotiate a grade crossing. Beside highways, overheated cars squatted like gaping-mouthed monsters, vomiting steam in angry clouds.

But, according to the news media, relief was on the way in the form of a cold front edging down from the north.

Because cold air is heavier than warm air, the front clung to the earth as it moved. It was an invisible wedge that pried the warm, damp air from the surface of the ground and sent it rolling skyward on the back of more cool air that came piling in behind. TEMPERATURES DUE TO DIVE, said the newspapers. They were correct. A second front of even cooler air was following on the heels of the first.

Meanwhile, the warm humid air kept rising, pushed relentlessly, impatiently from below. Soon it found itself ten, fifteen, even twenty thousand feet high. And suddenly the air became cold. Like steam from a kettle, the moisture in the air underwent a rapid transformation. It had no choice. It became visible: tiny droplets of water that clustered together as if fearful of their strange new environment. They had become clouds. Cumulus. Cumulonimbus. And, far below, the invasion by the cool air continued, thrusting even more warm, moisture-laden air to undergo metamorphoses that became increasingly violent as they took place at greater and greater altitudes in colder and colder environments.

Nature was busily setting the scene for the storm.

In the 1930s five German glider pilots flew deliberately into a thunderstorm to study its effects at close quarters. They were brave men, but foolhardy. Within minutes their gliders were being tossed around like feathers; soon they began to break up. The pilots jumped for their lives. But they made the mistake of opening their parachutes too soon. The storm's violent up-currents took their open chutes and sent the men hurtling upward. They were powerless. Gasping for air, they found themselves becoming coated with ice. Now, heavy with layers of the stuff, they plunged earthward, until the up-rushing torrent of warm air found their chutes and sent them up again. Incredibly one of the five men survived, though he was horribly frost-bitten. The others continued to be playthings of the storm until at last it subsided. Then, finally, they returned to earth: human hailstones strapped to ripped parachutes.

Thunderstorms commanded the utmost respect from any pilot possessing more than a glimmering of intelligence. Thunderstorms were killers, capable of generating awesome energy; they had torn apart more aircraft—commercial, military and private—than any official agency cared or dared admit. By far the most sensible thing to do with thunderstorms was to avoid them. To that end, passenger airliners carried radar capable of detecting storm precipitation up to two hundred miles ahead.

In the old days of piston engines, it was the practice to fly through severe turbulence at speeds only just above the stalling mark. In that way the worst of the bumps could be smoothed as much as was humanly possible, for the benefit of both passengers and airframe. The trouble with jets was that they were designed to fly high and fast. At low speeds they were ill-mannered and sulky—and prone to snap into nose-dives.

The cells of the storm sped upward, ebullient with energy. Behind them swept tides of air. The unholy process was accelerated: as the storm cells climbed, still more damp, warm air was sucked up from below. The conversion to clouds was now so rapid and taking place in surroundings of such extreme frigidity that the process produced a kind of friction—which in turn produced static electricity; and heat.

A dark, threatening hand of cloud was spreading across the sky. By now water particles were being propelled to such altitudes that they promptly froze. They fell. They melted. And then, as water droplets again, they went careering upward once more. And once more they froze. And fell. And still more moist, warm air came surging up from below. It found itself surrounded by countless crystals of ice bouncing on up-currents like ping-pong balls at a fairground rifle range. Quickly the ice crystals grew, nourished by ever more moist air from below. Each crystal developed fresh layers and assumed a different form. But as they grew, the crystals became heavier. The up-currents could no longer sustain them. They fell. And again stronger, newer updraughts packed with moisture halted their tumbling and sent them spinning towards the heavens once more.

It was a madly industrious factory in the troposphere. And at last its product was ready. The ice particles were now so heavy that even the strongest up-current could no longer stay their plunge. Down they went, billions of them, at speeds ranging from sixty to one hundred and twenty miles per hour, weighing a fraction of an ounce to well over a pound. They were an avalanche that smashed its way down through the warm up-currents, dragging wave after wave of frigid air in its wake.

It was the storm's catalyst. Now the winds began their battle.

'Local turbulence is becoming severe,' Toronto reported.

The storm could be seen on radar screens: crackling areas of white dots that glowed with each sweep of the scanner needles as if they were wands giving them life.

Conditions deteriorated with terrifying speed. Suddenly the barometric pressure soared. As if someone had pressed a button, the winds abruptly shifted. As hail thrashed the earth, the sky became a battleground. Up-draughts and down-draughts fought in deadly proximity, creating windshears like guillotines that were capable of slicing an aeroplane's wing from its body.

25

'Holy Christ,' said Henry Peel loudly and distinctly.

He gulped, his eyes wide. He was utterly motionless for a moment, frozen in horror at the sight. He stared. Absurdly, he thought of moths. Now he knew how they felt when hands of gigantic proportions came looking around them, seeking to crush the life out of them. The clouds were enormous. Blue-black. Seething with anger. Henry Peel started to explain to himself how he got into this predicament. He hadn't noticed the clouds forming. He had been looking out over the Lake, thinking of it as the Atlantic, imagining himself flying it, becoming a famous hero, lionized in every city....

The sun disappeared. It was night. Henry tore his dark glasses off and dropped them somewhere on the floor of the cockpit. Never had he felt so tiny, so inadequate. Never had he experienced such utter, complete loneliness. There was, he realized, no one in the entire world who could help him. He had no radio, no means of contacting anyone until he landed. *If* he landed. He clasped a hand over his mouth. I may be dead in a few minutes, he thought.

The realization calmed him to a degree.

'What do I do now?'

He asked himself the question twice, aloud. He could just hear his own voice over the clatter of the motor.

The storm-clouds had formed a huge wall, a mobile wall that seemed bent on forcing him out over the Lake. But he couldn't let it. He had to turn inland. Ten o'clock direction. Over there, the sky seemed a bit lighter. With a morsel of luck he might find somewhere to land.

He pushed the stick forward, instinctively seeking the proximity of *terra firma*. The tiny aircraft bounced and tilted, bravely pushing its way through the hostile air. He passed over the shoreline with its ribbon of busy highway. Hurrying traffic. Some cars already beaming their headlights. Expecting the worst. But the ground was still dry. The storm hadn't really begun, but he could feel its anger already.

No field in sight. Where the hell was he? Why in God's name hadn't he paid attention? Wandering around the bloody sky like a hobo ...

'Why,' he asked himself, 'didn't I stick to the territory I knew? And why didn't I check on the weather?'

Mistakes never to be repeated.

Please give me a chance to prove it.

Henry had been told by flight instructors and ground-school lecturers of the dangers of wing-tip vortices and thunderstorms. Avoid them. Never, ever, try to fight them. If in doubt, turn around.

'But I can't, damn it,' Henry snapped as if the instructor was in the back seat, 'the damn storm is behind me too!'

It was his own fault. He knew it. He had been on top of the world, imagining himself a latter-day Lindbergh. Now the elements were paying him back for his conceit, showing him who was boss, demonstrating the fact with a tidal wave of sheer, savage power.

He pushed the throttle lever full forward and sped towards the hazy doorway in the cloud. He flew across rows of houses and roads on which people walked, their feet firmly, sensibly planted on good, solid earth. A shopping plaza: cars in dense, neat rows, the store lights bravely defying the gargantuan shadow above.

It was densely built-up. Nowhere to land. Good God, he thought, it must be Toronto!

It had to be! There was no other city of this size in the area. Lord, how he had wandered. 'You goddamn idiot.'

The first drops of rain hit the windshield.

Almost simultaneously a giant hand grabbed Henry and his Aeronca. Up he went. Madly. Suicidally.

He opened his mouth as if to protest. Nothing, absolutely nothing he did made the slightest difference. It was as if he no longer sat in the pilot's seat. Stick fully forward. Rudder pedals hard left, then right. Throttle forward. Back. They were all futile, quite pointless actions. The Aeronca still zoomed upward, rocking, slipping, bouncing on a torrent of boiling air. The ground vanished. Above was nothing but blue-blackness.

It took Henry precious seconds to realize his helplessness. The elevators *had* to raise the tail; the rudder *had* to turn the nose. It was what he had learned. But it was no longer true.

His head jerked back as the boisterous air tossed the aircraft's tiny nose. The left wing dropped. The Aeronca was in the attitude of a steep bank. But still she was unable to escape the up-current. Her control surfaces were just so much useless metal and fabric and wood because the air was no longer streaming over them to be shaped and formed and given strength.

'God ... oh, God.'

Now the Aeronca was almost vertical. Stupefied with fear, Henry found himself looking straight at another world: a world of black, seething cloud.

And now it was dark. Utterly, completely dark. It was the end. It had to be. Henry was conscious of violent movements. He felt his body banging against the side of the cockpit. Something hit him on the head. In a moment of semi-light, he saw his sun-glasses pinned to the roof of the cockpit. He shook his head. He was sure he wasn't upside down. But, upon numbed reflection, he wasn't sure at all. He wasn't sure of anything. The air had turned on him. He had thought it to be his friend, his companion in adventure; now it was doing its level best to kill him.

With the realization that he was utterly helpless came a kind of peace. He could do absolutely nothing but sit there and wait for the end. In all probability the aircraft would shortly come to bits. A thousand fragments would flutter down to the ground. He would be one.

'It's going to be all right,' Frederick Cox assured his wife, patting her hand that had become a fist. 'A few air-pockets, that's all. Nothing to get het up about.'

She groaned. Her face shone dully and was the colour of full-cream milk. 'Fred,' she gasped, 'make him put this thing on the ground.'

'Make who?'

'The driver.'

'Can't do that, old girl. He's got his hands full up there, you know. We don't want to interfere with his work, do we?'

She nodded dumbly; yes, she did want to interfere. She told her husband that she would without doubt pass away if she wasn't deposited back on solid ground in the next two minutes. She said she had never felt so ill in her life; it was even worse than the time she had that dubious curry in the place in Soho and had tried so gallantly to keep it down during the show at the Palladium which seemed to last a fortnight or more.

Mr Cox kept patting. He wished Else would shut up. He wanted to get on with the book. And there wasn't much time left.

Len Sparrow was thinking what a godsend this rough weather would have been if only he had been sitting in the right ruddy seat! A bit of the old strong-silent-comforter would have worked wonders. Relax, baby. No sweat. Just an air-pocket or two. This bucket'll get us down, you'll see. No, don't mind a bit if you want to put your head on my shoulder. You go on and do it....

Then, without the slightest warning, Len Sparrow's lunch came up. All over his skin-tight denims.

He heard the girl say, 'Oh, you poor little chap!'

Poor little chap!

Aggrieved, ashamed, he hurled himself out of his seat and rushed for the toilet.

'Is he all right?' Miss Hardcastle enquired.

'He was sick,' said Julie. 'It's quite bumpy.'

Miss Hardcastle smiled. 'Yes, I did notice.'

Julie blushed. 'Of course you did. How absolutely stupid of me.'

'Don't mention it, my dear. People do have the funniest ideas about blind people. An astonishingly high number tend to talk very loudly, for example. They apparently think that loss of sight affects the ears also. I suppose it does, really, but in a positive way. One's hearing is, I believe, rather more acute than that of the average person with sight.'

'You're very nice about it,' said Julie.

'Do you think so? Actually, I often think how nasty I am about it. I get dreadfully annoyed at times because I can't do what I feel sure I could do so awfully well if only I could see. You'll laugh,

I'm sure, but ever since I was a child I have been convinced that if I had my sight I would be a great artist. And yet I have never seen a picture. I have an idea that my concept of what a picture looks like is totally different from what it really looks like!'

Vaughan took a deep breath as he gazed at the thunderheads. Dark, angry cells throbbing with unimaginable power, they proliferated forming enormous mountains in the sky.

'That stuff,' said Cutshall, 'looks kind of shitty.'

Vaughan turned to Garten. 'What's Toronto calling for now?'

The report was substantially the same as before: bands of thunderstorms, moderate to severe. Heavy rain and hail periodically. Winds gusting up to fifty knots during the storms.

Vaughan leant forward and looked around him to see as much of the sky as possible through the cabin windows.

'Toronto, TranState 738.'

The controller's voice replied: 'Go ahead, TranState 738.'

'We'd like to orbit until the worst of this stuff has gone through.'

'Roger, TranState 738. Stand by, please.'

A minute later, the controller called again, advising the flight to orbit the Ash beacon where the storm was not active. Soon the aircraft's path became smoother. Nearby, the sun sparkled on the choppy waters of Lake Ontario. Vaughan turned the yoke and applied gentle rudder. Towns on the far shore appeared in the windshield panels then slid away as the turn was maintained. Ahead lay a hundred miles of water; the Canadian shore huddled beneath glowering storm clouds. Occasionally, lightning flashes streaked jaggedly between sky and ground. A hundred thousand amperes, give or take a few score. Lightning was spectacular when seen from an aircraft, but hail could do more damage. Hail could batter a jet until it was fit for the junkyard. Hailstones ingested by jet engines could result in deadly flame-outs and wreck delicate turbine blades. Conceivably, a sufficiently intense hailstorm could knock out all an aircraft's engines simultaneously.

He pressed the PA button. 'This is the captain speaking, ladies and gentlemen. I'm sorry to have to tell you that we're going to be a few minutes late landing at Toronto. The reason is the weather. They're experiencing some pretty rough stuff at the airport at the moment but it should be through the area shortly. Then we'll put down. We apologize for the delay, ladies and gentlemen, but we think you'd rather be a few minutes late than ...'

Than what? Dead? Like Lee?

He winced. No, he hadn't intended to say that. He thumbed the PA button again. 'Er, we'll let you know just as soon as we have clearance to land. Thank you.'

Lake Ontario turned smoothly below.

In the passenger cabins, heads nodded approvingly. The captain was smart. Dumb to take chances in weather like this. No Kamikaze pilot, this guy.

There was no way for any of the passengers or crew to know that it would almost certainly have been safer to have attempted a landing during the storm.

26

Beatty sat back and watched as Corfield guided the 707 between the towering thunderheads, gently banking to the left and right, anticipating his path in order to avoid sudden movements—and added discomfort for the passengers. The shapely wing-tips sliced the churning clouds like rapiers then darted out over air that was clear almost to the ground; through the haze Beatty could see the Thousand Islands and the eastern extremities of Lake Ontario. Then cloud obscured his downward vision again.

Beatty was on top line.

It was curious how extravagantly well he could feel after a bout with whatever-it-was. Perhaps, he thought, the turbulence had shaken his troublesome electrics back into working order; perhaps he was like an old radio set that responds to a kick in just the right spot at the right time. Three rousing cheers for Doctor Hoke's Magic Pills. Results Guaranteed Or Money Cheerfully Refunded.

Lewis came in, balancing himself with the assurance of one who has spent a major part of his adult life walking around aircraft in flight.

'How are the passengers?' Beatty enquired.

Lewis grimaced. 'There's a bit of puking going on back there, sir, but we're coping.'

'We should be down in about thirty minutes,' Beatty told him.

'Glad to hear it, sir. Can I trouble you for your empties?'

Webb handed Beatty a card on which he had written his estimate of the aircraft's landing weight and the correct power setting in case of an overshoot. Jordan was busy with cabin depressurization and fuel balance.

'Runway 32.'

'Roger.' Beatty pulled the approach plate for that runway at Toronto International.

Descending towards Toronto, the 707 passed through the 18,000-foot level. The two pilots reset their altimeters to the airport reading. Beatty consulted the manual which informed him of the safe approach speed for the aircraft at its landing weight. One hundred and thirty knots. He leant forward and rotated the 'bug' on the two airspeed indicators to that figure.

The radar operator frowned. Was that an echo? It vanished. Then seemed to reappear. Then vanished again. The operator shook his head. It was impossible to sort things out properly with storms popping off all around. If that was an echo, then it would be from a small aircraft, judging by its size. But no small aircraft were in the vicinity—at least none had announced their presence on the Toronto Advisory frequency, 119.3.

The voice from the ground battled with the static. 'Amory Ten-Ten. you are clear to descend to and maintain 15,000. Over.'

Beatty repeated the instructions. The aircraft was descending at a rate of 2,000 feet per minute, slicing through the turbulent air, shrugging off the repeated blows. The thunderheads loomed on either side, glowering at the impudent little intruder.

Beatty turned to Corfield.

'What are your intentions?'

'Sir?'

'You're the skipper. Do you intend to go straight on in through this clag and land?'

Corfield thought a moment. 'The visibility is almost down to minimums on the ground. The storms are severe. I heard a couple of aircraft saying they intended to wait it out. I say we should do the same.'

Beatty said, 'Thunderstorms can go on for a hell of a long time in this part of the world.'

'Yes, sir, but I still think it would be preferable to wait.'

'We're badly behind schedule.'

'I realize that, sir,' said Corfield, reddening, knowing that he had come up with the wrong answer.

'Don't you think we owe it to our employer to make every effort to get down and get the passengers disembarked so that we can get ready for the next trip?'

'Of course, sir, but if conditions make it dangerous ...'

'Don't you think it would be a good idea to continue our approach and plan on landing until it becomes absolutely obvious that we can't?'

'If you say so, sir.'

'What do you say?'

Corfield swallowed. 'I think you should fly the aircraft, sir.'

'I have the utmost confidence in you.'

Corfield said awkwardly. 'I don't feel I have sufficient experience of conditions like this, sir. I'd rather you took control.'

Beatty nodded. 'Very well.'

Corfield abruptly raised his hands from the yoke as if it had suddenly become too hot to hold.

Beatty smiled to himself. Very tight-lipped, friend Corfield. He knew how the poor blighter felt. Probably thinking fierce thoughts at that very moment, about rotters of captains who give a chap command and then take it away again on a whim. He sympathized with Corfield and, silently, told him: We've all had to go through it, old chap. Although you probably don't believe me, I can assure you that it used to be a damn sight worse. There were captains who would never deign to address a ground-crew bod directly. Indeed there were some who would only communicate with the crew through the first officer. Some of the old-time captains would have made Bligh look like a holiday-camp counsellor. One fellow —what was his name? Armitage? Armstrong?—whatever his name, he would never permit his first officer to handle a landing or take-off. Never. He tore the most frightful strip off me one day because I forgot myself and said, 'Thank you, *sir*,' to a tower operator who had been particularly helpful. 'Never, never, under any circumstances,' said the captain, 'can an R/T man be considered the equal of a pilot—or even a navigator—and thus worthy of the appellation "sir" from such a pilot or even navigator.' It was, in that captain's opinion, the worst of form to give the blighters the slightest reason to think of themselves as anything other than the serfs they most assuredly were. Another captain was informed by the control tower that his wings and tail unit appeared to have collected a film of ice while the passengers were boarding; the control tower thus presumed that the captain would wish to delay his take-off while the ice was removed. But the tower was informed in the most acid of tones by the captain that only he would decide whether or not to take off; he had no need of mere control-tower wallahs telling him about the airworthiness of his aircraft. He took off, promptly collected more ice during his climb through the low clouds, stalled and spun into a schoolyard, killing a dozen passengers and injuring four children on the ground. Such captains were the air-age equivalent of the mulish Royal Navy admiral who, during Fleet manoeuvres, managed to sink his ship and a couple of others and drown a hundred sailors by autocratically refusing to countermand his order to turn to port when it was obvious, even to him, that he should have turned to starboard.

Toronto said, 'Amory Ten Ten, we're not reading your transponder squawk.'

Which, thought Beatty, is hardly surprising.

Corfield was staring ahead, rigidly.

Beatty made a show of switching to the back-up transponder. Predictably, the ground controller reported a continued lack of response on his radar screen. His task was now to make sure which of the flickering dots on his screen was the Amory 707.

'Turn on a heading of three three zero.'

'Roger, turning to three three zero.'

'OK, Amory Ten Ten, we have you identified now. Please advise your intentions.'

'Landing Toronto.'

'Roger. Stand by.'

Beatty scratched the tip of his nose. He felt absolutely confident of his ability to land the aircraft—or, if conditions were impossible, he would know when to abandon the attempt. No question. The flight was dreadfully behind schedule; it would be a damned poor show to delay it even further. Old Amory was relying on the crew to do everything possible to keep the show on the road, so to speak. As he had said, he had a great deal of money riding on Flight 1010.

'Let's have the preliminary check-list, shall we?'

'Roger.'

'Seat-belt sign.'
'Sign is on.'
'Window heat.'
'Window heat is on High.'
'Anti-ice?'
'Anti-ice checked and OK.'
'Emergency brake pressure?'
'Brake pressure OK.'
'Gross weight and IAS bug?'
'Set and checked.'

One by one the aircraft's systems were checked. No problems—
except for the unserviceable transponder. Even that was no longer
a problem; Toronto radar had identified the Amory flight. The
flickering dot on the screens now had an identity.

Time had no meaning. If Henry Peel had been asked to state
how long he had been tossed and pummelled by the storm, he
might have said half an hour, even forty-five minutes. In fact, it
was less than three minutes. A 180-second-long lifetime. For much
of that merciless interlude he was upside down. At one point he
emerged from a wall of cloud as if propelled through a door. The
Aeronca was spinning. Henry saw a blur of sky. Black cloud
tumbled across his line of vision. Then, without warning, it was
dark again. Dark and wet and lonely. He had no way of deter-
mining the little aircraft's attitude. He felt no pressure forcing him
down in his seat or thrusting him out of it. His brain had room
only for scenes of the Aeronca exploding against the earth in a
welter of blazing fuel. But, slowly, gradually, it seemed, he realized
that it was becoming cold. He was holding on to the rim of the
instrument panel; his shoulder was hard against the door. There
were moments of partial light. But it didn't help. He saw nothing
that made sense. Light came from every direction simultaneously.
Then promptly vanished. Nothing helped—throttle or controls.
The instruments had gone mad, the needles spinning one way then
the other. Rain pelted the windshield. It was immediately followed
by hail that caked his tiny world with a layer of frost. Moments
later the frost melted and flew away in jagged chunks. There was
no sign of the ground. Did it still exist? Was this, Henry wondered,

the end of the world? Had the world split into hundreds of billions of fragments that had gone spinning in every conceivable direction? And was he the only living soul left, being tossed around in the storm that caused it all? Was there no earth for him to return to ... ?

Suddenly, gloriously, he was free.

And the earth was there below. Beautiful earth, full of gorgeous human beings. He could see the earth quite distinctly, through a break in the clouds. But he couldn't see the gorgeous human beings.

'Good God, I'm out of it,' he said.

It was as if the storm had tired of playing with him and had tossed him away.

'Good God,' he kept saying. 'Good God.'

A kick somewhere in the region of the stabilizer reminded him that the storm was still close by. And still angry. He discovered that if he didn't do something about the turn at once he would simply fly back into the cloud again.

'Good God,' he said. If there was one place he did not want to go it was back in that cloud.

He kicked the rudder and jammed the stick to one side. The Aeronca obediently righted herself. Throttle right forward. Escape!

He came to the conclusion that he was smiling at the tone of the engine. It sounded oddly tinny.

He also came to the conclusion that it was remarkably cold.

He looked at the altimeter.

It took him moments to interpret the positions of the needles. It took him more moments to absorb the significance of their positions.

'Good God,' he said.

He was at 17,000 feet.

'Fred, I'm going to die.'

Mr Cox shook his head. 'Don't you believe it, old girl. You'll be as right as rain the moment we're down on the ground.'

'I'll never see Joycie again.'

'You will, my dear, I promise.'

Mrs Cox groaned. She told her husband that she wanted her

body shipped back to dear old Britain for burial.

Automatically, Mr Cox patted her arm and said, 'Anything you say, old girl,' whereupon she burst into heartfelt sobs.

Mr Cox sighed. There were times when it was physically impossible for a bloke to say the right thing.

Corfield watched the instruments on the panel shivering with each thump of the turbulent air. On this trip there was no need for the mechanical vibrator which ensured that needles didn't stick. Nature was doing the job quite efficiently.

Corfield regarded the towering, boiling thunderheads with a combination of awe and professional interest. This display of 'clag' was something to store away in one's memory, a standard against which future storms could be measured. The cumulonimbus mountains were closely packed, uncommonly so; and the turbulence was bordering on 'severe'. Corfield remembered hearing of some superstorm back in the old piston-engine days. It was said that a DC-6 found itself surrounded by cumulonimbus of such ferocity that the captain elected to attempt a landing on the 3,000-foot strip of a flying-club field directly below rather than attempt to find or fight a way through the storm. He landed safely. Corfield had heard veteran pilots say that they would never attempt to fly through a thunderstorm under any circumstances; others maintained that there was always a way through if you took the trouble to find it.

The TranState flight was correct to wait out the storm, Corfield thought. It was the sensible, cautious decision. But gallant Captain Beatty was undeterred by the storm. Press on regardless. These old Bomber Command types were all the same.

Henry's consciousness was swimming. He could hear his own voice instructing himself to shove the stick forward. The reason, his voice explained, is not too hard to comprehend. You are in the process of flaking out. You are suffering from oxygen starvation; perhaps you recall; the doctor told you all about it at ground school. If you don't do something about it, you will die. And yet it was a shame to leave. Up near the heavens the colours were soft and the sounds sweet. A man had time to ruminate. All the conundrums became unravelled. It was like watching someone crocheting in reverse. The girl on the sun-ray lamp box was smiling at him, saying something.

He opened his mouth to answer her.

Then his eyes began to focus on something. It was difficult because the something refused to stay still.

He blinked. Good God. It was a layer of cloud. Hurtling at him. It looked solid enough to shatter the Aeronca. And him. But then he realized that he was through the layer of cloud. Below, there were more layers, layer upon layer. Befuddled, he thought of an enormous theatre with umpteen strata of seats, all packed, everyone eagerly awaiting the command performance by the Rolling Stones and The Holy Ghost.

What?

Reality returned with each breath of denser air. One by one, as if there was all the time in the world, the facts of his situation thrust themselves upon him.

He was diving. Rapidly. He had to pull out. If he didn't he would be killed.

For an instant he wondered if he was speeding earthward in a fuselage, without wings or tail. Was it not highly likely that they had been ripped off by the storm? He looked, left, then right. Everything was still attached.

The joystick pumped against his hand as if trying to escape.

Good God! Henry discovered that the engine was blasting away at full throttle.

He pulled the throttle back to idle.

My, it's quiet, he thought.

Sweetly, the little aircraft began to come out of her dive. She bounded through a bank of grey cloud. There was a moment of damp blackness. Then a glimpse of something far below that looked like houses and streets. Then more fog. Drops of moisture raced across the windshield.

Now the Aeronca's speed was down to a hundred knots. She was almost on the level again and still retaining her wings. Henry didn't force her to hasten her levelling-out. She was coming out of the dive in her own good time. She knew best.

Now the clouds below were thin, semi-transparent. Through them, Henry caught glimpses of the ground and, farther on, the lake. But which lake? Ontario? Erie? Simcoe? He hadn't the faintest idea where he was. He smiled. He was above cloud, therefore breaking the regulations pertaining to VFR flight. 'Sue me!' he burbled happily. He looked around looking for a landmark.

Instead, he saw a Boeing 707.

27

The tiny Aeronca suddenly materialized, popping out from behind the cloud like some suicidally dangerous toy.

It was there, mere feet away: a flimsy thing, wobbling in the air, a great flap of torn fabric beating the side of the fuselage just behind the cabin, its little doughnut-like wheels still spattered with mud. Inside, clearly visible, sat a young man in a bright check shirt, sleeves rolled up past the elbow. His face was turned towards the hurtling 707. He looked disbelieving.

Corfield had time to utter a strangled croak of warning.

Beatty had already jammed on aileron and rudder. But there was so little time. In a fragment of an instant, the jet had consumed the space between the two machines. The Aeronca loomed in the windshield, insanely huge and close. And then it was gone.

In the passenger cabin, Len Sparrow had just emerged, rather weakly, from the toilet. He was closing the door behind him when, without warning, everything tipped over. Len was tossed back into the toilet to sprawl, dazed and sickly, on the seat.

A stewardess named Dee was also on her feet when Beatty threw the 707 into a violent bank. Instinctively her hands grasped for something, anything. Her fingers encountered Mr Cox's book and whisked it away just as he was getting to the bit where, tiring of charades in the nude, the party decided upon musical chairs in the same state.

'We're crashing,' gasped Mrs Cox.

'No ... quite normal manoeuvre just before landing,' her husband muttered bravely but unconvincingly.

Pillows and blankets tumbled from the overhead racks. A Polaroid camera, artfully stowed up there when the stewardess wasn't looking, came bounding down and fractured its owner's skull.

The 707 plummeted.

'Give me a hand, man!'

Corfield nodded jerkily, his eyes bright with the horror of what was happening. His hands gripped the yoke. Together the two pilots fought the aircraft's plunge. Every instant made it harder: enormous weight and aerodynamic form combined to create a kind of mechanical death-wish.

Every muscle, every fibre was concentrated on the task of forcing the 707 back to level flight before it smashed into the frigid waters of Lake Ontario. Layer after layer of cloud rushed past. Somewhere a radio voice was yelling something in agitated tones. Someone else was calling out altitudes. It was Jordan. Sensible chap.

Beatty didn't know whether he had hit the Aeronca. Would a frail little thing like that make any sort of impact? But it might have wiped off the tail in which case all this effort would go for naught.

Why was the stupid bastard *there, then*?

I wonder, he thought, if the wings will fold up. What will the G-force be on the airframe at the moment of pull-out? More important, will there be such a moment?

'Easy. Don't force her.'

Corfield was pulling too energetically. In his eagerness to live, he was practically guaranteeing an early demise.

Oh my God, thought Beatty, I think we might make it.

He felt the savage force of gravity thrusting him down in his seat, trying to squash the life out of him. He saw the waters of the lake tipping, straightening then screaming towards him at a crazy, impossible pace.

'Bloody marvellous!' yelled Corfield, beaming. 'Good girl! Good girl!' He kept patting the instrument panel as if it was the back of a faithful hound.

Ahead there was a shaft of sunlight piercing the clouds like a searchlight.

The waters sped below. Three masses of water: the centre mass hurtling along, blurring with its pace, the flanking masses turning, twisting as they attempted to catch up with the centre mass.

Beatty realized that he was smiling, about to laugh out loud. Reprieved again! How many lives did he have left now?

'Are the bloody wings still on?'

Corfield elaborately gazed out of the windows. 'All wings present and accounted for, sir. Better luck next time.'

'What's that din?' Webb said.

'Undercart horn. Shut it off, will you?'

It screeched at the crew, nagging them like a cantankerous old fish-wife, telling them that the undercarriage was still retracted although they had brought the aircraft down almost to ground level.

The control column heaved against Beatty's hand. Gentle back pressure. Up a bit, old girl. We need a spot of height. Don't strain yourself, though. Easy does it. No hurry.

'Four seventy knots.'

'Too bad they haven't got a race on. We'd bloody well win it.'

The ground controller sounded vexed. Deal with him in a jiff.

'Would someone go and see how the passengers are coping? And, Corfield, be a good chap and apologize for the aerobatics, will you. Tell them it was a near miss . . .'

Near missmissmissmissmiss . . .

The dials on the instrument panel began to move like ameoba beneath a scientist's microscope. Beatty had time to think: God, I'm going to have another attack and mumble, 'Take over,' to Corfield and then the world became a blur of revolving lights and shadows and dull, insistent sounds.

Charles Vaughan was talking to Walt Przeczek.

'I'm trying to be honest,' he was saying. 'I'm aware of a change in my emotions, a sort of shifting of the balance. I'm not very proud of it but it's what's happening. A little while ago I could think only of that sweet girl, dead. I didn't have room for anything else. But now I'm able to realize that I haven't seen my children, the girls, in a long time and I've missed them. I've missed Susan too.'

'So it was lucky for you that the broad in Toronto got killed.'

'Christ, no.'

'Are you sure?'

'It was a tragedy.'

'Sure it was. But it was fortunate, in a way.'

'No.'

'Absolutely sure?'

'No.'

'An honest man speaks. You have to face it if it's a truth, buddy. And this is. There's a morsel of gratitude in there, uh?'

'Yes,' Vaughan admitted at last, 'I think there is.'

'You're grieving for the girl and yet you're grateful because fate has stepped in and dragged you out of a situation you couldn't handle.'

'Yes, I admit it,' said Vaughan. 'That's exactly what is happening. I'm as ashamed as hell of it, but I can't deny it.'

Walt Przeczek was chuckling. 'In your own fumbling way, buddy, you're a genius. You've done something very clever. You could start a whole new trend. From now on, guys who are breaking up affairs anyway can make all kinds of yards by calling their wives and telling them that their mistresses have met with untimely ends. Suddenly you undergo a metamorphosis! One minute you're the all-American son-of-a-bitch who's screwing around with loose women, the next you're someone to comfort because you've suffered a great loss! Beautiful!'

The controller's face was ashen. His radarscope had become a nightmare. The bright green blips—each representing a jet packed with humanity—were like wilful little creatures bent on self-destruction.

Frantically he tried to create a perspective of the situation—and what the situation would be in ten seconds and thirty seconds.

The errant blip on the left side of the screen had to be Amory. But what had caused it to dive? Now it was streaking out across the lake.

And climbing.

Mother of God!

'Amory Ten Ten, make an immediate left turn!'

He's had a bloody heart attack, Corfield thought.

He turned. 'Have a look at the skipper, will you?' he asked Webb.

Christ, whatever the hell next?

As if in answer, the controller's voice rasped through his earphones.

But Corfield didn't react. He was gazing appalled at Beatty's mouth and its pathetic attempts to move, to form sounds.

Then Jordan snapped, 'They're calling us!'

'What?'

Precious, irreplaceable seconds slipped by.

The controller's voice cut through the static again, edgy and harsh with urgency.

'TranState 738, make an immediate right turn! *Immediate!*'

Vaughan heard the controller's order. But for an instant, a mere fragment of time, he didn't react. The words of the controller had somehow become part of what Lee was saying. Her voice was sharp and urgent. She was reaching out to him; her fingers were parted; the skin on them was taut and white. And he wanted somehow to answer her and tell her that there was meaning in it all, that it wasn't just a mindless sexual ritual; there was significance in what had happened. . . .

An instant.

Then he was thrusting control yoke and rudder hard over, obeying the 'immediate' command, hurtling the big machine towards a gigantic wall of cloud.

'TranState 738, turning ninety to the right.'

The cloud enfolded them. A second later, they were in the sunlight.

And then Amory Flight 1010 hit them.

28

Simultaneously, scores of people saw different things happen.

Grant Hobbs saw the row of seats immediately in front of him rise as if lifted by giant hands. A fraction of an instant later there was a shuddering bang that stunned the senses. It exploded out of the very walls of the aircraft. At the same moment he saw a second wing suddenly materialize beneath that of the DC-8. Absurdly the thought flashed through his mind that the aircraft had become a biplane. Then, instinctively, frantically, his hand was reaching for the emergency exit handle.

Jane Meade, the chief stewardess on the TranState aircraft, opened her mouth to scream. Then she checked herself. Screaming wouldn't help. But what had happened? The DC-8 seemed to have been halted in mid-flight. It was coming to pieces before her eyes. Passengers were falling about, smashing into each other. The first rows in Economy were hardest hit. It was as if a volcano had erupted beneath the floor; the deck had reared up and broken; the seats spilled passengers who were not strapped in; those that were, tried immediately to free themselves. She kept saying that everything was going to be all right, but her words were drowned in din the instant they were uttered.

Earl Gasparac saw the sides of the aircraft bend and buckle; ahead the seats seemed to spring as if suddenly alive. He clutched at his wife's arm and buried her head in his chest.

He saw a stewardess emerge from the flight deck at the moment the Amory aircraft collided. The girl's legs buckled and she slammed into the floor. She skidded along the aisle her arms and legs flopping as if the bones had turned to rubber.

An emergency exit—a great door-like panel in the side of the jet —suddenly opened beside Lillian Dumont. Shocked, she turned.

She saw Grant Hobbs—but only for an infinitesimal fragment of time. He was suspended in mid-air, a foot or two from the aircraft. His thin face wore an expression of mild surprise. His hand still gripped the emergency exit handle. Then he vanished, a charcoal-grey blur. Lillian screamed as a tidal wave of air grabbed at her. She was able to resist it; her seat belt held her securely. Her purse wasn't so fortunate. Snatched by the boiling-yet-icy gale, it made a distinct turn to the left as it departed from the aircraft and rocketed away out of sight.

Inconsequentially, she thought: I wish I'd spent the goddam money in Des Moines.

Aboard the Amory aircraft, the passengers were already strapped in their seats. It was fortunate, for the impact caused them to half-rise, their heads involuntarily bobbing, doll-like, up at the roof that was abruptly crumpling in upon them in a mess of decorative plastic sheeting and soft metal fittings.

There was an appalling din, a grinding and smashing, an end-of-the-world eruption of sound.

The aircraft staggered, shuddered, shook itself; it squealed in pain from every stringer and spar.

Mr Cox looked up to see a section of the roof disappear, exposing the underside of another aeroplane. It was a dreadful-looking tangle of metal and, incongruously, baggage. The impact had opened up the DC-8's luggage compartment. The flimsy material of a night-dress fluttered like a threadbare flag; it was entangled in a smart blue and white tie.

'Good gracious,' exclaimed Miss Hardcastle, as if the aircraft had done something in questionable taste. 'Whatever has happened?' she asked Julie.

'I think we ... hit another aeroplane.'

Julie looked up through her window to find an enormous shimmering mass of metal bearing bright red letters spelling TRAN-STATE. She blinked as if what she had seen was imaginary and would go away if she willed it.

In front of Mr Cox, the wall separating the flight deck from the passenger cabin suddenly folded and collapsed. Mr Cox saw four men sitting in the cockpit. He had always thought transatlantic jets carried more than four airmen.

A child asked: 'Mummy, what's happened?'

Corfield realized something appalling.

The instruction to turn right had been given to a TranState aircraft, not to Amory 1010. He had obeyed the wrong orders. He had turned right instead of left.

He was to blame.

Vaughan held up his arms to protect his head as the floor of the DC-8's flight deck heaved and broke in a confusion of metal, wires, switches and levers. Part of the nose section broke away. An icy hurricane tore through the flight deck. Garten, in the right-hand seat, tried to shield his eyes from the blast.

Vaughan felt the wind tearing at his earphones. But it was oddly disciplined gale: it didn't touch his face.

He looked down. 'Sweet Jesus,' he breathed. The torn wing of the Boeing 707 could be seen. It looked close enough to touch.

A mid-air. It had happened to him.

But why was the aircraft still flying? Why wasn't everything exploding and burning and tumbling?

A hand touched his shoulder. Cutshall, was crouching beside him, his grey eyes blinking in the torrent of air.

Mouths opened to form words. But they were snatched away to be dashed against the crumpled walls of the flight deck. Vaughan leant back out of the wind.

'Check the damage!'

Cutshall nodded.

Vaughan turned back to the controls. No time to wonder about the passengers or the cabin crew. There was nothing he could do for them at this moment. The only thing that mattered was getting the aircraft down safely, if that was possible. Worry about other problems later—if there was a later.

First; find out what still worked.

He clutched the control yoke. It was loose, like a broken limb.

God.

He touched the thrust levers but dared not move them. The rudder pedals were jammed.

Vaughan swallowed. His brain reasoned: of course the controls are useless; the linkages of the hydraulic-boost system run through the floor beams, under the flight deck. How could they be expected to work, for Christ's sake? Icy, panicky fingers grabbed at his intestines. He had no controls. He was powerless to do anything to control the aircraft.

In a moment, he thought, the whole goddam thing will come apart.

The 707's wing was streaked with dirt.

But, incredibly, the ground and sky remained in their proper places as moment succeeded moment.

Dazed, groggy, Beatty thought the aircraft had hit something on the ground. He kept seeing Johnny Torbin's Wellington and a front turret full of hay. And a West African village store cut in half by the right main landing-gear unit of an Anglo-World 747.

'Mid-air,' Corfield was croaking. 'We've had a mid-air.'

His face glistened; his mouth was slightly open.

Beatty struggled with his consciousness. 'What did you say?'

'We hit another bloody aeroplane!'

As Corfield spoke, Beatty's eyes were scanning the instrument panel. The speed was falling off! Why? For God's sake, why?

'Look behind you.'

'What?'

Then, through the side window he saw the unbelievable sight of the DC-8's wing, snuggling up to the 707's wing, the tips almost touching. The metal was torn and folded back, curiously neatly as if done with care. Fuel poured out, in a wind-battered mist.

'You passed out,' said Corfield accusingly.

'He hit us,' said Webb.

'No, we hit him,' said Jordan.

The flight-deck roof was a shambles. It had semi-collapsed; buckled, broken, it sagged over the heads of the crew. Beatty saw that the bulkhead at the rear of the flight deck had disappeared. The passengers could be seen: rows of faces, white and terrified, with imploring eyes. Do something, they seemed to plead. Get us out of this horrible situation. Quickly he turned forward as if chastised by them.

Then he heard the voice of the TranState pilot on the VHF radio.

29

By chance, sheer miraculous chance, the two aircraft had been travelling in almost exactly the same direction and at similar speeds when they came into collision. This alone saved them from instant destruction.

Angled upward a degree or two, the 707 had thudded into the belly of the DC-8. Thus the roof of one aircraft slithered along the underside of the other. Contact was relatively gentle. But speed exacerbated its effect. Like voracious predators, the jetliners bit through structural metal and skin, spars, cables, tubes, longerons, bulkheads. Sections of metal plating crumpled and fluttered away, flimsy momentos of the contact. A great section of the Amory aircraft's wing folded and snapped amid a haze of excaping fuel.

At last the awesome forces of momentum were tamed.

Joined by a tangle of tortured metal, the two splendid aircraft had become one.

They had become a monster. An aeronautical aberration. A sagging, heaving catastrophe that had no right to remain in the air but for the single fact that its wings were still capable of creating power from the speeding air. To this end, the wings were shapely, the curves even more generous on the upper surfaces than on the lower. Thus the air was compelled to flow more rapidly over the wing than under it. Since low static pressure accompanies high velocity pressure, the arrangement resulted in a net force acting upward, a force known as lift.

As an aircraft, the monster was inefficient because its two sets of wings did not meet the air at precisely the same angle; and it lacked lateral stability because of damage to its vertical tail surfaces and because the sides of its body were torn and broken, spoiling the smooth flow of air. Like a heavy ship without a keel, it kept wobbling, on the point of tumbling. But fuel continued to pour to the damaged engines that still functioned. They provided thrust.

The monster staggered towards the shore. For the moment—the immediate, terrifying moment—the pilots were little more than passengers. Still struggling to grasp the enormity of their predicament, they dared not attempt more than tiny, exploratory movement of the controls. God knows what the result might be.

The passenger cabin of the DC-8 had become a nightmare. The wind swept into the narrow hull of the aircraft and snatched at anything moveable, hurling it down the length of the cabin with lethal force. You ducked these objects or tried to deflect them. Not all such attempts were successful. A section of metal pannelling smashed into Earl Gasparac's forehead. A million lights burst before him; they burned intensely for an instant; then they went out.

The maddened winds, gulped in through the torn nose, collided with walls and seats and people and scattered in umpteen directions, desperately exploring the flanks of the aircraft, seeking escape.

Lillian Dumont had managed to transfer herself to the aisle seat of the next row back. She was now its only occupant. Lillian sighed. At last she was safe from the wind. But she wished she had been sucked through the hole in the plane's wall to follow the classy man and her purse and her $16,821.37. She was broke. Flat broke. And what could she do about it? Sue the airline? She shuddered. Was there a way to explain it all to Herman? Why did she have to write him that goddam note, for Pete's sake? It was then that her foot touched the attaché case. On the floor, wedged against the seat, it had survived the hurricane. Lillian guessed it had belonged to the nice man. Well, it surely wasn't much use to him now. She reached down. A classy case, real leather, just the sort of thing you'd have expected him to own. She tried the latches. They opened readily. The case contained a little over one hundred and three thousand dollars in slightly soiled tens and twenties. Lillian quietly relatched the case. Then she began to chuckle. She found it hard to stop, despite the inquiring glances from other passengers.

The TranState stewardesses had been well trained. They knew that passengers in an emergency urgently need leadership and liberal doses of reassurance. But it was impossible to provide either because it was impossible to communicate except by pointing to the emergency landing instructions in the seat-pocket literature. You couldn't talk to anyone in this fiendish hurricane; it was hard enough even to stand up.

Jane Meade managed to half-drag, half-push an injured girl to an unoccupied row of seats. Jane Meade kept telling her that everything was going to be all right; she had repeated the phrase over and over again and she wondered whether she was really talking to the girl or to herself. She wondered how long it would be until the aircraft tore itself into pieces and whether she would be brave in the moments before she died. She felt sick and weak with fear; her self control was a slender vein, impossibly stretched. In a moment it would snap and she would scurry across the aircraft's shattered floor, mindless with terror. But in the meantime the girl had to be helped.

Earl Gasparac was only dimly conscious of the icy wind that battered his face. But he could feel his wife's fingers pressing insistently on the side of his head. He knew something heavy had hit him. It might have been a Mack truck, the way it seemed to smash through everything. But, he thought painfully, it couldn't possibly have been a Mack truck, not up in an airplane. Whatever it was, he knew it had cut him up badly. But his wife was tending to the problem. She knew what to do; she had been a nurse for a dozen years.

'I have no aileron or elevator control,' Vaughan reported.

'How about rudder?' asked the controller. He sounded calm and matter-of-fact.

'Negative. Jammed.'

'Roger. Your controls, Amory?'

Beatty said, 'Our controls seem to be working, after a fashion.'

He and Corfield had the control yoke hard over to the left, compensating for the missing wing section, persuading the angry, confused forces to balance. The controls pounded against their hands as if frustrated by what they were being asked to do.

It was odd to think that the TranState pilot was only a few feet away, inside that aluminium cocoon that couldn't be seen from the flight deck.

'Amory to TranState. We seem to be temporarily wedded. If you've got any ideas on how we might get this thing down, let's hear them by all means.'

The American answered at once. 'Negative, Amory. She's all yours. All I can do is sit and watch.'

The airspeed indicator registered 250 knots.

What, Beatty wondered, is the stalling speed of two crashed jetliners?

There was so much to decide, and so little time. The seconds fled, bounded away, lost for ever. The shoreline was already near. The airport, shrouded in fitful rain showers, was only a few miles distant.

Christ, why was the thing still flying?

'TranState to Amory. You're doing a great job. Wish I could help.'

Beatty thanked him. He sounded incredibly casual about the whole thing. Typical Yank. Beatty felt the sweat trickling over his forehead. His arms ached. The monster was appallingly unstable; it wobbled through the air like a top-heavy tightrope-walker. One couldn't relax for an instant. The turbulent air kept jogging, trying to tip the whole contraption off balance and send it tumbling out of the sky like the mountain of junk it was.

'Amory to TranState. I'm just aiming it at the airport and I plan to plonk it down as rapidly as I can.'

'Roger, Amory. We can maybe help you with a little power if necessary. I haven't tried the engines yet but they may be OK; they're still delivering right now.'

'Thanks, TranState. I think we'd better leave things as they are for the moment. I'll let you know if we need any more power.'

Ground control reported all runways clear for emergency landing. There was not, however, time to foam the runways.

'Anything else we can do?' asked the controller.

Webb said flatly, 'Ask him if he knows a good prayer.'

'Shut your bloody mouth!' snapped Corfield.

'Go aft,' Beatty told Webb. 'See if you can do anything for the passengers.'

He winced. Hell, the speed was falling off! Gently, timorously, he edged the nose down. He was tempted to apply more power. But he shook his head. No, the application of power was too dangerous: it was liable to drag the Amory aircraft free of the DC-8. And the DC-8 had no controls. It would simply tumble several thousand feet to the ground, its pilot unable to do anything to prevent the disaster.

He felt dizzy from the effort of holding the controls hard over. The monster wanted to roll up and die. It had had enough of this idiotic game. It was tired of pretending to be an aeroplane.

'The bloody fuel's simply pouring out!' Jordan yelled from the other side of the flight deck. He sounded as if he was commenting on an interesting phenomenon, a fascinating sight they all should see. But the poor sod knew only too well the appalling probability of everything suddenly becoming a giant bonfire in the sky.

Fast, though; it'll be bloody fast.

Beatty pressed the PA button. He cleared his throat, hastily deciding what to say and how to say it. The right words were important.

'This is the captain speaking. I don't have to tell you what has happened. I *am* telling you, however, that we have control of the aircraft and we are heading straight in for a landing. But it could be rough, so prepare yourselves. The cabin crew have given you instructions. Please obey them. We'll be touching down in a few minutes. Everything will be OK provided you do as you are instructed. Thank you.'

What, he wondered, am I thanking them for? For not storming the flight deck and lynching him for being a criminally dangerous pilot?

Upcurrents kept jarring the monster. Tons of metal shifted, crunching, folding, in tenuous contact.

Lewis came forward. For the first time in anyone's memory, he was grubby and dishevelled.

'Passengers are all set for crash-landing, sir.'

Beatty nodded, still straining at the controls. 'How are they?'

'Not too bad, sir. Some of 'em a bit scared, you know.'

Beatty nodded again. Yes, he knew.

He called the TranState pilot. 'I think my undercarriage and flaps will still work. I plan to use them.'

'OK,' said the TranState pilot.

'I'm going to leave them until the last possible moment, though.'

'I understand,' said the American. 'If we try it before, we might stall out, uh?'

'Exactly. She's frightfully wobbly even now.'

'I bet she is.'

For the first time, it occurred to Beatty that his conversation with the TranState pilot was being heard on the ground; indeed it was at this moment being taped, every word recorded for posterity and the accident investigators.

The rain stopped in the typically sudden manner of a North American summer storm. A patch of blue sky appeared.

Heading in from the lake was an incredible sight: two big jets in what appeared to be the tightest formation in the history of aviation. Torontonians looked up, aghast. What the hell were those dumb fliers doing? Didn't they know how dangerous that kind of stuff was?

In the control tower, binoculars were in suddenly short supply. One controller hastily loaded his camera with film. Another man found that he was all out of film; he dashed for the nearest airport shop.

On the field, emergency vehicles cruised warily along deserted runways, their crews watching and wondering.

A curious tension became apparent in the terminal buildings. Passengers looked around to see what was happening. But everything seemed normal. Checkers, red-caps, rent-a-car desks, insurance booths: business appeared to be carrying on as usual. What *was* it?

'No,' said Mrs Cox, 'I won't.'

'No one will see,' said her husband. 'And it's for your own good.'

She shook her head. 'If I'm going to die it's going to be with me teeth in.'

Moments before, the pale-faced stewardesses had hurried from seat to seat, instructing their passengers to fasten their seat-belts over their hips rather than across their stomachs. Hold your arms under your knees, were the orders. Protect your head with a pillow. Take off your shoes and glasses. Loosen your collars. Remove pens and other sharp objects from your pockets. And take dentures from your mouth.

'Suppose you lose them again,' said Mr Cox.

'What d'you mean?'

'Well, let's suppose we hit the ground with a bit of a bang—I'm not saying we will, mind; I'm just saying we might—anyway, your dentures will go flying out of your mouth. And then someone might tread on them. And then where would you be?'

'What d'you mean?' his wife asked again.

'I mean you'd be facing your daughter without any teeth. Think of it: three weeks of bare gums. You couldn't get any replacements 'till we got home again.'

She paled. 'You're right, Fred. It never crossed me mind. I'll take 'em out.'

'Good girl,' he said approvingly.

'We have you in sight,' the ground controller announced. 'You are cleared for a straight-in approach to runway three two.'

'Good,' said Vaughan, 'because we sure as hell can't do a circuit of the field.'

'The wind,' said the controller levelly, as if this was a normal, everyday, deadly dull landing, 'is two eight degrees at twenty knots.'

'Roger,' said Vaughan. 'OK, Amory?'

'Piece of cake,' came the Englishman's voice.

Vaughan gazed ahead. It was weirdly terrifying to sit in a cockpit and see the runway approaching and yet be powerless to control the approach. Now his flying had started to resemble his life: all he could do was watch; he was no longer directly in control of anything any more.

The runway could be seen. Was this to be his last landing ever? Every pilot had his last landing some-time. Never again to have to judge height and rate of descent.

He wiped the sweat from his forehead.

What the hell will happen when we hit the ground?

Vaughan realized that there was no one in the world who could answer that question. No one in the world had ever done this before.

Suddenly the Englishman's voice cut through his ruminations.

'We're sinking too fast! Have to have some more power!'

'OK.' His hand was on the thrust levers. 'Let's go. Now!'

'Roger!'

Vaughan's heart pounded. There was a frightfully real possibility that a surge of power would tear the two aircraft apart. Then what? It was only too horribly clear.

Christ, she was sinking. Gingerly, Vaughan pushed the thrust levers forward. Pages of manuals and text books seemed to flip before his eyes: thousands of erudite words about too-sudden demands for thrust resulting in over-fuelling and, inevitably, over-heating with subsequent surging, which was why fuel control units restricted output until an rpm level was reached at which response could take place without problems....

It took time. Three seconds, four seconds, five. Row upon row of houses wobbled nearer. Coloured roofs. Orange, blue, green. Then, with a terrifying heave, the engines began to deliver more power.

The metal and plastic world oozed and buckled. You could hear the metal groaning, stretching. The monster tottered precariously in the sky, trying to tear itself into two.

Vaughan said aloud, 'Hang in there, baby. For God's sake, hang in there. Please.'

The pungent smoke-smell came seeping up through the floor from the shattered electrical and radio compartment beneath the flight deck. Garten had emptied a portable extinguisher into it; but still it smoked; acid, putrid stuff. Hydraulic fluid sloshed over the floor; the hurricane still screamed in through the torn nose.

Jane Meade appeared between the two pilots, hair plastered flatly across her grimy, sticky forehead. She reported that the passengers were in crash-landing positions.

'How are they?'

'Pretty good,' she yelled. 'But it's as draughty as hell back there. Mind if we close the window?'

Vaughan smiled, acknowledging the attempt to ease the tension of the moment.

'Good girl,' he said. But she had already returned to her passengers.

'Still there, old boy?' The British voice sounded as if it was taking orders for whiskys and soda.

'Affirmative. But only just.'

'Good show. I think we might start bleeding off a little of that power now, don't you?'

'OK. I'm easing back on my thrust levers. Now.'

'Good, let's hold her there for the moment, shall we?'

He sounds just like David Niven, Vaughan thought numbly.

'How does she feel now?'

'Could be better,' David Niven replied, 'but we'll cope.'

'Sure you will. Your approach looks real good now, from up here.'

'Right. Hang on if you can.'

The runway was a strip of grey. The light-toned airport buildings flanked the runway; highways lacerated the ground all around the field. Somehow the Englishman was bringing this airborne abortion in on a reasonable facsimile of a final landing approach. He's one hell of a fine pilot, Vaughan thought.

Was there anything left to do? The passengers had been readied for a crash-landing; they had been told to expect a rough one. Everyone else was strapped in position.

David Niven said: 'She's feeling very dicey and I have no idea what will happen to the trim or the stalling speed when we put on flaps and gear.'

'I understand,' Vaughan replied.

'Let's hope for the best, shall we?'

Vaughan said, 'Seems to me we don't have one hell of a lot of choice.'

Earl Gasparac realized that he was dying. Although he had known that he was hurt, the possibility of his dying hadn't occurred to him; but now he knew it; there wasn't a shadow of doubt about it. Life was dissolving within him. Soon, he knew, the last fragments would be gone. He accepted the fact without regret. He was content. He managed to squeeze his wife's hand.

She looked down at him. Her eyes were gentle, brimming with love. Without speaking she was able to tell him that she knew he was happy. And she understood why.

*　　　*　　　*

Len Sparrow came to his senses. Where the hell was he? In a box? That was what it looked like. What was he doing in a box? And why was it so ruddy noisy? Everything was rattling. Then he remembered. He was in the toilet in the jet. That was it. Only from the floor it looked like a box. But a bent box. What had happened to it? It looked sort of squashed and creased. He reached for the door. The handle turned but the door wouldn't budge. He bit his lip as the truth hit him. He was trapped.

Mr Cox grasped his wife's hand. He braced himself; it had to be said.

'There's a chance, Else—just a chance, mind you, but a chance, nonetheless—that we won't get out of this, er, in one piece, if you know what I mean.'

She clutched her jaw with her left hand and stared at him. 'I know what you mean, Fred.'

'Do you? Yes, well, 'course I think it'll be all right ... but, well, in case it isn't ... I just want to say ... I've always loved you, old girl. I'm saying it ... just in case, you know.'

She nodded and released her jaw. 'Me too, Fred. You've been a good husband and father. I couldn't have asked for better.'

'Good of you to say so, old girl.'

'And,' said Mrs Cox, 'that business with George Harris didn't mean anything at all, really.'

' 'Course it didn't,' said Mr Cox comfortingly. Then, as the unfamiliar terrain of Southern Ontario appeared in the cabin window, his eyes grew big. Had he heard a-right? What bloody business with George Harris?

30

The nearer to touchdown, the more viciously the monster fought, twisting, nosing, one instant dipping a torn, trembling wing, the next skidding like an overloaded truck on an icy road. A frustrated suicide, it was angered by the efforts expended to keep it alive.

Beatty felt weak. Christ, I mustn't pass out, he thought.

The runway was dead ahead.

'Fifteen hundred feet,' said Corfield. The altimeters still worked. 'Will we ...?' Corfield didn't complete the question. It was a stupid, unanswerable question. And unprofessional.

'Piece of cake,' Beatty made himself say. Then he wondered whether the phrase meant anything to airmen of Corfield's generation.

A tottering: a loss of a few more feet. A flexing and stretching of the ungainly structure. Sullen, temporal obedience.

Beatty thumbed the transmit button.

'TranState, let's start peeling off some of our power, shall we?'

'Sure thing,' came the reply.

Beatty grinned wryly. Both he and the American were trying to sound quite unconcerned by the catastrophe and its imminent consequences. And neither man was fooling the other. Beatty thanked God he had the controls. He couldn't imagine how the poor sod in the DC-8 could simply sit there and wait, powerless to do a thing except work the throttles.

Below, cars breezed along neat roads as if all was well with the world.

It will be all over, Beatty thought, in a few moments, one way or the other, win or lose.

Rain spotted the windshield. Too late, rain. You can't mess up my approach now.

Like an enormous, mobile tapestry, the buildings, roads, people and vehicles swept below.

Half a dozen men in shirt sleeves and hard hats stood beside the steel chain-link fence that marked the boundary of the airfield. Their heads moved in concert as they followed the progress of the aircraft. Their arms were semi-extended; the men looked ready to run for their lives at a moment's notice.

The American pilot said, 'You're doing just fine, buddy.' He spoke slowly, casually, as if he had all the time and not a care in the world.

Beatty realized that there was an odd smell in the 707's cockpit. It was the smell of vomit. How clever of the vomit smell, he thought, to manage the journey forward from the passenger cabin.

He blinked as the airfield blurred for an instant.

Just sweat in the eye, thank God.

He spoke to the aircraft: Please behave for another few seconds. I know it's a hell of a thing to ask but please, just a few seconds more.

The window panel at his left shoulder suddenly began to vibrate, shivering as if terrified by the imminent return to earth.

'Stand by!'

As he uttered the words he wondered what they meant. Surely the crew didn't have to be reminded that touchdown was only seconds away.

The American said, 'Real nice, buddy, right on the button.'

'Roger,' said Beatty. 'Flaps and undercarriage coming. Good luck, old boy.'

'Same to you!'

Corfield's hands were on the flap and undercarriage levers.

Beatty nodded. 'Now!'

He grimaced as the monster bucked and swung.

Oh my Christ, he thought, only half the bloody flaps are working.

Controls hard over and forward. Power off on one side.

He saw the thing in his imagination: the whole silly contraption separating into half a million individual components thirty feet off the ground, all fluttering to the earth like metallic Autumn leaves.

The ground tilted and swayed. The strip of dark grey concrete swept towards him: a sword plunging into him. The white centre-line stripes flicked below. He found himself remembering the nights of thirty years ago when tracer and flak floated through the darkness. He thought: When the speed drops off another few knots, the wing will suddenly drop. It's really bloody obvious when you think about it. The poor thing can't do anything else. And when it does, we're really going to be up the creek. We'll be cartwheeling all over the bloody aerodrome, which is singularly unhealthy under any circumstances whatever.

Whereupon he corrected, even before the wing began to drop. At his side, Corfield thought he had gone mad; he tried to cancel out the control movements.

Beatty shook his head. 'We've got to,' he explained as the ground whirled past. 'I know I'm right,' he added quite mildly.

The monster wobbled threateningly.

And then its wheels touched the concrete.

The tyres held for approximately five seconds. Then the first blew. The other followed in rapid succession, abused far beyond their design limits. An instant later the nose wheel and the right main undercarriage unit collapsed.

The monster slewed off the runway in an explosion of dirt and turf. A JT3D engine snapped off its wing mounting and tumbled end over end like a circus clown, demolishing an unoccupied Piper Aztec parked near a hangar.

Simultaneously, the TranState DC-8 tore herself free, thrusting her shapely nose forward as the 707 dipped. For a fragment of time, the two aircraft were bridged by an afterbirth of torn metal, tubing, cables and wires. Then they separated.

The DC-8 hit the ground tail first. A wing snapped cleanly and spun sideways as if flicked away by a giant finger. To horrified watchers, it appeared that the wing of the 707 had sliced into the TranState machine; in fact the two aircraft missed each other by several feet. The 707 skidded in a virtually straight line over the sodden grass, crossing Runway 28, shedding sections of wing and fuselage while fuel cascaded from the torn wing tanks. The rear of the fuselage broke away. The DC-8 ground-looped, describing a semi-circle, gouging a trench with a wing tip. There was nothing that either pilot could do to control his aircraft. The tools of control

—ailerons, elevators, rudders, flaps, spoilers, slots—were now just so much more weight to charge the relentless impetus.

Inside the aircraft, passengers and crew-members huddled in their seats, dazed and stupefied by the battering and the din. It was incredible, merciless, beyond imagination. Eyes seemed about to pop out of shivering sockets. Muscles turned to jelly under the pounding. All the world's dust-bin lids were being beaten simultaneously by lead pipes; a billion drummers were hitting a billion cymbals. The noise enveloped one, consumed one, reduced one to quivering semi-consciousness. It seemed to come from within: it hurtled along veins and erupted from every trembling nerve-end.

And then, suddenly, miraculously, the world was quiet.

31

The wind, damp and unseasonably chilly, pulled and probed at the sombre clothes of the mourners. From the tall trees surrounding the cemetery, a few leaves were torn; they were hounded across the wet grass like small, frightened animals. Dr T. Roydon Goodall shivered. He felt sick at heart—as he had felt for days, since he had read the appalling news of the crash at Toronto. 'MAJOR AERIAL DISASTER ... DEATH IN THE SKIES ... BRITISH AND U.S. JET AIRLINERS COLLIDE.' Wincing, he had scanned the story for the name he intuitively knew was there. He was correct, horribly correct. 'The British aircraft was a 707 charter belonging to Amory International, piloted by Captain F. N. Beatty, 49, of Royston, Herts,' said *The Times*. Hoke had telephoned Mrs Latham and had instructed her to cancel his appointments for the next few days; he wasn't well; he would be out of town, incommunicado. To his relief, she had made no mention of the crash. The fact had puzzled him until he had remembered that the name Beatty meant nothing to her. She remembered a man named Carter.

Now, cold and miserable, he stood amid a hundred strangers and watched as the white-haired minister intoned his sacred words at the graveside. But the words were lost, borne away by the uncaring wind; only occasional syllables, disconnected and meaningless, reached Hoke's ears.

At last the prayer book was closed. The service had ended. The congregation stirred.

Hoke watched as the minister spoke to the widow and her son. She kept nodding to the old man, as if accepting instructions from him. Her eyes glittered.

Hoke smoothed the ruffled wisps of hair across his pink skull. It was, he supposed, time to leave. He had paid his respects; he could do nothing more; he knew no one; he was just another small man in a black suit. God, but one felt so *helpless* at such times....

The flowers on the grave bowed low to the wind, their petals fluttering desperately.

Briefly Hoke wondered whether he should speak to the widow. But what would he say? What *could* he say? What comfort would it afford her to receive the sympathies of a complete stranger, an ageing relic from schooldays?

He observed a man speaking to her, a man in an airline pilot's uniform. Someone said it was the pilot of the American jet. Hoke looked at the man again. He was tanned, a pleasant-enough-looking individual. Was he telling her how proud she should be of her husband's memory? Was he talking about her husband's skill and gallantry? The papers had quoted him; his name was Vaughan, if Hoke remembered correctly. He had spoken of an 'amazing feat of piloting' in managing to coax the two airliners back to the ground.

Hoke shivered as, for the umpteenth time, he imagined Frank's aircraft slithering and smashing its way across the field on its belly, fire gobbling away at the torn wings, the crew hurling open the doors and hatches, inflatable escape chutes prancing out like great, dangling tongues, passengers slithering down them to land in graceless piles in the mud. And then the frenzy to run from the flames. A hurrying, slipping, stumbling, sprawling, crawling. And after the passengers, the crew: choking, coughing, the stewardesses, hair awry, pretty faces smudged, the men with white shirts singed and bloody....

'Everyone made good their escape,' *The Times* reported, 'except for Captain Beatty and a passenger, twenty-year-old Leonard Sparrow of Streatham, who had become trapped in the wreckage of the crashed jet and who had been overlooked by the other members of the crew. Captain Beatty, without regard for his own safety, remained inside the burning, smoke-filled hull in order to assist Mr Sparrow to escape.'

The words evoked the most sickening images in Hoke's mind. The dreadful, searing heat; the dense, poisonous fumes. Frank tearing at the scorching metal with his bare hands, dragging the lad free, then shoving him out of the aircraft so that he slid to safety down the escape chute.

The papers said that Leonard Sparrow was in satisfactory condition in Toronto General Hospital, suffering the effects of smoke inhalation, minor burns, cuts and contusions.

The paper also rued the fact that Captain Beatty didn't make his escape at the same time. 'He returned to the interior of the hull,' they said, 'presumably searching for more passengers.'

Does Leonard Sparrow realize how lucky he is? Hoke wondered. Does he have any inkling that his rescuer would undoubtedly have remained in the burning aircraft even if there had been no one to rescue?

The papers had no definite information as to why the two machines collided. The matter, they said, was 'under investigation'. One account hinted at 'electronic problems, possibly caused by the severe storm conditions'. Another speculated that a third aircraft might have been involved.

A 'full-scale investigation' was being initiated by the Canadian authorities, since the incident had occurred over Canadian territory.

What would it uncover? Hoke didn't know; he didn't care. The reason for Frank's death seemed unimportant now; only the fact of it mattered.

He watched as Frank's widow and son entered the black Daimler. The door snapped shut behind them. Gravel crunched and groaned as the big car moved silently away. Behind it, a score of engines started; doors slammed like the rattle of a machine gun. A convoy of cars followed the Daimler towards the road.

A handful of people remained. Hoke was one: an insignificant figure, his sad eyes fixed on the grave. What a pointless, bloody business living seemed to be if it all added up to a few charred fragments in a wooden box.

He turned and thrust his hands in his overcoat pockets. Unhappily he shook his head as he walked slowly along the gravel path. On the way he passed two men in airline uniform. One said that Frank Beatty was a good pilot, a damned good pilot.

Hoke was inclined to agree; Frank had indeed been damned.

Advertisement in *Canadian Aviation*:

TECHNICAL NOTE

It is an astonishing fact that the first mid-air collision between airliners on scheduled flights took place more than half a century ago. On that overcast day in April 1922, navigation aids were almost unknown. The DH 18 of Daimler Airways and the Farman Goliath of Grands Exprès Aèriens were flying north of Paris— and navigating by the elementary means of following a main road. Unfortunately, they were following it in opposite directions. They collided head-on; seven died.

Today, there is little chance of two airliners blundering into one another under similar circumstances. Navigation has become electronic; beacons guide aircraft from point A to point B; ground controllers monitor their charges' progress by means of radar. In theory, collisions between airliners should never again take place. The problem is that the number of aircraft has grown at an incredible rate; and they operate in almost all weather conditions. Equipment sometimes fails; and human beings occasionally err. And private aircraft—often with inexperienced pilots at the controls —roam more or less at will. The result: hundreds of 'near-misses' are reported every year; it is estimated that hundreds more go unreported. And from time to time, everyone's luck runs out and a collision takes place—usually with carnage of appalling proportions.

But not always. People *can* survive mid-airs. On a perfectly clear day in the 1950s, a Cessna descended upon a DC-3 of Continental Air Lines. Instants before, the Cessna pilot had been busy showing his four young passengers a view of their home from the air; the DC-3 crew-members were preoccupied with their pre-landing cockpit checks. No one, it seemed, was much concerned with other traffic. Suddenly the DC-3 crew found they had a private aircraft astride their fuselage. Damaged but still airworthy, the DC-plus-Cessna combination came in for a safe landing. The important fact, of course, was that the two machines were travelling in the same direction at the moment of impact. Sheer chance prevented a disaster. The tiny airport at Sandwich, Illinois, was the scene of a similar incident some years later. A Cessna 150 flew into the rear fuselage of a Fairchild 24 while both aircraft were on final approach to landing. Again it was a question of two machines heading the same way, vastly reducing the severity of the impact. And again, there was a safe, if bumpy, landing of two interlocked aeroplanes; and no injuries or deaths. World War II provides a further example. During a raid on Hamburg, a B-17 abruptly climbed and hit the underside of another. In a crunching, crumpling second, the two bombers had become one. Eleven crew-members parachuted, but the pilots of the upper Boeing discovered to their considerable surprise that they still possessed some semblance of control. Gingerly, only too aware of the imminent danger of tumbling away in an uncontrollable spin, the pilots managed to steer the interlocked bombers to a successful crash-landing in a German field. They stepped out, unhurt.

The ability of the Boeing 707 to fly *sans* major portions of wing has been dramatically demonstrated on at least two occasions. A Pan-American 707 took off from San Francisco International Airport on 28 June 1965. Shortly after lift-off, number four engine exploded and ripped away, taking with it twenty-five feet of the starboard wing. On fire, listing suicidally, the 707 made a safe landing at nearby Travis Air Force base. On 4 December of that same year, a TWA 707 collided with a Constellation of Eastern Airlines over Carmel, New York. The 707 lost a phenomenal thirty feet of the port wing plus one engine, yet the captain succeeded in setting his aircraft down safely—as did the pilot of the Constellation. All praise to the awesome skill of the airmen involved.

SOURCES: R. A. Freeman, *The Mighty Eighth*. (Macdonald)
A. J. Jackson, *British Civil Aircraft*. (Putnam)
A. Luanay, *Historic Air Disasters*. (Ian Allan)
Plane and Pilot. (May 1970)
B. Power-Waters, *Safety Last*. (The Dial Press)
B. J. Schiff, *The Boeing 707*. (Arco)